IMMORTAL PASSION

"Tell me to stop, my Tabitha. Because If you do not . . ."

"Do not stop. Teach me. Help me. Sergio, do not leave me needing . . . needing . . ."

"This," he said softly, and bent to take her lips with still more passion than when they had first kissed. His hands wandered more freely, gradually raising her gown, pushing it up farther and farther, his fingers burning along paths which, previously, no hands but her own had touched. "Touch me, *mia cara.*"

He murmured words of love as she obeyed by pushing her hands under his coat and then, when that was not enough, tearing at his shirt until it came loose from his trousers and she could press her palms to bare skin. Hot skin.

Passion blossomed rapidly, forcing them to greater and greater intimacy until finally, when Tabitha felt she could no more, he came to her . . .

From *Dark Seduction*, by Jeanne Savery

HIS ETERNAL KISS

KARLA HOCKER

JUDITH A. LANSDOWNE

JEANNE SAVERY

ZEBRA BOOKS
KENSINGTON PUBLISHING CORP.
http://www.kensingtonbooks.com

Contents

A Lady of the Night

Karla Hocker

Prologue

The last entry in the old journal—several pages removed from previous entries in bold, masculine strokes—was written by a different hand. The letters were unformed, childlike. But it was no child who had written the words.

> It is Anna ye must court
> My goode friend Anna
> Ye will find the ringe
> She will find herself

Chapter 1

A Ghost Revived

Throughout the performance, Anna felt his gaze on her, but, blinded by the too-bright lamps circling the stage and proscenium, she did not catch a glimpse of him until the final tableau. All but three of the stage lamps were doused, and those burned opposite her, illuminating the spectacle that had drawn a full house since the play opened six weeks ago. The man of the intense gaze would be the only one of the almost exclusively male audience whose eyes were not on the nude-appearing female shrugging off a ghost's white shroud, but were drawn to the dim corner where Anna stood.

She turned and scanned the seats to the left of the proscenium. The Venus Theatre was nothing but an ancient posting inn, where the stables, connected to the main structure, had been converted into an auditorium of sorts. There were no boxes, only crude benches or, for a higher admission, wooden chairs; no chandeliers to be raised or lowered, only stable lanterns atop iron posts to shed constant light upon an audience that could, at times, become too roisterous for comfort.

Anna saw him almost instantly—and stumbled backward as if knocked by an invisible hand. Her mind spun, whirling her back in time close on ninety years, and she was staring at the man she had sworn to punish, but who had escaped her vengeance: the hateful Fourth Viscount Darringford.

"An uncanny likeness, is it not?"

Anna heard the voice, so soft, yet commanding instant attention. Vladim Szeben. Her mentor. Her eternal enemy. Her only friend.

With effort, she closed her mind to Szeben. She did not want his intrusion. Not now, while her mind was in turmoil and her body trembled worse than that of the "revived" ghost on the stage. It had been so very long since she'd experienced such a passionate emotion, she could not be certain whether she was shaking from the emotion itself, the rage invoked by Darringford's face, or from relief that she was still capable of deep, human feelings.

Somehow, Anna made it through the applause, the bows, the smiles. Somehow, she found her way to her dressing room, a former bedchamber on the second story of the adjoining old inn. As always, it was dimly lit, balm to her eyes after the bright stage lights. And, of course, Szeben was there. In his inimitable style, he lounged on the bench in front of her dressing table, a dark, austere male with soulless eyes. His pale fingers clasped a goblet of ruby liquid. At her entrance, he raised the goblet in salute before putting it to bloodless lips.

Anna shuddered. But when she did not smell the heavy, metallic scent she abhorred, she squeezed beside him on the bench and faced the mirror. She saw herself, not as clearly as she would wish, but unmistakably the Anna she had known for two centuries. As happened every time she gazed into a mirror, relief flooded her, and also fear. She would swear her image had paled just a shade since she'd applied the heavy makeup prior to the performance. Soon she would be like Vladim Szeben, totally without mirror image.

"Not soon enough for me," Szeben responded to her thought. "You need to feed, my love."

"You saw him."

"Darringford's great-grandson."

With a soft cloth, Anna wiped the rouge off her face. Great-grandson. Of course. The shock of seeing that hated visage had so numbed her mind that she had imagined the villain himself watching her so closely.

But since it was not—could not be—the Fourth Viscount himself, why the interest in her?

"The ring," said Szeben.

Anna looked at her right hand, where a ruby, the size of a robin's egg, glowed bloodred against her pale skin.

A knock fell on the door. Old Marthe, the costumer, poked her mob-capped head into the dressing room.

"Gent ter see ye, Miss Anna."

Before Anna could turn or respond, the man whose face had shaken her so badly stepped inside. She saw him in the mottled mirror: tall, dark like Vladim Szeben, but without Szeben's austerity that bordered on the moribund.

"Good evening." His voice was deep, beautifully modulated; his bow courteous, neither mockingly low nor arrogantly curt, as was so often the practice of gentlemen thrusting their uninvited presence upon an actress. "My sincere apologies for the intrusion, ma'am, but I would beg a few moments of your time."

Anna could barely nod as, once more, the heat of rage

engulfed her. Neither could she deny him. Something in her demanded that she speak to him. After all, her anger and hate were irrational. He was not the man who had destroyed the only human she had loved since she lost her family at the beginning of her immortal existence.

"I am Darringford," he said, unwittingly twisting the knife in the still-raw wound.

Szeben rose and stood some distance away from the mirror. "Vladim Szeben, at your service, my lord."

Darringford acknowledged the other man's greeting with a nod, then returned his gaze to Anna, still facing the mirror, still holding the rouge-stained cloth.

"Gareth Rossiter," he elaborated. "Seventh Viscount Darringford. May I know your name?"

Not an unreasonable request, since Anna was billed only as "The Divine Anna."

"Anna von Hermannstadt." She picked up her brush to smooth her unbound hair. "And, no," she added, "you need not twist your tongue around that name. Addressing me as Miss Hermann will do very nicely."

Szeben said, "Why do you wish to speak to Anna?"

Darringford's gaze was on Anna's hand wielding the hairbrush. He took a step closer. "Ma'am." His voice was crisp, almost sharp. "How did you come by that ring?"

How . . . How . . . ?

The question pounded in her mind, knocking down the barriers she had erected around that bitter memory. She saw Marika, on the ground, struggling with Darringford. Heard Darringford's laugh and Marika's sobs. She saw—

She rose so violently that the bench toppled. "Leave! And do not dare show your face again in this theater!"

"My apologies, Miss Hermann. I had no intention to

distress you. In truth, I fail to see how I did with the simple question I posed. Unless, of course—" Dark brows knitted in a frown. "Unless you came by that ring dishonestly?"

Fury, red-hot and violent, engulfed her. No longer could she distinguish between present and past. She saw only the Darringford face and knew only the urge to have his blood at last.

The heavy, silver-backed brush dropped with a clatter as she flew at him. He looked surprised, caught her by the shoulders, and held her off.

Then cold fingers touched her cheek, her neck. Vladim Szeben's voice, silky and cool, doused the fire of her rage.

"Anna, my love. Restrain yourself."

She stumbled back, sick with shame . . . and fear. It had happened. She was turning into a monster!

She heard Szeben talking with Darringford but did not take in what the men were saying. Only when Darringford bowed, with an unreadable look at her, did Szeben's last words to the retreating viscount penetrate her mind.

"You have my word, my lord," Vladim Szeben was saying. "I shall pass on your apology and plead your case. I do not doubt that Anna will be pleased to speak with you at length."

Nausea racked her body. See him and turn into a monster again? She snatched a shawl from one of the wall hooks just as the door shut with a soft click. She sank to the ground and was violently ill.

The faint rattle of china woke Anna. The narrow bed-chamber of her basement lodgings was dark, but from the door to her sitting room came a sliver of light. She heard Marthe's off-key humming, smelled the savory aroma of soup, and knew it was time to rise.

How did you come by that ring?

Anna's breath caught as memory, clear and sharp, of Darringford's visit to her dressing room returned and caught her unawares. And with it came the memory of her monstrous reaction.

She could not stir from the bed.

"Rise and shine, Miss Anna!" Marthe called from the sitting room. "I made 'tater soup, just the way ye like it, with carrots and leeks."

Obediently, Anna rose and performed her ablutions. As she slipped into a gown, Marthe entered the bedroom, a basket dangling from the crook of her arm. A dart of sunlight followed the older woman.

"Market's about ter close, Miss Anna. So I'll be off." With quick, determined steps, she approached the windows. "Just let me pull them drapes back a mite."

"Not yet, Marthe. When you return is soon enough. And please draw the sitting room curtains on your way out."

Muttering under her breath, Marthe retreated. With much clatter of brass rings, the thickly lined velvet curtains banished what little daylight two small windows had allowed into the sitting room. Then the outer door closed with a distinct snap before the key turned in the lock.

Anna grimaced wryly. They had had the same exchange since Marthe replaced Old Sara ten months ago. And Sara had fought the same battle, as had every costumer-cum-chaperone Vladim Szeben had engaged during Anna's long life as an actress. The costumers were always elderly, so that after three or four years, they could be granted a cottage and small pension.

If only Anna could be granted a cottage and stipend. She was growing weary of subterfuge and pretense. Of loneliness.

As she entered the sitting room, now lit only by two candles on the credenza, she once more heard the key. The outside door opened, and Marthe said, "Ye go right in, my lord. Ye'll find Miss Anna in the room straight ahead."

"Marthe!" Anna rushed into the minuscule, dark hall, colliding with a tall, solid shape just as the door to her lodgings was locked again.

Firm hands steadied her. "I do beg your pardon, ma'am. I had no intention of barging in like this, but your maid—"

"My maid," said Anna, instantly recognizing the deep, modulated voice and dreading a return of that ungovernable rage, the bloodlust, of the previous night, "is an impertinent, stubborn old woman whom I ought to dismiss on the spot."

"But you won't." His voice held conviction. "You're not that unkind."

"You know nothing about me, my lord," she retorted, turning, and taking the few short steps into the sitting room.

She could send him on his way. Should.

Or face her demons.

She hesitated for only an instant. "Since you're here, you might as well come in, I suppose."

"Thank you."

She darted a look at him as he followed her into the cramped room. It was impossible to see his features clearly, but, perhaps, it was better so. Safer. Safer not to see his face too sharply, the face that held the power to tear down her defenses and plunge her into purgatory.

He was walking slowly, almost hesitantly, touching the back of the sofa as he approached her.

"Pardon the dark, Lord Darringford. Since I bask in the light, so to speak, most of my nights, I prefer dimness during the day."

"Not to worry, ma'am. I, too, prefer—" His gaze fell on the low table, where Marthe had placed Anna's luncheon. "But I am interrupting your meal. My apologies. I shall leave immediately. Only tell me when it will be convenient to receive me."

Last night, even a little while ago when memory of the previous night had returned, she would have replied, "Never." But something was different. Perhaps, at last, reason prevailed.

She motioned him to a chair. "I . . . lost my temper last night. I need to prove—never mind. I promise I shall do my best not to . . . fly into the boughs again."

"I provoked you, ma'am, and I do beg your pardon. What I said, more or less accusing you of theft, was inexcusable."

She did not correct him. Could not. How could she explain what had happened to her, that sudden transformation. If Szeben had not stopped her—

Anna banished those dark thoughts. "Perhaps you'll join me in a bowl of soup, my lord?"

"Thank you."

"Then, pray excuse me for a moment."

She fled to the small kitchen adjoining Marthe's chamber. She did not understand herself. Certainly, it was comforting to know that she was no longer governed purely by emotion where Darringford was concerned. But that did not mean she must share a meal with him, for goodness's sake!

"You need him, Anna."

The soup bowl slipped from her fingers as Szeben's voice invaded her thoughts. She stared at the shards scattered on the gray tiles.

"Discover what he wants. What he knows about the ring. And stay calm, Anna. Friendly. Remember, you need to feed soon!"

Nausea threatened. How she detested the mere word "feed," let alone the deed. Hands clenched, eyes shut against the light streaming from the open kitchen window, Anna gathered her strength and thoughts.

"Don't bother me now, Vladim!"

"I am guiding you, love. Protecting you. If left to your own devices, you'd be doomed already."

This was indisputable, but it was because of Szeben in the first place that she was doomed.

"I'll brook no interference with Darringford. I am locking you out, Vladim."

"No! You must not be alone with him."

She did not reply, but closed her eyes even tighter. It had taken her decades to master, and still required willpower and concentration, erecting the mental block that would stop Vladim Szeben from invading her mind. But she could do it, even when he fought her. Breathing slowly, deeply, Anna channeled her energy until she had deflected his determined assault, and the barrier in her mind was impenetrable.

She was trembling from the effort when she opened her eyes. Taking another bowl from the cupboard, she set it on a plate, picked up a spoon, and returned to the sitting room.

Darringford was still standing.

"I heard a crash," he said. "Are you all right?"

"Quite, thank you. Merely clumsy."

"I did not know what would be the greater mistake—rushing to your assistance or remaining here. I hope I made the right choice?"

"That depends on what you wished to achieve, my lord."

"I did not wish to be shown the door. My sense of consequence still has not recovered from last night."

"My lord? You sound amused. I fail to see what was so funny about last night."

"What is a man to do but laugh at himself when he acts the fool. And what could be more foolish than barging in on you a second time?"

She was not convinced that he spoke the truth but allowed him to seat her, then started ladling out the soup while he took the chair opposite hers. His movements were slow and cautious, not as if hampered by the dark, but as if he were in pain.

"Did I hurt you when I ran into you in the hall?"

"No," he said quickly. Too quickly.

"I did. I am sorry. My elbow, I believe. I seem to remember poking your side."

"I assure you, Miss von Hermannstadt, it isn't your fault. Just a small memento from the Peninsular War that acts up now and then. Please let us not mention it again."

She nodded. "You have no trouble with my full name, even apply the German pronunciation of the 'st,' the way my ancestors did."

"I heard it pronounced thus when I traveled in the Carpathian Mountains." He sipped a spoonful of soup, but his gaze remained on her. "I spent a fortnight in Siebenbürgen. In Hermannstadt."

Anna's heart pounded. Hermannstadt was the town of her birth, the place she had lived until her marriage.

Now she did regret the sparse candlelight. An aching head and smarting eyes were a small price to pay to see his expression. His voice was casual, but the way he kept looking at her so steadily imbued his words with special meaning. But, surely, her imagination was running away with her. He could not know anything. 'Twas a coincidence that he had been to her birthplace. A coincidence. Nothing more.

"I stayed at the *Adler* Inn," he said. "Parts of it are three hundred years old, as old as the castle perched above the town."

The castle, her home. If she had been there, with her husband and small daughter, when the attack came—

Anna felt cold all over as the terror of her last moments as a mortal threatened to overcome her. Forcing her mind to stay riveted on the here and now, she, too, partook of a spoonful of soup, which she could scarcely swallow.

"Miss von Hermannstadt? Are you feeling quite well? Have I once again said something to distress you?"

"Dear me, no!" She gave a gurgle of laughter. She was an actress, wasn't she, and a very good one, too. "I am fascinated, that is all. Imagine staying in a three-hundred-year-old inn! I only hope the beds weren't quite that ancient."

"That would have been torture, indeed. Straw pallets are not my preference. Fortunately, the ancient parts of the hostelry are two of the chimneys and half of the public room."

"Ah, that's all right, then. Would you like a glass of wine, my lord?"

"No, thank you. 'Twas a rogue band of Turks, you

know, who destroyed the inn—most of the town, actually—and the castle."

"Indeed," she said, trying to shut out the clash of sabers, the screams of humans and horses. The Turks had been allies against Austria's greed. The attack had taken town and castle by utter surprise. "Perhaps a cup of tea, then?"

"No, thank you." He idly stirred his soup, then looked at her again. "The town was rebuilt, but not the castle. Do you know what the castle was called, Miss von Hermannstadt?"

Why would he not abandon the topic, the dratted man!

"Dare I guess?" She kept her tone airy. "Seated above the town of Hermannstadt, I'd say the castle was called Hermannsburg. Or, perhaps—" Her hands clenched. There was no reason to continue, but something indefinable made her go on. "Perhaps, *Schloß* Hermannsfels?"

"Hermannsfels it is. Miss von Hermannstadt, why do I have the feeling that you are sparring with me?"

"*I* am sparring with you?" Indignance overrode caution. "If that doesn't beat the Dutch! If you believe that I am familiar with the history of a Carpathian town or castle, why do you not say so?"

"Well, Miss von Hermannstadt? Are you?"

The challenge hung between them, impossible to ignore. Anna sat up straighter. "I am, indeed! And I'll thank you to stop tossing my name about in that annoying manner."

"My apologies, ma'am. Are you a descendant—"

She rose, forcing Darringford to follow suit. "My lord, I must ask you to leave now."

"Why are you afraid of my questions?"

"Do not be ridiculous. I am merely pressed for time."

"Just tell me about the ring, then."

Heat engulfed her.

He stepped toward her. "At least permit me to take a close look at it."

"I'm not wearing it. Some other time, perhaps."

"But where, how did you come by it? And—"

A heavy knock on the entrance door cut short Darringford's questions.

Szeben shouted, "Anna, my love! Let me in!"

Torn between relief and annoyance, Anna admitted her mentor.

"I happened across Marthe," said Szeben. "She told me that you're here, *alone* with Darringford."

She knew full well that he would not have been abroad at this time of day to "happen" across Marthe had she not closed her mind to him.

"And how dark you have it. Scandalous, my love! Have you no regard for your good reputation?"

"Whatever are you talking about, Vladim?" she said impatiently. "If an actress of the Venus Theatre has a reputation at all, it certainly does not qualify as 'good.' "

Szeben faced Darringford. "My lord, I gave my word that you would speak with Anna at length, but you presume too much by forcing this tête-à-tête. You will be so kind and leave now. And in the future, if Anna is agreeable to see you again, any meeting will be arranged through me."

The two men, both tall and dark, measured each other. Darringford said, "Are you, sir, the lady's guardian?"

"Indeed. And I'll thank you to remember it."

"Nonsense!" snapped Anna. "I am well past the age requiring a guardian. Or chaperone, for that matter."

"In that case, Miss von—I beg your pardon, ma'am. Miss Hermann, I would like to invite you to supper after your performance tonight. And if you do not wish to answer any of my questions, you need only say so."

"Thank you, my lord. I fear I must—"

"Decline," Szeben cut in, taking her hand and holding it possessively. "Anna is promised to me for supper. However, if she is agreeable, you may join us."

Darringford looked at her, and she, who had indeed been about to decline his invitation and intended never to see him again, found herself wavering. Szeben was forever making decisions for her. It was nice to be deferred to. And Darringford did promise not to interrogate her.

"My lord, I would prefer, then, if you would take me to supper some other night."

"I'd be delighted, Miss Hermann. I have some urgent business, which will take me out of town for a day or two. Three at the most. You will hear from me on Friday."

"Decline!" Szeben commanded silently, gripping her hand more tightly when she tried to remove it from his clasp. *"Or include me."*

Smiling, she extended her free hand to Darringford. "I have never had supper at the Piazza."

"Then, that is where we shall go."

He bowed over her hand. How warm his touch, how human, compared to Szeben's, which chilled her with its iciness. She had a sudden, startling need to cling to that warmth, to capture it, make it hers to savor during those dark moments that were her lot for eternity.

But he had already released her hand. Darringford inclined his head at Szeben. "Good day, sir."

He left the sitting room, his movements still slow, a little stiff. He retrieved his gloves from the hall table.

But he had no hat, Anna noted as she saw him out. Only a cane, which had leaned in the corner close to the entrance.

Chapter 2

The Players

Gareth Rossiter, Seventh Viscount Darringford, had proceeded no more than a few dozen paces from Miss von Hermannstadt's Tavistock Street lodgings before he was hailed from the doorway of a tobacconist's.

"Well met, Gareth!" His cousin, Henry Rossiter, resplendent in white pantaloons and a coat of palest green, minced up to him. "What a wonderful coincidence. You're just the man I wished to see."

"Wonderful, indeed," Darringford replied dryly, "since it was you who told me where to find Miss von Hermannstadt at this time of day."

"Von Hermann—? Ah, you're speaking of 'The Divine Anna.' Did you see her, then? More importantly, did you see the ring?"

"I saw her."

Usually, Henry had to hurry to keep up with his cousin's long stride, but not today. However, he knew better than to refer to Darringford's slow pace, or to his cousin's use of a cane. Twirling his own, he said, "So? Are you not pleased now that you finally listened to me and attended the theater last night? Knew 'twas the Darringford Ruby the moment I clapped eyes on it. Knew you'd be grateful."

Darringford raised a brow. "How much do you need, Henry?"

"You misunderstand!" Henry protested, doffing his hat while Darringford stopped and bowed to two matrons passing in a barouche. "I say, Gareth! You really mustn't be out and about without a hat. Bad *ton*, don't you know. And Lydia says your head would ache much less if you covered it. Or if—"

"Much obliged," Darringford cut in. "You must thank Lydia for me. Her concern is most gratifying, and I shall strive to adhere to her advice. Now, Henry, how much do you need?"

"I assure you, Gareth, I want nothing from you." Henry once more fell into step beside his cousin. "All I wish is for *you* to recover what's yours. Did you see the ring?"

"Miss von Hermannstadt was not wearing it."

"Dash it all! Did you not ask her to show it to you?"

"I'll see it soon enough. Besides, there's no doubt in my mind that it is the ring our great-grandfather lost, and when I meet the lady again, I shall offer to purchase it from her."

"Purchase it! Why waste your blunt? The ring is ours. When do you see her again?"

"The end of the week." They had reached St. Martin's Lane, and Gareth hailed an approaching hackney. "Good day, Henry. I shall keep you apprised."

"I suppose you'll be 'out of town' until then," said Henry with a sapient look at Darringford's cane and the coach coming to a stop beside them. "Perhaps Lydia—"

"No, thank you! I'm told my pantry is already overflowing with jars of your wife's restoratives."

"Just as well, I suppose. Young Gareth is ailing, and Lydia is busy—"

"What's wrong?" Darringford cut in.

"Just a cough. Nothing much to fret about this time."

"That's all right, then. He'll be in good hands with Lydia." Concern and love for his five-year-old namesake were probably the only sentiments he would ever have in common with Henry's wife. She was a devoted mother—perhaps even obsessive since her first child's, little Jane's, death. And she would personally nurse her son.

He climbed stiffly into the coach. "Upper Brook Street," he told the jarvey, then gave Henry a jaunty smile. "Do give Gareth a hug for me. And my regards to Lydia."

The smile faded as soon as the hackney started to roll. His side felt hot and sticky, as if the old saber wound was opening again. And his head ached unbearably. Yes, he would, indeed, be "out of town" for a while, and he must count himself fortunate that Miss von Hermannstadt had not been available that evening. But see her again, he must. And would.

Darringford rested his head against the musty-smelling upholstery and closed his eyes. What an enigma the actress was proving. He had expected—in truth, he had had no notion what to expect, but it wasn't what he had found. His mystification had nothing to do with her appearance, though he couldn't be certain of that either; her basement lodgings were too dark. Except under bright stage lights, where her features were enhanced with rouge and kohl, he had never seen Miss von Hermannstadt clearly. She was not tall, but her figure was splendid, "The Divine Anna" not a misnomer. Her hair was the color of Spanish sherry. *Olorosa*, he thought, but only daylight could confirm his estimation. He did not know the exact color of her eyes, only that they were light. Gray, perhaps, or blue, or somewhere in between. Her skin, when she gave him her hand, was soft and smooth. . . . And what the devil did it matter?

Darringford sat up, wincing, then stared out the coach window to judge how soon he could hide in his chamber. Nothing mattered except sleep and the quiet ministrations of the faithful Wheatley, who had been his companion when they were carefree lads, his batman on the Peninsula, and now served as his valet.

The only pertinent facts about Miss von Hermannstadt he must not forget were the facts that she reacted quite strongly to any mention of the ring, and that not once had she asked *why* he was questioning her.

And no matter how good an actress she was, she could not hide her agitation when he spoke of Hermannstadt, or the castle high in the Carpathian mountains that had been destroyed by Turkish marauders.

Indeed, she was not at all what he'd expected.

Vladim Szeben faced Anna. "What are you about? If you see him alone, you'll botch it."

"What is there to botch?" Now that Darringford was gone, Anna felt tired, dispirited. "I'm not even certain I *will* see him again. And if I do, I may just give him the ring."

Szeben was silent.

"Well?" she demanded. "Did you not always tell me I should forget my thirst for revenge?"

"So I did. I never imagined, however, you'd meet the very image of the fiend."

"But he's not the same man." Anna sat down and tasted a spoonful of the now cold soup. No matter. She wasn't hungry anyway.

As always, Szeben knew her thoughts. "You're never hungry," he said. "But you tire easily, and your sensitivity to light is more pronounced. You know what that means. Have known for years."

She looked up at him. "Vladim, is there no alternative? No end to this . . . existence?"

"Why ask?" His voice was harsh. With a sweeping gesture, he indicated her bedchamber. "You own and have read more books on us than anyone. Or did you think I would not know?"

"No, and it was never my intention to hide the books from you. Vladim, it's so discouraging! There is nothing definitive. There is no science, even if the work is written by a scholar, which is rare in any case. Much of what I found was written by sensation seekers more bloodthirsty than witch hunters ever were. Some so-called 'facts' stated by them are so ludicrous, I do not know whether to laugh or cry over such gross misrepresentations."

"All I know is that you must feed more frequently than you do, or you will turn into one of the monsters that kill and maim for the sheer lust of it—as described by the sensation seekers."

Her throat tightened. "As almost happened last night?"

He seemed about to speak, then shrugged and shook his head.

"And there is no reversal of this state, Vladim? There is no way I can turn mortal again, grow old, and—"

"And die?" Szeben finished. He drew a chair close and sat down beside her. "You can die, Anna. By fire."

She was silent, remembering the inferno that had devoured the town where she had been born, where she had lived until she married and moved into the castle. She had been in Hermannstadt the day the Turks attacked.

Szeben said, "Why can you not be like me, accepting that the taste of blood is essential to our well-being? You ought to be like me. I turned you into what you are."

She spoke without heat. "And I have hated you for it ever since."

"No, Anna. You resent me at times. You would have died had I not drunk your blood and healed your wounds, and you feel guilty that you survived . . . and your family did not."

Again she was silent. How could he call her existence survival?

She *had* hated him. Of that she was certain. She had despised him. But now? Perhaps, over the years, her feelings had, indeed, mellowed to resentment. Certainly, from necessity, she had grown comfortable with his constant presence. Most of the time, at least.

"You see," said Szeben. "I know you better than you know yourself."

"So you would like to believe."

"Admit that you hold admiration for my abilities," he coaxed. "Just think how diligently I contrive to shift members of our company to other theaters when they begin to question your eternal youth. And how I have moved our company from country to country, from theater to theater."

"Alas, how low we have sunk with the Venus Theatre and *A Ghost Revived*. Now *that* is scandalous! And scarcely enough lines to merit the definition 'play.' "

He waved a dismissive hand. "We will move on in a month or so. Remember, instead, the admirable deeds I've performed. How I provided us with a long, distinguished line of thespian forebears to explain the similarity in looks to an actress many years earlier."

"Making me grandmother and granddaughter all in

one." A chuckle escaped her as, no doubt, Szeben had planned. "That poor old gentleman—some *Conde* or other, in Spain, was it not?"

"Portugal."

"The looks he gave me! How we threw him into utter confusion."

"So resentment is not all that you feel for me."

"No, of course not. Perhaps you have forgotten what it is like, but there is intricacy in feelings. Why, even my husband, whom I loved deeply, could provoke me to exasperation. And I hated it when Walter arranged a bear baiting."

"Anna." Hands pushed against his thighs, Szeben leaned forward. "I want you to marry me."

"Marry!" She all but choked on the word. He had asked her to be his lover more than once, and she had refused. But marriage—

"I want to do it right, Anna. You still suffer from human emotions—more than any of us I've ever known. And for some reason, you have not shaken off the conventions and regulations governing humans. You still remember what your mother taught you, do you not?"

"Oh, indeed." Anna savored the warmth evoked by thoughts of her mother. "I remember so very well. When I turned fourteen and Walter started to pay me marked attention, she took me aside and said—"

"That a man who can have his milk for free, need not buy a cow."

"A goat, Vladim. We had only goats and sheep. And I truly dislike it when you invade my mind."

"I did not. At least, not this instant. I culled that bit of information the first time I invited you to be my lover."

He reached out, clasping her hands in both of his. "So, Anna, what say you? Will you marry me?"

She heard a strange note in his voice. If it had not been Vladim Szeben asking the question, she might have imagined a plea. But, perhaps, even Szeben could plead. Perhaps he, too, suffered from the devastating aloneness that dampened the spirit and choked all joy.

The chill of his skin transferred to hers until she felt cold all over. Unbidden, the memory of Darringford's touch leaped to mind. Such warmth.

She freed herself and rose. "I am sorry, Vladim. I cannot marry you."

"It's Darringford!" Szeben's chair scraped harshly against the floorboards as he stood. "I knew the man was trouble the moment I laid eyes on him."

"You're talking rubbish. Darringford has nothing at all to do with my decision. Who knows, if I had survived as a widow in Hermannstadt, I might have married again. But as it is . . . as I am . . . no! I promise you, I'll never marry again."

"Then, remember that promise. Make it a vow. Because with Darringford, you'd find nothing but unhappiness."

Szeben strode quickly down Tavistock Street. Perhaps, if he hurried, he would catch up to the man. Darringford had been in pain, and slow. His lordship was injured; Szeben had caught the faintest whiff of blood. As Anna should have—would have—if she weren't so inept.

Szeben shielded his thoughts from Anna. She rarely tried to communicate with him, but with Darringford's appearance on the scene, this might change. Her composure was badly shaken by the man, so badly that she had not yet caught on just how much he knew about Darringford; that he had kept up with the Rossiter family ever since the Fourth Viscount had ravished that young gypsy Anna had taken such a fancy to. Marika, the wench was called. The same name as Anna's daughter.

His Anna. He had made her one of them. The cursed undead. Doomed to walk the earth throughout eternity. But, somehow, he had erred; Anna's transformation had not been perfect.

When Darringford had appeared so suddenly at the theater, Szeben had hoped the man would be Anna's salvation. Anna's attack on Darringford had been a good sign, but it was all wrong. She had been in pain, in a mindless rage. If she had tasted Darringford's blood then, she would, indeed, have slipped into the state she most dreaded. No, it must be done a different way, the right way.

Oblivious to the complaints of pedestrians who felt the thrust of his elbow as he pushed past, and the curses of drivers who had to rein in sharply as he dashed across streets, Szeben forged on until he reached Grosvenor Square and could see down the length of Upper Brook Street. There was no sign of Darringford.

Szeben stood and stared at the imposing building he knew to be Darringford House. At last, he turned away. 'Twas for the best. Accosting Darringford in the street might have caused that gentleman to pay more attention to him than was desirable. Demanding admittance to Darringford House and an interview most definitely would arouse suspicion. But, for the time being, Szeben preferred to remain in the background.

And he had better remember that the next time Anna said or did something unpredictable. Which she would. He knew her too well not to recognize just how strongly she was drawn to Darringford. She might believe it was the man's courtesy, his charming manner, that held her enthralled. Szeben knew better. Darringford was human. That was what drew Anna.

It had happened with the gypsy, Marika. The reason was simple then: Marika had reminded Anna of her daughter. It was more difficult to see what it was about Darringford that touched a chord in Anna. Not the likeness to the Fourth Viscount; that could only spawn anger and disgust. But whatever it was that drew her, Anna was not for Darringford.

Chapter 3

Shadows Past . . .

The moment Anna stepped out of the hatmaker's establishment, she knew she had made a serious mistake in venturing outside on an April day. It had been overcast and gray when she left her lodgings, but while she was trying on bonnets and hats, the sun had come out. She felt dizzy and weak, even though a midnight-blue parasol shielded her from the direct light.

How very long Bond Street was. And where were the hackneys when one was in need of their services?

She swayed, brushing against someone, and muttered an apology, then stopped. She was almost at the corner of Conduit Street. About five or six doors farther down was a stationer she patronized frequently. If she could make it to the shop, surely the clerk would summon a coach for her.

The pavement beneath her feet was shifting, undulating, making every step a hazard. Szeben had warned her more than once that she would be less able to face daylight the longer she postponed feeding, but since she hardly ever went out, except at night, she had ignored him for years. Now she knew that he was correct.

Or was he? What if a more frequent taste of blood would merely make her more like him? Was that what he wanted?

Why, oh why, had she ventured out?

It had been vanity that drove her, pure and simple vanity, she admitted. Tomorrow was Friday, and she had awakened at noon wanting a new hat if Darringford was taking her to the Piazza for supper. She had not cared about fashion in such a long time that the sudden, irresistible desire had startled her. It was such an amazingly *pleasant* feeling. And the results of her venture had been more than satisfactory, although, right at present, the wide box tied with string seemed to weigh as much as a millstone.

Anna became aware of a carriage and pair drawing to a halt beside her. She knew, with certainty and an immediate and totally inexplicable lifting of spirits, even before she looked around, before she heard the greeting, that it was *he*.

"Miss Hermann! Good day to you. May I offer you a seat in my curricle?"

"You may, indeed. And I thank you for your kindness, Lord Darringford."

"You'll pardon me for not getting down, but the pair is fresh. My cousin will assist you. Miss Hermann, allow me to present Henry Rossiter."

Only now did Anna notice the second gentleman, a Tulip of the first stare, who stepped down, doffed his hat with a flourish, and bowed low before her.

"Pleasure to make your acquaintance at last, Miss Hermann. You never stop in the Green Room, and I've been waiting for weeks to tell you that I'm your most ardent admirer."

"Indeed?" murmured Anna, her gaze held in fascination by his waistcoat embroidered with brilliantly hued parakeets. "Please accept my gratitude for giving up your seat to me."

"My pleasure, ma'am." With courtly grace he handed her, along with parasol and hatbox, into the curricle. "And if you'll permit Gareth a gander at your ring, I'll be more than repaid."

"The ring." She looked at Darringford. "We're back to that, are we?"

He drove off without another word to Henry Rossiter. "I shan't deny it, Miss Hermann. I still need to know how you came by the ruby, but there is something else as well."

He was looking at her so intently and for such a length of time that she became alarmed. "What are you about, my lord? Pray pay attention!"

"I am. And I was correct. Your hair is the color of sherry. *Olorosa.*"

"Pay attention to the street! Look where you're driving! And slow down. You're about to run over the crossing sweep!"

"My grays know their way about town."

But, flipping a large silver coin to the urchin with the broom twice as long as he, Darringford did turn his eyes upon the road. "Shall I take you home, or do you have other errands?"

"Home, please." She adjusted the hatbox at her feet. "I did not expect to see you today. Was your business completed satisfactorily, my lord?"

"Quite. And sooner than I deemed possible, which is why I called at your lodgings. Your maid told me that I would find you in Bond Street."

"How fortuitous."

"Will you sup with me tonight, Miss von Hermannstadt—beg pardon—Miss Hermann?"

"Never mind about Miss Hermann. You may use my full name if you wish." She gripped her parasol so tightly that the carved ornamentations of the handle cut into her palm. "I suppose you'll want to discuss the ring tonight?"

"I said I would not press you, and I shan't."

"But you are determined to interrogate me at some point. So, I suppose, it might as well be tonight."

"Or, perhaps, now?" With a light touch of the reins, he guided his pair into Haymarket. "Then we need not spoil our supper with a topic that is so obviously distasteful to you."

"Or we need not even take supper together at all."

"That would not be my preference, but, I promise you, it will be your decision alone."

Anna switched hands on the parasol. "And what do you wish to know, Lord Darringford?"

"To start with, Miss von Hermannstadt," he said, his voice remaining light and pleasant, "why do you not demand to know what business of mine your ring could possibly be?"

She was glad that she was seated now, or her knees surely would have buckled. Of course he must wonder!

"My lord, I have always known that the ring in my possession is the Darringford Ruby."

Again he turned his gaze on her. "You puzzle me, ma'am. I did not think to get the truth from you in such a blunt and straightforward manner."

"Why not, pray tell?" She sat up straighter. "What *did* you expect? *Lies?*"

"In a manner of speaking . . . yes."

"I may be an actress, my lord. But I am not a liar. At least," she added, "not an accomplished one."

This drew a wry chuckle. "Truth, indeed, Miss von Hermannstadt. I noted your lack of accomplishment in that quarter when we spoke of my visit to the Carpathian Mountains."

"*You* spoke of it. I merely listened. And I did not lie! When you asked if I was familiar with the town and castle, I told you yes."

"So you did. And then you asked me to leave."

She had no reply to that, and for a while they rode in silence. They were already in the Strand, would turn off for Tavistock Street presently.

She was about to speak when she remembered Szeben and willed herself to bolt the mental barrier against his intrusion.

"Lord Darringford—"

"Miss von Hermannstadt—"

They had spoken simultaneously, and simultaneously they fell silent.

Anna saw they were passing Southampton Street. "Should we not turn here?" she asked. " 'Tis the most direct way to my lodgings. I was about to ask if you would like to take a dish of tea with me. I am determined, you see, not to avoid your questions again. In fact, I wish to pose a few of my own."

"Sauce for the goose, Miss von Hermannstadt?"

She saw Somerset House looming to their right. "Where are we going?"

"I could not fail to notice that sunlight gives you discomfort, so I was planning to take you to a shady spot by the Strand Stairs. But that was before you invited me. Now I shall leave the decision to you."

"How kind. And before my invitation, you meant to simply abduct me?"

"Abduct? Yes, I daresay that is what it would have amounted to if you would not agree, but I doubt it would have been a *simple* undertaking."

She slanted a look at him, saw that he was smiling, and felt quite unaccountably lighthearted. In the sunlight—he still wore no hat—he did not look quite so much like that other Darringford. Or did he? Perhaps it was merely the smile that made him different. And he had a scar. About an inch of it was visible on his left temple, but in the bright light she could see it continue under the thick, dark hair above his ear.

She said, "Let us proceed to your shady spot, then. I doubt you'd have found a competent lad in Tavistock Street to mind your horses. We've turned into quite a thieves' den there, I fear, and you might have lost both the curricle and pair before you'd enjoyed your first sip of tea."

"I shall keep that in mind when I call upon you next."

She had no response to this and watched in silence as he guided his pair into a narrow lane leading south, to the Thames. He stopped beneath an ancient chestnut tree, already in leaf and splendid to look at with its white blooms dashed with red.

She wrinkled her nose. "I'd forgotten how bad the river smells."

"You do not venture out much, do you, Miss von Hermannstadt?"

"Rarely. And I won't complain. It's not quite as bad here as the odor around the theater. And now I smell lilacs. How delightful." She looked around. "I wonder where they grow?"

"Will this do, then?"

"Very nicely, thank you." Shutting her parasol, she placed it beside the hatbox at her feet.

"The shade is dense enough?"

She was very aware of him, so close that their shoulders almost touched. She moved a little, turning sideways to look at him, and found that she was facing him squarely, since he had turned as well.

"I shall not swoon, my lord, if that is what you fear."

"I did. And if you had seen yourself when I encountered you on Bond Street, you would not wonder at my concern. You looked as pale as a ghost. At least, as pale as the one you revive so dramatically in your play."

"Pale, indeed, then, since her costume consists of hose and bodice knitted of fine, bleached wool and a white shroud. And what little skin is showing is covered in white paint. But I am quite well now. Pray let us get to the point."

"Certainly. Though I fear the topic of the Darringford Ruby is as discomfiting to you as the topic of your sensitivity to light."

Her breath caught. "My lord? I'm afraid I do not follow you."

"No?" His gaze was probing. "Then, I must beg your pardon."

Momentarily distracted by one of the horses taking exception to a bee buzzing close to its ear, Darringford turned away from her.

She studied his profile, the strong, capable hands that held the reins so lightly yet controlled the shying horse without difficulty. How different the outing would be if their topic of discussion could be other than the ring. If they could be . . . friends. If . . .

What madness possessed her to entertain such notions! No, if she was in need of a friend, Szeben would have to do.

When the bee had returned to higher altitudes and the horse quieted, he said, "Miss von Hermannstadt, if you knew the ring belongs to my family, why have you not tried to return it? We are not very difficult to find, you know."

The ring.

"The Fourth Viscount Darringford," she said stiffly, "and, therefore, his descendants, forfeited any rights to the ring."

His brow furrowed. "How? And are you saying it has been in your family ever since my great-grandfather lost it, close on ninety years ago?"

"He did not lose it, my lord. It was taken from him."

"Stolen? But then you *should* have—"

"It was *taken*," she repeated, her whole body suddenly bathed in perspiration.

"Why?"

"In payment for the life he took." She struggled not to succumb to memories, not to allow emotion to color her voice. "If he had valued his own life, then he would have been condemned to death. But he was so completely uncaring whether he lived or died—whether *anybody* lived or died—that it was decided to take the only thing he did value: the ring."

That had been the gypsies' vote, and theirs had prevailed. Szeben had wanted Darringford's death. And Anna—she had wanted his blood and to change him into one of them. To her, there was no greater punishment.

Darringford was staring at her. "Whose life did he take?"

"She was a young gypsy woman." Anna's voice was toneless. The ribbons of her bonnet seemed too tight all of a sudden. With unsteady fingers, she retied them. "Her name was Marika."

He frowned at her but did not speak. And Anna was glad he did not interrupt. The sorry tale must be told quickly, lest pain and anger overpower her once more, as they had done the night she met Darringford at the theater.

"Darringford raped her," she said quickly, baldly. "Marika was pledged to a young man of a related tribe. The rape not only dishonored her, but him and both tribes as well. She killed herself."

Again, he frowned. "Are you certain?"

"Of course I am certain," she snapped. "Her slippers, shawl, and the gold bracelet given her by her betrothed were found atop the cliff and, when the tide receded, shreds of her skirt among the rocks below."

For a brief yet oddly reassuring instant, he placed a hand atop her clenched fists. "I am sorry."

After a brief silence, he said, "It happened a long time ago, yet you are affected as if it was only yesterday. Almost as if . . . you knew the young woman personally."

The image of Marika, singing, dancing, laughing, flashed through Anna's mind. Marika, of the wildly curling auburn hair and sparkling green eyes . . . so like Anna's own little Marika an eternity ago. For a while, she had been able to pretend that her daughter lived, that she had grown into a beautiful young woman with life, love, and happiness awaiting her.

Anna fleetingly touched the locket inside her gown, companion piece to the locket Marika had worn. She looked at Darringford and once more saw the man who'd held the struggling girl pinned to the ground. The man who, sated and triumphant, had laughed in Anna's face when she came running to Marika's aid.

Pain and rage engulfed her. She saw his face, so close. The hint of vein above his neckcloth. With a cry, Anna would have lunged at him, but he caught her arms and held her fast.

"No, Anna," he said quietly. "I am not the one you seek to punish."

His very calm doused the frenzy consuming her.

"I beg your pardon," she said shakily, feeling ill and not a little frightened.

He released her, picking up the reins he must have dropped. "And I beg yours. Please believe that I do not deliberately set out to distress you."

She saw only sincerity in his gaze, and concern. But she was all right now. She could look at him and feel nothing but gratitude for his calm acceptance of her sudden rage.

"And I apologize for using your given name. I meant no disrespect, Miss von Hermannstadt. It merely seemed right at the moment."

Again, his sincerity was clear, and she nodded. She forced herself to ask, "Do you have more questions, my lord?"

He gave a wry chuckle. "My dear ma'am, if only you knew how many questions. And how long they've plagued me!"

She steeled herself. "Then, ask away."

"Only if you're certain you are stout enough for further interrogation."

"Quite stout," she lied.

"Miss von Hermannstadt, how did you learn the

story of the ring? Were you told—" He broke off, scowling. "Tarnation! I beg your pardon, ma'am, but I see the one I'm beginning to think of as my nemesis. And he's approaching in a hurry. What do you wish me to do?"

Filled with foreboding, Anna turned. From the direction of Somerset Place, Vladim Szeben came striding toward them. She had blocked him from invading her mind, but there was no way to prevent his finding her if he was determined to do so. And he would be upon them in another minute or two.

"Shall I send him on his way?" asked Darringford.

If Szeben were a mere mortal . . .

But even then she would not have Darringford try. It was best if she was not in his company, at least for a while.

"No. Allow him to accompany me to my lodgings."

"You would have to walk!" he protested.

"Pray don't argue, my lord."

"Then, permit me to collect you at the theater tonight. We shall have that supper I promised. And no questions about the ring."

"No? But I was under the impression your questions were urgent."

"They can wait." He caught her gaze and held it. "Now I am quite content to string them out from meeting to meeting if that gives me the opportunity to see you frequently."

She felt as flustered as she did as a young girl when Walter asked her for the first time to ride out with him, and called herself sharply to order. "My lord—"

"Anna!" Szeben was still several paces away, but she knew him well and recognized the dangerous note in his usually expressionless voice. "I've been looking for you."

She gave Darringford her hand. "Good day, my lord. I thank you for coming to my rescue on Bond Street."

"My pleasure."

All of a sudden, the horses grew restive. Darringford gave a curt nod to Szeben, who had reached the curricle and stood with his hand imperatively extended to Anna. "One moment, Szeben. Let me steady my pair. Don't know what got into them. They're not usually so skittish unless something spooks them."

When he had the grays under control, he turned once more to Anna as she gathered parasol and hatbox, and murmured, for her ears alone, "One question I would like answered tonight."

"Yes, my lord?"

"Miss von Hermannstadt, what is Szeben to you?"

Chapter 4

. . . and Shadows Future

The question startled Anna. Were it not for Szeben's presence, she would have demanded that Darringford explain himself. As it was, she murmured another thank-you and allowed Szeben to help her from the curricle.

Darringford's gaze was on her. "Miss von Hermannstadt, I cannot like it that you will have to walk. If necessary, I can take you both wherever you wish. It'll be a bit of a squeeze, I daresay, but not impossible."

"Unnecessary." Szeben took Anna's hatbox and parasol. "I have a hackney waiting at Somerset House. If you wish to be of assistance, direct the driver here."

Darringford's gaze did not waver from Anna. Upon her nod, he said, "Very well. I shall send the hackney. Until tonight, then, Miss von Hermannstadt."

Anna did not watch him drive off. She could not. Seeing the distance widen between them would only magnify the sensation of heaviness that settled on her. But what one had to do with the other, she did not understand, since every moment in Darringford's presence was filled with apprehension of what he would ask or say next.

Not *every* moment.

"You're besotted," said Szeben.

She rounded on him. "And you presume too much! What has come over you that you must watch my every step? And say horrid things that are absolutely untrue!"

Anna started up the lane to the Strand, uncaring whether Szeben followed with her parasol or not.

He did, taking her arm and shading both of them. "Do you deny that you are attracted to him? And don't lie. I can always tell."

"I have no reason to lie, and I'll tell you precisely what I feel when I am with him. I feel alive! I feel . . . like a woman again. A flesh-and-blood woman, Vladim! Not the empty shell I've been so long."

A dangerous light flared in his usually flat, obsidian eyes. He blinked, and the spark was gone. His voice was silky cool. "You've seen him twice, nay, thrice, if you count that first meeting. That night, you certainly came alive. But not like a woman, Anna. You were pure, vengeful immortal."

She winced. Not only that first meeting, but also today.

"That reaction was not to *him*. You know it, Vladim! If only he did not look quite so much like that other Darringford."

"He cannot change his looks."

"Of course not. And I shall prove to you and, more importantly, to myself that I can master the demons in me. I vow, I will!"

"Such passion, my love."

"Don't call me that!"

He merely continued as if she had not interrupted. "It's admirable but, I fear, quite misdirected."

A hackney coach turned into the lane from the Strand, wheels and horses' hooves noisy on the cobbles. Darringford had been as good as his word.

More calmly, Anna said, "I am not changing into a monster, Vladim. I am *not.*"

The coach stopped.

"Not even when you want his blood?" Szeben asked.

"I do *not* want his blood."

The hackney driver shouted, "Do ye want me services, or not?"

The man's demand had followed her words so promptly that Anna gasped. Her sense of the ridiculous took over, and she choked on a bubble of laughter. She whispered, "Is he offering his blood?"

"To Tavistock Street," Szeben told the driver. He opened the coach door. "Get in, Anna. You've been in the sun too long."

"Don't sneer. It does not become you. And it is uncivil." She climbed into the hackney. "Darringford treats me the way I used to be treated. Not as if I were an imbecile, the way you're wont to do."

"Never that. I merely give you the guidance you so woefully need."

Anna did not even hear him. "And not like an actress either, to be ogled and subjected to improper advances. Darringford treats me as if I were the lady I was meant to be."

"But you're not a lady, Anna. You are one of us." Szeben adjusted the tattered and begrimed window shades before sitting down beside her, just in time to avoid a tumble as the coach started off with a lurch.

"How old do you think he is, Vladim?"

"Past thirty. Why do you ask?"

"Do you know if he is married?"

Szeben gripped her shoulder. "What is this, Anna? Why this fervent interest in a man who can be nothing to you?"

"And why *not?*" She shook off his hand. "He is . . . warm. And kind. And—"

"And he wants the ring."

"He can have it."

"And if he wants you as well? Will he have you, Anna?"

She drew back from the icy cold in his voice.

"Will you be his lover, Anna?"

"You forget yourself. What I will or will not do is my concern alone."

"And mine. I have looked after you for two centuries. You cannot expect me to be indifferent now."

She held her temper in check. "You do not own me, Vladim. What I expect is a measure of privacy."

The rest of the short distance to Tavistock Street was covered in silence.

When the coach stopped, Szeben helped her out. "You forget how well I know you. And I can promise you that any liaison between you and Darringford will only lead to eternal damnation—for both of you."

Having been duly forewarned by the footman that Mr. Rossiter was awaiting him in the study, Darringford's mood was not precisely charitable when he entered the room. Henry, immediately after Szeben, was too much to bear for the most stalwart of men.

Darringford went straight to the tray of decanters and glasses on an octagonal pedestal table next to his desk. "What is it, Henry?" His hand tightened on the decanter he was about to pick up. "Not Gareth, I trust?"

"Told you earlier that the young rascal's fully recovered, didn't I? Stop fretting so much over the boy. Between you and Lydia, he'll be mollycoddled to no end." Contrary to his words, Henry looked gratified. "Won't let him out of her sight now. Takes him wherever she goes. Took him to call on Lady Sefton this morning!"

Concern laid to rest, Darringford said bitingly, "In that case, to what do I owe the pleasure of your unexpected company?"

Henry squinted at him, then nodded sagely. "The Divine Anna got under your skin. Still not wanting to show you the ring, eh?"

"Shouldn't you go home?" Darringford poured. "Lydia must be wondering where you are."

"I've *been* home. Here, I say, if that's the claret I had last time, you might offer me some. Devilish good stuff. Where'd you find it?"

Darringford poured another glass. "Drink and return to your wife."

"No need to be uncivil, coz. Just came to tell you that Lydia will see Miss von Hermanntal and—"

"Hermannstadt," Darringford corrected curtly. "And I'll thank Lydia not to poke her aristocratic nose in my affairs."

"Hermannstadt, of course. Dashed awkward name, if you ask me." Henry sampled the claret appreciatively. "In any case, Lydia says what you need is a woman's touch. She'll—"

"Lydia will do precisely nothing, Henry."

Henry opened his mouth, but Darringford forestalled him. "Drink up. And not another word on the matter."

Henry stared at him, then finished his wine, and rose. "I understand, Gareth. Lydia warned me. Said you'd left your sickbed much too soon and would suffer the consequences before the day is out. And Wheatley said you did not even take your cane today."

When Darringford only opened the study door, Henry reluctantly minced off, patting him on the shoulder in leave-taking. "I'll look in on you tomorrow. Wouldn't be surprised if I found you prostrate again."

Darringford shut the door. He took a key from his desk drawer. For a moment, he only looked at the key, but not really seeing it, as he considered his next move regarding Miss von Hermannstadt. He had not been quite truthful with her, but neither had she told him everything he needed to know.

"And you, sir," he addressed the gentleman in a portrait above the mantelpiece, "you have lied by omission. That was not at all well done."

Except that the man in the portrait wore his hair tied back and his clothing was of a different era, it could have been Darringford himself posing with his lady. But it was William Rossiter, Fourth Viscount Darringford, in the painting, and Darringford told him, "I should have suspected your history was worse, I suppose, since you admitted yourself to being a rogue. But that is neither here nor there. I do believe it is advisable to hasten the pace. Our Anna has a mighty inconvenient protector. Dangerous, too, I should think."

He strode to the back of the room, where, framed by windows overlooking a narrow stretch of garden and the mews behind the house, stood a mahogany cabinet.

Glancing over his shoulder at the portrait, he raised a brow. "You're quite correct, sir. A spot of danger has never yet deterred me. That much, at least, we do have in common. And speaking of Szeben, that's precisely what had me mystified. That Anna is not like him. Not at all."

Darringford unlocked the cabinet doors and opened them. On the middle shelf sat eight slender, leather-bound volumes. His great-grandfather's journals.

The tiresome performance was over at last. Anna had not seen Darringford, or sensed his presence, and was glad of it. He had attended the performance once, and that was more than enough. She did not want him to carry a stage image of her when they went to supper. *A Ghost Revived* was such an embarrassment, poorly written, with the thinnest of silly plots and the most ridiculous of characters. It was more scandalous than anything they had ever presented, and Szeben would not hear of changing the billing, since *Ghost* was raking in more profits in a few short weeks than they had seen this past twelvemonth. Not even the Lenten season and threat of fine or incarceration made him change his mind. They must be in dire straits, indeed.

Somewhat to her surprise, Szeben was not in her dressing room when she rushed in to change.

"Marthe, where is Mr. Szeben?" she asked breathlessly, already shrugging out of the low-cut scarlet gown that far from turning her into the witch the play demanded, only made her look like a disreputable "lady of the night."

"Haven't seen him. Not for an hour at least. Want me to look fer him, Miss Anna?"

"Not at all." Donning a robe, Anna sat down before the dressing mirror. She wiped off rouge and kohl, then brushed her hair before twisting it in a loose knot at her nape.

"Do you have the warm water?" She slid the ruby off her finger. "Hurry, Marthe! I want to scrub off the rest of this greasepaint."

"Won't hurt to keep his lordship waitin' a minute or two, Miss Anna." The costumer splashed water into a basin. "Won't hurt neither if ye'd wipe that keen look off yer face. Don't want him to think you're a plum, ripe an' ready for his pickin', do ye?"

Speechless, Anna stared at the older woman. At last, she looked at herself in the mirror. And, heart suddenly racing, she picked up the candle and held it aloft for a closer, better look. Did her image seem crisper? There was color in her cheeks, the result of a brisk scrubbing, no doubt. Her eyes, though. . . . That bright sparkle could not possibly have anything to do with the removal of kohl.

Walter used to say that her eyes always told him what she was feeling. Had she looked like this when she was expecting him? How vague, at times, her recollection of life with her husband, while every moment with her daughter was etched in her memory. Painfully so. Which was why she did not often permit herself to think of those all too few years when she had been a mother.

"Miss Anna? Water's cooling."

Anna rose, washed, then donned the only elaborate gown she owned, of gentian blue silk, with an overskirt of midnight blue lace. Her new hat, wide-brimmed and shallow, matched the silk of her gown. It had seemed like a good omen when she saw the hat. The only alteration it had required was the removal of a spray of silk lilies of the valley. Even the hatmaker had agreed that the resulting simplicity was stunning.

A knock on the dressing room door sent her scrambling for gloves and wrap while Marthe admitted Gareth Rossiter, Seventh Viscount Darringford. Anna did not pull on the gloves. Instead, she put the ring back on her finger.

"Good evening, Miss von Hermannstadt." Darringford's appreciative look made her feel warm all over. "Would you care to take supper with me at the Piazza?"

"I'd be delighted, my lord."

Taking his proffered arm, she walked beside him—it felt like floating—down the ancient, creaking stairs, through the public-cum-Green Room thronging with raucous males and giggling actresses, dancers, and the occasional lightskirts whose catcalls during the performance were lewder than those of their male companions. She caught a fleeting glimpse of Henry Rossiter with a female so out of place that Anna took a second look. But Mr. Rossiter and the aristocratic-looking lady beside him had disappeared.

"Miss von Hermannstadt." Darringford's voice was rueful. "How have I offended?"

"Offended? Whatever are you talking about?"

"I am talking about being ignored, Miss von Hermann-stadt."

"I beg your pardon." Spontaneously, she made up her mind. "Lord Darringford, I feel obliged to make a confession."

"Yes, Miss von Hermannstadt?"

It seemed to her that he sounded inordinately interested, making her wonder what he expected to hear. From an actress, most likely something scandalous.

"I am a widow, you see. I shouldn't be using the title 'Miss' at all."

There was the slightest pause, but when he spoke, his voice gave no hint of surprise or disappointment, or whatever it was that made him hesitate. "Indeed? If your bereavement is recent, permit me to express my condolences."

"No. Not at all recent, my lord. I merely mentioned it because—"

It was her turn to hesitate. Why did she feel compelled to tell him?

"Because?" he prompted, steering her across the street to a waiting carriage. "Because you're incurably honest, perhaps?"

"In truth, I do not know."

She breathed deeply. The air might be sooty, but the dark of the night was soothing, reviving. Especially, since the moon was hidden and could not remind her of time passing inexorably.

She studied the crest on the carriage door. "How splendid, my lord. But I would have preferred the curricle."

"So would I. However, there's always the awkward question what to do with it while we partake of supper."

He handed her into the carriage. The coachman, apparently, knew where to go, for they started to roll as soon as Darringford had shut the door and settled beside her.

"Is von Hermannstadt your maiden name, then?" he asked. "Or was it your husband's?"

"My husband's."

As soon as she said it, she wondered if she had made a mistake. But Darringford had already changed the topic and was asking if she was agreeable to lobster patties and champagne at the Bedford Coffeehouse, or if she would prefer something else. She dismissed the feeling of unease and assured him that she liked lobster patties very well.

Covent Garden and the Piazza weren't far from the Venus Theatre, and before long, she was handed out of the carriage again and escorted into the famed old coffeehouse. Darringford had arranged for a corner table. He was holding her chair and about to seat her, when she saw his jaw tighten. It was for such a fleeting moment only that she would have missed the expression if she had not been looking at him directly. She followed his gaze to a nearby box.

Seated there, with a young female of great beauty and little discretion in her selection of a gown, was Vladim Szeben. Nothing could surpass the urbanity of his smile— or the coldness of his eyes—as he rose and bowed to Anna.

She rarely initiated silent communication with him, but she did now. *"You're vile, Vladim. How did you know Darringford would take me to Bedford's?"*

"You are lovely, my Anna. But you're not for him, remember that."

The words chilled her.

She became aware of Darringford's hand on her arm. He said, "Will you not be seated, Miss von Hermann-stadt?"

Firmly, she barred Szeben from invading her mind. "If it is all the same to you, my lord, may we go some-where else?"

His gaze flicked once more to Szeben; then he bowed and without further ado led her out into the night to wait beneath the lighted colonnade.

"My coachman has instructions to circle the square, so the carriage should be here presently. Miss von Her-mannstadt—" Darringford hesitated. "Are you afraid of Szeben?"

"Afraid? No, not at all. At least not for myself."

"But for others? Then, I wonder you did not warn that young woman."

Her breath caught. She had not considered the woman, but him. Her apprehension was on his behalf, but she could scarcely tell him so.

In any case, he believed the woman in some danger. Anna did not dare look at him. What did he know? Nothing, surely. He could not possibly know how Szeben used the females he sought out from time to time.

Darringford was watching her keenly; she had been silent too long.

"Szeben is most generous," she said hastily. "The young woman will be well compensated, even set up with some small shop, if that is her wish. Which is more, I daresay, than she might expect from many a lord."

"But no more than she deserves?"

While Anna once more searched for words, he turned away from her, toward the rattle of a carriage ap-proaching.

"There we are. Knew we would not have to wait long. Miss von Hermannstadt—" Darringford faced her. "Anna, is Szeben your lover?"

This question, or the reply, required no thought. "No, Lord Darringford. Much as he might seem so with his manner toward me, Szeben is not my lover."

A jaunty smile lit his features. "That's all right, then. I had to know."

"Why? It is none of your concern."

"But it will be." He opened the carriage door and let down the steps for her. "Home," he told the coachman, and settled beside her on the plushly covered seat.

Anna stood up. "How dare you? Merely because I am an actress, it does not mean—"

"I beg your pardon." He steadied her as the carriage started to roll. "Only please sit down again before you fall. I have no designs on you other than to give you the supper I promised. And to show you something. Won't you trust me, Anna?"

She could not distinguish his features, but the deep voice was, indeed, trust inspiring.

She sat down. "Why do you call me by my given name? Do I no longer merit formality and respect?"

"Definitely respect. But I hope you will agree to dispense with formality. Anna is such a beautiful name."

"Thank you. Lord Darringford—"

"My name is Gareth."

"Lord Darringford, before I enter your house I must know why my connection with Szeben will be your concern."

"The reason is simple. Because, my dear Anna—and I hereby give fair warning—I plan to court you."

Chapter 5

The Truth Revealed

Anna sat bolt upright. "You are mad!"

"Yes," he said so cheerfully that she began to doubt his reason in earnest.

She thought back over their meetings. Twice she had attacked him, and never had he flinched. Only a madman would consider her behavior nothing out of the ordinary. And only someone as scatterbrained as she would have noticed nothing amiss with his lack of concern.

But he had shown concern. For her. He was kind, and seemed utterly reliable. Warm. And he said he would court her. Was this madness? Yes, but only because the thought of being courted made her pulse race.

She glanced out the carriage window. "Is this Piccadilly? How much farther do we go?"

"Darringford House sits in Upper Brook Street. Patience, Anna. What I have to show you will explain much."

She said no more but sank back into her corner of the seat and listened to the clatter of the carriage wheels and the horses' hooves. If he was mad, she ought to jump out. But, of course, she did nothing of the kind.

Instead, she allowed herself to dream of continued meetings, of companionship, of long talks that would bring them to close understanding of each other, of touches that kindled warmth and longing, of kisses. . . .

With a start, she recalled her errant thoughts. What she had shared with Walter, that beautiful, breathtaking courtship an eternity ago, she could never have again.

She glanced at the man seated beside her. He was looking out the window on his side of the carriage, his profile briefly illuminated by a street lamp. How pensive he looked. How serious all of a sudden, almost grim. Yet she was not afraid. Not of him.

Szeben, she acknowledged, was correct in one respect. Not totally, of course, for she was *not* besotted. But she would admit to being strongly drawn to Darringford.

And he could be nothing to her. Ever. For his own sake.

Yet, surely, there could be no harm in entering his house, in seeing what he wanted to show her. No harm in continuing their acquaintance, in being a woman again. A lady. Just for a short while, until Szeben decided that they must move on.

When the footman opened the door, Darringford ordered a light supper to be served in half an hour, then led Anna straight into the study.

The room was well prepared, not too dark and not too bright, lit by a candelabrum on a low table flanked by two chairs at the back of the study, and by a bracket light on either side of the portrait above the mantelpiece. Although he could not have known that they would be taking supper here, he had planned all along to bring Anna to Darringford House. Into the study.

And now, how was he to proceed? He was almost certain that he knew who Anna was. What she was. Originally, he had meant to confront her with his supposition, but already in their second meeting he had changed his mind. He now wanted her to trust him, to tell him of her own volition. But she would need prompting.

Darringford wavered between one course of action

and another. What he should have done was plan this meeting like a military action and settle on a strategy in advance. He was still weighing his options when Anna spoke.

"You call this your study, my lord? Why, it's as vast as a reception chamber." She had dropped her gloves and wrap on a chair and was strolling around the room, admiring a glass-fronted cabinet here, bending to trace the delicate inlay on a table there. "What lovely furnishings!"

"Made by Thomas Chippendale, well before he reached fame. I believe it was 1746 or thereabouts—it's recorded somewhere. My great-grandfather decided to refurbish much of this house for his second wife. They had lived secluded for over twenty years, but then it was time to present their son at Court."

"Your great-grandfather?" Her eyes had widened. She looked as if she was ready to flee. Then she gave a little shrug. "It does not matter. You will not get a rise out of me tonight. This is simply too beautiful not to be enjoyed. How much I miss the spaciousness, the loftiness of a—"

When she did not continue, he said, "You did not always live in cramped lodgings?"

"No." She gave him a bright smile. "Is it time for supper yet? I am famished, Darringford."

"Thank you."

"For what? Being famished?"

"For at last dropping the 'Lord.' "

She smiled, took up her stroll again. How well she suited this setting. Her walk was graceful, her bearing proud. She would be the perfect mistress of a grand house.

Anna turned and faced the fireplace. She looked up

at the portrait—and stumbled. He was at her side in an instant, but she had regained her equilibrium and was drawing away from him.

"That—" She pointed a not too steady hand at the large painting. "That is Darringford. And . . . and Marika."

"Yes."

She stepped back, until she came up against a chair. Without taking her eyes off the portrait, she sat down.

"How is it possible? Marika and Darringford? She did not kill herself?" A lone tear slid down her face, but she did not seem to notice. "I do not understand. He . . . made her his mistress? But, no. She would not be in the portrait."

"They married. Marika was my great-grandmother." Darringford poured claret into two glasses. He approached Anna. "Will you drink this? It's bracing."

She looked at the glass as if he were offering poison. "What is it?"

"Just a little wine. Claret. It'll do you good, Anna."

She accepted the glass but only held it. "Why did you not tell me this morning?"

"I should have. I was about to speak when you mentioned Marika, then decided to hear all you had to say. I did not know he had raped her."

"Then, what *do* you know?"

She looked so small and vulnerable in that large, claw-footed chair that he wanted to put a supportive arm around her, but he knew that would be a grave mistake.

He said, "I was under the impression that he had seduced her, then, when he learned that she was with child, decided to marry her."

Anna sniffed in disbelief.

"I know he was a rake, a profligate, at least for part

of his life." Darringford drank some of his claret. "I suppose he was capable of the dastardly deed you accuse him of, and he probably would not admit his misdeed later on. What man would want it known just how low he had sunk?"

"So you know part of the story. How did you learn of it?"

He looked at the portrait. "Well, sir? Do we tell her?"

"You . . . talk to a painting?"

"Alas. A foolish habit I picked up when I first read the rogue's journals. I was a stripling then—which might be considered an excuse for talking out loud? I offer no excuses now."

"His journals?" Anna's interest was caught. She no longer looked as if she was about to swoon. "What did he say about Marika? May I read them?"

"Of course."

Setting her glass down, Anna rose, stepped closer to the portrait and gazed at it intently. "How beautiful she looks. And . . . not unhappy, I believe. But how strange to think of her married. To *Darringford.*"

"No, Anna. *I* am Darringford. And I prefer to hear my name without that touch of disdain you apply to the rogue. Let us call him William, shall we?"

Anna faced him. "What happened? How did they meet again? Why would Marika agree to marry Darr—William?"

"I can only guess at the answer to your last question. She was with child. That is indisputable. Henry, my grandfather, was born seven months after their marriage. Would that not be reason enough?"

"Perhaps. No matter how innocent she was, she had been the instrument of dishonor to two tribes. She could no longer live with her people." Anna's look turned fierce.

"But Marika had friends outside the tribes. She *knew* she was welcome there. They believed she chose death—a painful blow! But to think that she chose *Darringford!*"

"I would not say it was by choice that she ended up with William. You see, he found her unconscious."

"Then, she did jump off the cliff?"

"Yes. She was grievously injured. William took her home."

"And nursed her back to health?" Anna said scathingly. "Why would he? Neither he nor Marika would have known about a child that day."

"I should hope it was remorse that drove him," said Darringford, looking at the portrait of his ancestor, so like a mirror image of himself. "And, to set the record straight, it was the housekeeper who nursed Marika. William did not go near her until she had recovered."

Anna drew a long, ragged breath. "Where are the journals?"

He indicated the table at the back of the study. "There are eight volumes altogether. I've set out the five that pertain to William and Marika. The earlier ones are about his life in India with his first wife and children. They were killed in an uprising."

Anna did not speak but approached the table. For a moment she merely stared down at the journals. Slowly, almost reluctantly, she sat down and picked one up. She flipped through the pages, then set the journal down again as if she could not bear to look at the words penned in bold, masculine strokes.

She looked at Darringford. "Is that what made him so uncaring of life? The death of his first family?"

"I am convinced it is. He loved them deeply." Darringford took the second chair at the table. He tapped one of the journals. "It's all in here. His final entries in

India. There are no entries for the next two and a half years, merely a reference or two later on about having led a life of dissipation in Paris, Venice, London. He starts writing again the night he finds Marika at the foot of the cliff near Darringford Keep in Scotland."

"Yes," Anna said tonelessly. "That is where it all happened."

Her gaze rested on the journals, but Darringford doubted she saw them. She appeared to be looking and listening inside herself, and whatever it was that she saw and heard was obviously painful. If he could spare her pain, he would, but by approaching her that night after the performance, he had set something in motion. Something that he could not define but knew was as inexorable as the change from day to night.

"Anna? What are you thinking?"

She blinked, focused on him. "The ruby. Why was it more precious to William than his own life?"

"You know, of course, that the ruby is valuable by its sheer size and perfection. It was a gift from Queen Elizabeth to one Henry Rossiter upon his creation of Baron Darringford. We weren't viscounts until Charles II, you see, but that is neither here nor there. Suffice it to say that the ruby was worn by the titleholder, down the line to William. But in honor of his wife, he decided to make it a ring that would be worn from then on by all Darringford wives. He had the band tightened, planning to present it to his beloved on their anniversary. He never had the chance. She was killed the night before the anniversary."

Anna looked at her hand where the ruby glowed bloodred against her skin. She picked up another journal, flipped through it.

"That is the last one, Anna." And it might be better if she did not see it just yet. "You should read them in order."

He reached for the volume, but before he could take it from her, it opened to a page that held but a single entry, written in a totally different hand from the previous entries. The letters were unformed, childlike.

> It is Anna ye must court
> My goode friend Anna
> Ye will find the ringe
> She will find herself
> *Marika Darringford*

Anna dropped the journal. "Marika wrote this!"

She looked at him, her eyes accusing. "Is that why you will court me? To get the ring?"

"No, Anna. Dash it, I had planned this quite differently! Or, perhaps, *not* planned would be a better term. If I'd had any forethought, I wouldn't have set that particular volume out until the time was right."

"Why, you're no better than William, and I have a good mind not to give you the ring at all!"

Contrary to her words, she began to tug off the ruby.

Darringford caught her hands. "Keep it."

"No! It feels wrong now!" She withdrew her hands from his, hastily, jerkily, as if she could not bear his touch. "Not that I have forgiven William, don't think I have! And *you!* How could I have been so mistaken in your character!"

"Anna, keep the ring. At least until you've read the journals."

He saw her hesitate and said, "Don't you want to know what William wrote about Marika?"

"I don't understand why she would have married him. If she was injured, unable to leave on her own, she could have sent word to . . . to her friends. They would have fetched her."

"I admit, William should have sent word. But he did not, and Marika lay unconscious for weeks."

"Weeks?" Anna paled. "How long precisely?"

"Just over three weeks."

When she spoke again, her voice was so low that he could not be certain he heard correctly, but he believed she said, "Three weeks. . . . By then we were long gone."

Very softly, Darringford asked, "Anna, were you there?"

She gave a start and looked at him, her eyes wide and frightened. But the fear he saw was at odds with the very convincing astonishment in her voice. "I beg your pardon, my lord?"

"In his journals, William mentions a troupe of players led by a black-haired man with dark, soulless eyes. The players were friends of the gypsies, particularly one actress." He watched her closely. "Her name was Anna von Hermannstadt, and she was teaching Marika to read and write and to speak like a lady."

"That would have been . . . my great-grandmother."

Darringford reached into his coat pocket. His gaze unwavering on Anna, he set a small gold locket and chain on the table.

Anna leaned over the table.

"Marika's," she whispered. A statement, not a question.

He opened it. The miniature inside was water stained, but the resemblance to the woman seated across from him was unmistakable.

"Is this you, Anna?"

"No!" She sat back, brushing an elbow against one

of the journals but caught it before it could slide off the table. "It is my . . . great-grandmother."

"You're such a poor liar."

"And you show a severe lack of civility, my lord." Anna rose abruptly. "I have the companion piece to your locket. Mine contains a miniature of Marika. My great-grandmother commissioned them a few months before . . ."

Letting the words trail, she once more approached the fireplace and gazed up at the portrait. The light from the bracket lamps bathed her in a soft, golden glow, but nothing could soften the pain etched in her every feature.

Darringford went to her. "If William had sent word, you would have seen her again. Is that what you're thinking, Anna?"

She turned, tears streaming down her face. She looked at him for a long moment, an eternity, while he willed her to trust him.

She straightened, an idiosyncracy he had noticed before when she was about to say something unexpected.

"Yes." Voice and look were defiant. "Yes, it is what I am thinking. If only—" Her voice broke.

Throwing caution to the wind, Darringford enfolded her in his arms. She stood stiff and trembling but did not pull away.

"Lean your head against me, Anna."

When she complied, he drew her closer. Her head just reached the spot where his heart was beating. She felt so right. Or would feel right, if only she weren't trembling so hard or standing poker stiff—as if she was afraid.

A surge of protectiveness rushed through him. She

had admitted to being there, with Marika and William. Close on ninety years ago. Yet how hollow felt his victory. And how disquieting.

He stroked her thick golden brown hair. If only she hadn't twisted it in a dashed awkward knot. Now that he felt the silky texture, he wanted to feel it loose, run his fingers through the length of it. He grimaced ruefully. 'Twas what he had longed to do ever since he first saw her on the stage, only he hadn't been man enough to admit it. He had pretended his interest in her was purely because of the Darringford Ruby and everything that her possession of it implied.

And now that his suspicions were confirmed, he could only wonder what their fate would be.

He extended his gentle stroking to her neck and shoulders; but she remained unyielding and stiff, and her breaths came fast and shallow as if she was on the alert, listening, waiting for something disastrous to happen.

The only disaster Darringford could think of was Szeben, and surely the man would not dare intrude here. But, then, Szeben had already intruded, or he wouldn't be thinking of the eternal nuisance.

Bending his head, he placed a gentle kiss atop her head, wishing she would look up and offer her lips. He heard the thud of his heart and called himself all manner of fool. A fool who was about to plunge into an abyss.

His embrace must have had a soothing effect on Anna after all. Her body was pliant at last, melting against him, forcing him to admit how much her closeness mattered. But her surrender lasted only the fleetest of moments.

She pulled away, giving him an uncertain look. "Thank you."

"There's no need to thank me."

"But there is. No one has held me in such a very long time. And now I must go."

"Most definitely not." He caught her hand. "Anna, don't you see, now is not the time to cry craven. We must talk. And there's supper. I'm sure we shall be summoned any moment now."

As if on cue, there was a scratch on the door. The housekeeper entered just as Anna snatched her hand away.

The woman curtsied. "Supper is served, my lord. And I do beg pardon for the delay. Cook was having one of his tantrums, I fear, but he recovered fast and outdid himself with a—"

"Thank you, Mrs. Forge. Tell Cook I appreciate his efforts."

"Yes, my lord. And begging your pardon, but there's callers. I told them you're not at home, but they insist on seeing you."

Not his heart, then, Darringford thought ruefully. It must have been the thud of the knocker he had heard.

"Tell them I'm otherwise engaged, Mrs. Forge."

"No, please see your friends," said Anna, picking up her gloves and wrap. "I am leaving. I should never have come here in the first place."

Unaccountably, Darringford felt panicked—a strange feeling for a man who prided himself on his unflappable calm. But he did not want Anna to go, and he had not the simplest notion how to hold her.

"You're staying," he told Anna, then commanded the housekeeper to send the callers to the devil.

"But it's Mrs. Henry, my lord. And the other, well, I didn't catch his name, but—"

"It is Szeben, my good woman," said Darringford's nemesis, pushing past the housekeeper, and followed on his heel by Lydia Rossiter.

Chapter 6

A Courtship

Anna cast one look at Szeben, a quick look but so scathing it should have withered him, then stared—or, perhaps she was gawking—with undisguised curiosity at the woman referred to as Mrs. Henry by the housekeeper. The same woman she had briefly glimpsed with Henry Rossiter at the Venus Theatre.

The housekeeper had disappeared, and Mrs. Henry took the stage. Neither acknowledging Darringford's presence, nor waiting for him to greet her or to make introductions, she swept regally toward Anna.

She pointed an accusing finger at Anna's hand clutching a pair of long, midnight blue gloves and proudly displaying the Darringford Ruby. "That is *our* ring, and I'll thank you to hand it over this instant."

"Lydia!" Darringford's voice was sharp. "May I remind you that this is *my* house, and Miss von Hermannstadt is *my* guest."

"Fiddlesticks!" Lydia Rossiter did not look at Darringford but kept staring down her aristocratic nose at Anna. "I told Henry you'd make a mull of it, Darringford. And see if I wasn't right. She is still wearing our ring."

"*My* ring," Darringford said with dangerous calm.

His tone of voice gave Mrs. Rossiter pause at last. She did not speak for the length of time it took to draw three deep breaths, time enough for Anna to fling her wrap around her shoulders and walk away.

She extended her hand to Darringford. "Good night. Szeben will see me home."

"When will I see you again?"

He held on to her hand, as if he knew—and was determined to drive home—how much she craved the warmth of his touch. Yes, she wanted to see him again, but common sense must prevail.

"You won't. Please let go of me."

His grip stayed firm. "You know I must see you." He lowered his voice. "I've been searching for you ever since I saw the miniature of you."

Madness, to allow his words to quicken her pulse. And dangerous to acknowledge them. She had been foolish earlier, foolish beyond belief.

Mustering firmness, she said, "You're wrong, Darringford. That is a painting of my great-grandmother."

"Fibster." Soft as a caress, his voice touched her ear. "And if I were wrong, then you'd have no reason at all to refuse me. I shall call on you tomorrow."

She was painfully aware of Lydia Rossiter at some distance but, undoubtedly, watching avidly; of Szeben, quite uncharacteristically reticent by the study door.

"Not tomorrow, Darringford. Give me time to think."

Bowing, he drew her hand to his lips. The brief, warm touch on her skin left her trembling, wanting the feel of his arms around her again.

"I'll give you three days," he said, releasing her.

Immediately, Szeben was at her side.

"I'll have the carriage brought around," said Darringford.

"Quite unnecessary," said Szeben. "I have a hackney waiting."

With a nod to Mrs. Henry Rossiter, Anna left on Szeben's arm, aware of the woman's dagger-sharp gaze on her back.

The silence between them lay thick and heavy and lasted throughout the drive to Tavistock Street. Szeben dismissed the hackney and followed Anna into her rooms. She did not want to face him but knew it would be useless to tell him to go. All she could do was shutter her mind to him.

Szeben closed the sitting room door behind them. "You are placing us in danger, Anna."

Her hands were not quite steady as she lit the candles on the credenza and table. He could not possibly have overheard the low-voiced exchange between her and Darringford about the miniature, but his instincts were preternaturally keen. He always knew when they were exposed. She had seen it happen twice. With the gypsies, whom they had first encountered in Hungary; they became their friends. But, perhaps, it was not surprising that Szeben did not dare harm the old woman, Marika's grandmother, a soothsayer, since it was the power of a gypsy's curse that had created the first of them, the undead. Another time it was a tavern keeper in Spain. The man was about to denounce them; he had not lived to see the light of day.

Anna shuddered.

Setting down the tinderbox, she turned to face Szeben. "I saw Mrs. Rossiter at the theater. What kind of husband is Henry Rossiter to bring his wife to a performance like ours?"

"What happened with Darringford, Anna? How did he find us out?"

"Darringford? What are you talking about, Vladim? Do you suppose Mrs. Rossiter was the driving force behind the theater visit? She strikes me as a woman who—"

"Anna!" Szeben cut in. "What did you tell Darringford?"

Quite calmly, she said, "We spoke of the ring, of course."

"Of course," he echoed sarcastically. "And what did you tell him? That I would have feasted on his great-grandfather's blood and killed him if the gypsies had not found the pouch hanging from his neck and discovered that the ruby meant more to him than life?"

"Don't speak like a monster!"

"Then, stop toying with me, Anna. Tell me what happened. And remember, I always know when you're lying."

That was indisputable. Even Darringford could tell when she fibbed. But never had there been so much at stake. She had placed Darringford in danger. She must now guard his life.

With a tired sigh—not even pretense—she sank into a corner of the worn sofa. "Sit down, then. I am exhausted, and I have no wish to crane my neck staring up at you."

"Your exhaustion will be remedied. 'Tis why I came to fetch you from Darringford House." Sitting down beside her, Szeben withdrew a crystal flask from his coat pocket.

Anna recoiled at the mere sight of the flask. "No!"

He removed the stopper. "Drink, Anna."

The despised, familiar scent hit her like a physical blow. She thrashed out blindly with both arms, spilling the noxious fluid over Szeben's hand and her skirt.

"What the devil! Anna, have you lost your mind?"

Anna stared at the crimson stain spreading on lace and silk. The smell made her gag and threatened to bring back unbearable memories.

She jumped up and fled to her bedchamber, kicking the door shut behind her. Retching, she stripped off the gown. She needed water, cold water to erase the smell and stop the stain from spreading. She saw the slop bucket and thrust in as much of the skirt as would fit, then drenched it with water from the pitcher on the washstand, saving a little to scrub her hands.

Szeben knocked on the door. "Anna! Let me help you."

"Go away!"

She could still smell blood and opened the curtains and window.

Szeben commanded, "Anna, come out or I shall fetch you."

And he would be as good as his word. "Toss the flask and wash, and I shall be out presently."

Anna removed her hat, donned a simple gown, all the while listening for sounds from the sitting room. She heard nothing, save for a faint squeaking noise she recognized as the water pump in the kitchen. She could only hope that Marthe would not wake.

For a moment she sat on the edge of the bed, head in hands, trying desperately to collect herself. She would have to face Szeben once more, and she must be calm.

When she entered the sitting room, a faint odor of

blood still lingered. Gritting her teeth, she opened drapes and windows here as well. She picked up a candle and inspected the sofa.

"There was only a small stain," said Szeben, entering. "I have removed it."

"Thank you."

She faced him. He was angry, no doubt about it. But he was holding his temper in check.

"Why, Anna?"

When she did not answer, he said, "You are one of us. I made you so. The taste and smell of blood should be as necessary to you as the dark of night. Instead, you are repulsed. After two centuries, that should no longer be the case. What is it, Anna? What keeps you from accepting your fate?"

She had never heard him speak thus. Yes, there was anger. But there was also puzzlement, and something else. Something that sounded almost like fear. But she must be mistaken. Szeben was never afraid.

"Anna!" No fear or puzzlement in his voice now. "The least you can do is give me an explanation."

"Very well. And may it stop you from bringing more offerings." Steeling herself, she said, "The sight and smell of blood brings back the moment I saw the battered body of my daughter. My precious little Marika."

No matter how she prepared for the image, the pain was never lessened. Razor sharp, it sliced through her. She saw her daughter's face, the lifeless green eyes. And all that blood. On Marika's small, broken body, on the flagstones in the castle yard.

Doubling over, Anna stumbled to a chair and sat there, with her knees drawn to her chest and her arms wrapped tightly around them. If she did not, the pain inside her would balloon to unbearable proportion.

"Anna."

She shook her head. After a moment, she heard Szeben pace in the cramped room. Then his footsteps stilled, just in front of her. She felt his touch, the cold and mercifully brief caress of fingertips on her hair, her cheek, her neck.

"If I did not know better, I'd suspect you're a changeling."

She heard his footsteps once more, heard the sitting room door open.

She looked up and saw him standing in the doorway as if at a loss whether to leave or stay.

"Vladim, did you see the portrait in Darringford's study?"

"The Fourth Viscount and his lady."

"Yes, but did you see—"

"Of course I did. It was Marika."

He was so calm. So matter-of-fact. She stared at him, horrible suspicion dawning.

Slowly she rose and walked toward him. "You knew."

He merely cocked a brow.

"You knew and did not tell me."

He turned to leave. "Rest, my Anna."

"Vladim!" Disbelief and anger warred in her breast. "*Why* did you not tell me?"

"I did not know she had survived until a month after their marriage." He faced her again. "Should I have told you then? Think, Anna! Marriage to Darringford placed her outside the tribe. You could never be friends again—unless you wished to court exposure?"

She was too shaken, too angry, to speak. There was some merit in what he said, but—dash it all—he had no right to govern her life.

"But I do," he said calmly. "And the duty. You see,

you cannot even keep up your guard. I've known yo
thoughts these past few minutes. Without me, yo
would be utterly lost. And now, I bid you good night, n
Anna."

He would give her three days, Darringford had to
her.

On the first day, he sent a posy of forget-me-no

Anna buried her face in the delicate pale blue flo
ers. No, he need not fear that she would forget hir
Ever.

But forget-me-nots meant so much more to her.

In the kitchen, she filled a plain white jug with wate
As she placed the flowers in it and gently tugged the
into a pleasing display, she noticed a square of vellur
folded several times, tucked among the stems. One co
ner was wet, but when she opened it to its full siz
headed in the upper right with the Darringford cres
the bold, masculine scrawl was quite legible, even thoug
a few of the words had run a little.

> *Forget-me-nots—a simple token to signify the start*
> *of my courtship.*
>
> *Darringford*

> *Anna, below is an excerpt I copied from one of*
> *William's journals:*
> *28 April, 1738*
> *Forget-me-nots are in bloom, and Marika has*
> *taken both children down to the brook, as is her*
> *habit every spring. She says it is to celebrate her*
> *friendship with Anna. Anna von Hermannstadt,*
> *that little virago who would have killed me if she*

*could; that actress, who came across me in my
darkest hour. Would that I could apologize to her
now! She, too, had a daughter and would gather
forget-me-nots with the child.*

Yes, she would. Once more, Anna let the tiny blue
blossoms caress her face. Her daughter loved to run barefoot through the soft spring grass, down to the millpond,
where the forget-me-nots grew thick and plentiful, and
where their color was a deeper blue than anywhere else
around *Schloß* Hermannsfels. That last spring, they had
been to the pond on Marika's eighth birthday, and Anna
had woven a crown of forget-me-nots for her beautiful
little daughter.

And when she first saw the other Marika, the gypsy
girl had been twelve or thirteen years old and was gathering forget-me-nots for a crown. Anna's heart had
raced at the sight. She might have been gazing at her
daughter, grown a little taller and sturdier, still running
and dancing barefoot through the grass, long, riotously
curling hair streaming out like a banner. And the girl
had the same name as Anna's daughter. . . .

"Miss Anna?" Marthe had returned from the market
unnoticed and was looking at her in concern. "Why are
ye cryin', dearie? Surely the pretty flowers didn't make
ye sad?"

Anna wiped her damp face with a sleeve. "I'm not sad,
Marthe. Or only a little. I was remembering something
very beautiful."

And that was the truth, Anna acknowledged in some
astonishment. For the first time, memories of her
daughter and the other Marika had been sweet rather
than painful.

"And who sent the posy?" asked Marthe, never bashful. "Not Mr. Szeben, I daresay, or he wouldn't need to fetch an' carry for him."

Carefully folding Darringford's note in half, Ar frowned at the older woman. "What is this about] Szeben? What did he have you fetch and carry?"

"Well, there's this." Setting her basket on the scrubl kitchen table, Marthe lifted the cloth covering her p chases. "A nice, juicy bit o' red beef he bought whe told him ye were quite poorly on rising."

Anna hastily averted her eyes.

"And he said ye needn't come to the theatei you're still poorly. He'll have Maryann play yer pa Just rest up, he said, until the benefit next week."

"Mr. Szeben is too kind." Anna picked up the jug forget-me-nots and prepared to leave the kitchen.

"Wait." Marthe pumped water into another j larger than the one Anna carried. "Ye'll need this the flowers Mr. Szeben sent. I've set them on the sitti room table."

Small jug and Darringford's note in one hand, lai jug in the other, Anna swung the sitting room door op with her hip. She did not need to see Szeben's flowe She could smell them the moment she entered room: lilacs.

They were beautiful, three long stems of white a three of lavender lilacs. *Why?* thought Anna as she ị them in the large jug. Why must Szeben repulse l with one gift and kindle gratitude and pleasure with t other?

The second day was Sunday, and no performance the Venus Theatre. It was Marthe's day off, and thu: was Anna who opened the door when Szeben knock in the early afternoon. Behind Szeben stood a footman in the Darringford livery.

The man bowed and handed Anna a small tissue-wrapped package. "With his lordship's compliments, ma'am."

"Thank you."

Anna looked at Szeben. He raised a brow, then flipped a coin to the footman, who caught it deftly, expressed his gratitude, and bolted up the area steps.

"Will you ask me in?" said Szeben.

Anna stepped back. "This is the first time you're waiting to be asked. Why the sudden courtesy?"

He did not reply but followed her into the sitting room.

She said, "The lilacs are lovely. Thank you, Vladim."

"My pleasure. Did you enjoy the beef?"

"Yes," she lied.

She had placed the lilacs on the credenza, and the room was fragrant with their sweet scent. But she had left her bedroom door open, and Szeben's eyes went straight to the posy of forget-me-nots on the night table beside her bed.

His eyes slitted. "Darringford's?"

"Yes."

"And what did he send today?"

Anna heard the dangerous note in his voice, but it did not alarm her. She was in a strange frame of mind caused, perhaps, by the weakness and bouts of light-headedness that had been her lot these past days. She felt as if her mind had separated from her body, as if she was watching herself from a distance as she went through the motions of daily existence. Or, as if she was waiting . . . waiting for the Anna she observed to do something, though what that something was she hadn't the slightest notion.

She said, already stripping off the tissue paper, "I'll have to open it, won't I?"

Darringford had sent a small box of papier-mâché, painted and lacquered. Inside, atop a folded note, lay a locket.

Anna recognized it at once but made no move to hide it, nor did she protest when Szeben lifted it from the box.

He opened the locket. His face was expressionless. "The miniature you commissioned for Marika."

He said nothing else, asked nothing. Anna tried to read his thoughts but found that he had barred his mind to her. That did frighten her.

"May I have the locket back?"

He gave it to her at once. He said, "I, too, have a gift for you, my Anna. Since you said you plan to return the Darringford Ruby, I thought you might enjoy this ring instead."

Taking her hand, he slipped a wide gold band on her finger, a gold band studded with small diamonds and pearls.

She stared at it in disbelief. Her knees buckled, and she would have fallen had Szeben not caught her and assisted her to a chair. She could not take her eyes off the ring, and at last convinced herself that it was not a figment of her imagination. The diamonds and pearls did, indeed, present the entwined letters "W" and "A."

It was the ring given her by Walter when they pledged their troth and stripped off her finger by one of the marauders, believing he had killed her.

"Vladim?" Anna looked up to find the sitting room empty.

Szeben had left, and she had not even noticed.

Chapter 7

The Test

Walter's ring. She had not missed it until days later. Days and nights of mourning the loss of her family. Days of confusion that she had survived the attack with not even a scratch to show for the vicious knife wound that should have killed her. Days of struggle with Szeben, who would not let her join Walter and Marika.

Then she had noticed the ring gone, and it was insult added to injury. She was seething with pain and anger. She did not tell Szeben about the ring—those early days, she hardly spoke to him at all, except to berate him. But, of course, even then he must have read her every thought as if she had spoken aloud.

And he had recovered her ring. Szeben. Her mentor. Only friend. Eternal enemy.

But he had not given it to her until now. Two centuries later. . . .

When Anna finally picked up the note Darringford had sent with the locket, it was late night. Marthe had long since returned from her weekly visit with her niece in Hampstead and had retired. The street outside was quiet, the candles on the credenza had burned out, and the large candle on the table was guttering.

Anna rose stiffly and blinked away a spell of dizziness.

She replaced the candles, brewed a pot of tea, then once more picked up the note. As in Darringford's previous missive, there was no salutation.

> *I was sixteen when I discovered the locket and journals in the muniment room at Darringford Keep. As I told you, a mere stripling—and as any romantic stripling would do, I fell head over heels in love with the woman in the miniature. No doubt, I would have forgotten the miniature and my love in due course, but I also read the journals. Marika's entry after William's death struck me as a direct command. Not, as you assumed, to retrieve the ring, but to find Anna and help her find herself.*
>
> *No longer am I a stripling, in the throes of youthful infatuation. I am a man, matured in years of war, and I ask nothing more, nothing less, than leave to court you.*
>
> *Darringford*

Over and over, Anna read the note. *I ask . . . leave to court you.* Just as Walter had asked her father's leave to court her. And just like Walter's request, so did Darringford's make her pulse race.

At least, it did the first few times she read the note. Then disquiet crept in. She berated herself again for her utter foolishness the night she saw the portrait of William and Marika. *How* had Darringford known that it was Anna herself and not her great-grandmother in the miniature? Why on earth had she not asked him?

And he did not appear to fear her.

* * *

Anna was roused from sleep by a loud rapping. She sat up, wincing at a stab of pain in neck and shoulder, and realized she had fallen asleep in a corner of the sofa in her sitting room. Again, only the candle on the table was still alight, so she must have been dozing for several hours.

The rapping persisted—someone demanding entrance to her basement lodgings. She rose, but Marthe was already shuffling down the hall.

"Give over, do!" Marthe grumbled, clanging the night bolt and rattling the key in the lock. "Whosoever it be, ye better show good cause for makin' such a racket."

Anna remained in the sitting room. Again, she had the strange feeling of having left her body and watching herself. Waiting . . . for what, she knew not.

She heard a male voice. "Begging your pardon, ma'am. I am Wheatley, Lord Darringford's valet. It's very important, it is, that I speak with your mistress."

Anna was already out of the sitting room, in the narrow hallway. Marthe's candle illuminated the ruddy face of a large, towheaded man.

"What's amiss?" A horrible vision of Szeben and Darringford confronting each other made her voice sharp with apprehension. "Is Lord Darringford hurt?"

Twisting his hat in his hands, large, big-knuckled hands more suited to a farmer than a valet, the man bowed to her. "Yes and no, ma'am. It's an old injury, but it's not healing right. He came down with a fever today, so high it's made him delirious. Please, ma'am, can you come and heal him?"

She was already moving toward him. "You have a carriage? Or do we need a hackney?"

"The carriage is waiting, ma'am."

No longer did she feel as if she stood outside her body, watching her other self. The feeling of waiting for something was gone, replaced by purpose. Now she must prove herself. She must perform the one beneficial act no human could perform.

Cutting short Marthe's protest at her leaving with a stranger in the middle of the night, she hurried up the area steps to the carriage with the Darringford crest. When the valet had handed her into the carriage and would have shut the door, she told him to join her.

A small lantern dangling from a hook cast its erratic light on the man sitting stiffly opposite her. He looked honest and confidence inspiring enough, with a steady gaze and bulky shoulders. But he did not look like a valet.

"Your name is Wheatley?"

"Yes, ma'am." He was still gripping his hat in his hands.

"And Lord Darringford sent you to fetch me?"

"Yes and no, ma'am. He's feverish and calling for you, but he didn't say I should go and fetch you." The hat was mishandled so roughly that it would probably never regain its original shape. "But, unlike the other times when he was talking to you or about you in delirium, this time I knew that he had found you. And I also know that you can heal his wounds."

This was the second reference Wheatley made to her healing power. Only now did it occur to her how very strange that was. Dizzily, Anna leaned her head against the squabs. Not dizziness from physical weakness, but light-headedness caused by apprehension. What else did the man know?

He was still twisting and mangling his hat.

"Are you afraid of me, Wheatley?"

"Yes, ma'am," he said quietly. "You see, I know what you are."

She took a deep breath. Sitting up straight, she said, "Put your hat aside and listen. I will not harm you. In fact, I am just as afraid of you as you are of me."

This, he had obviously not expected. He peered at her, then set the hat on the seat beside him.

"There's no need for *you* to be afraid, ma'am. Lord Darringford swore me to secrecy when we found the journals and the locket. I'd never divulge a word about you to anyone."

"You've been with him that long?"

"Longer. His mother died birthing him, and we were nursed and raised together by my ma. I accompanied him when he traveled the Continent looking for you. I was his batman in the war. He would have bought me a commission, mind you, but I felt I could do more good as his batman."

"And now you're his valet. You're very fond of him." Anna did not make it a question, and Wheatley seemed to know that she required no answer.

He said, "I have no need to act valet. He's settled a nice estate on me, and I could be a gentleman of leisure were I so inclined. But he needs me still. Now, if you can heal him, it may be different."

"Did you read the journals, Wheatley?" Anna gripped the strap to steady herself as the carriage made a turn. "Is that where Darringford learned so much about me?"

"Most of what we know about you specifically, we know from the journals. Her ladyship, apparently, confided your story to his lordship—to William—because he was forever mentioning bits and pieces about you."

Her ladyship. Anna could not help but smile when

she tried to picture the exuberant young gypsy woman she had known as a dignified viscountess. Whatever Marika's feelings might have been for the man who raped, then married her, apparently she had learned to trust him, else she would never have divulged her friendship with one of the cursed undead.

Wheatley said, "When we traveled we picked up more specific knowledge about vamp—" He broke off, swallowing hard. It seemed, he even knew that the term vampire was tabu.

"Go on."

"The journals never mentioned where you're from, ma'am. But we knew her ladyship's tribe had come from Hungary. We started there, questioning other gypsies." Wheatley leaned close to the carriage window and peered out. He turned back to Anna. "Almost there. To make it short, we were pointed to Hermannstadt in Siebenbürgen by an old gypsy woman. A soothsayer. We got the impression that she was kin to her ladyship. To Marika. Don't quite know how, but, apparently, soothsaying runs in the family."

Anna nodded. Indeed. Marika, too, had shown great promise.

Wheatley said, "The soothsayer also told his lordship that no female child of his family would survive her eighth year until the woman he sought was returned to her mortal shape."

Anna's breath caught. "What? A gypsy told his lordship *what?*"

The carriage stopped.

"Here we are, ma'am." Wheatley snatched up his hat, opened the door, and let down the steps. "Will you come inside and heal his lordship? Please, ma'am?"

Anna delegated Wheatley's startling disclosure to the back of her mind. "Yes, of course I'll heal his lordship."

The bedchamber was dark and oppressively warm.

"Light candles and open the windows," Anna told Wheatley, then went straight to the large four-poster bed in the center of the room.

Darringford, clad in breeches and sweat-soaked shirt, lay on his side atop the counterpane. When Wheatley lit the candle on the nightstand, she saw that Darringford was shivering, even though his face was damp with perspiration. His hands moved restlessly, and he was muttering under his breath.

An ache filled her. How vulnerable he looked. How gravely ill. Gently, she placed a hand on his forehead. It was burning hot.

Her touch had an instant affect. Darringford quieted, lay motionless. It looked almost as if he had stopped breathing. Suddenly, his eyes opened, looking straight at her.

"Anna."

His beautiful voice was raspy and weak, and cut her to the quick with its yearning note. "Shh. Close your eyes again. I will help you."

A moment longer, the dark eyes clung to her, as if to draw strength, then closed.

"More light, Wheatley. I need to see where he is hurt."

But her fingers had already found the cut at the side of his head, where she had once noticed the scar. It felt sticky, and the familiar smell of blood assailed her nostrils. She flinched and withdrew her hand but stood her ground at the bedside.

"That's one of them. A piece of shrapnel did it." Wheatley stepped closer, carrying a candelabrum. He set it in front of the single candle on the nightstand. Opening Darringford's shirt, he said, "The other is here. A saber cut. It's not bleeding now, thank goodness, but it's looking mighty angry again."

And it was. Red streaks slashed from a raw-looking scar that curved from the breastbone to his left side. He must be in considerable pain.

"Ma'am." Wheatley hesitated. "Ma'am, will you have to drink his blood?"

She rounded on him angrily, but her anger died in view of his obvious concern. "No, Wheatley. It is my saliva that will heal him. Now, please step back."

"Shall I leave, ma'am?"

It was her turn to hesitate. Except once, when Marika had cut her finger, Anna had never used her healing powers. Healing Marika's cut had been as instinctive and quick as the many "kisses" she had placed on her daughter's frequent scrapes and cuts, but when faced with bleeding strangers, she had not been able to overcome her aversion. It was Szeben who at times worked as a "surgeon" and brought in additional funds. The injured was always unconscious; the family, banned from the bedside to prevent exposure of Szeben's methods.

Anna looked at Darringford, restless again and perspiring freely. The blood seeping from his head wound had started to trickle down his neck and soak the pillow. She steeled herself against nausea but felt only impatience with herself and fear for Darringford's life. If he had blood poisoning, and it spread, he would die. It was as simple as that.

"Step back," she repeated, then bent over Darringford.

She caught his restless hands and held them, but she did not need to fear that he would hit out or try to push her away. As soon as her mouth touched the wound on the side of his head, he quieted again.

Anna closed her eyes, willing her strength, her immortal good health, to flow from her mouth to his body. She willed him to fight off poison, putrefaction, and disease. To be whole.

She tasted the flavor of his blood, the dark quality of illness and infection, then the change to brightness, to health. For a moment, she lingered, making certain, giving more strength, smoothing tissue and skin so no scar would remain. At last, she released him.

Exhausted, Anna straightened. She had no notion how much time had passed, but her back was sore from bending at an awkward angle. She grimaced wryly. So much for eternal health. Though she might not suffer from cuts, the sniffles or a cough, she was not immune from common aches and pains in bone and muscle.

Wheatley handed her a towel, then went to stand by the bed. He stared down at Darringford.

"Thank you, ma'am." His voice held reverence. "He is healed. Quite healed."

Anna wiped her mouth and face. She still tasted his blood, but there was no nausea, only a return of her vigor. She felt stronger than she had in quite a while.

"I must heal the other scar."

"It looks better already, ma'am."

"I want the scar gone completely. If I did not transfer sufficient healing power, it might get inflamed again."

Wheatley retreated once more. Anna sat on the side of the bed. Tenderness filled her as she gazed at the peacefully slumbering man. He was probably quite healed, but it was best to make sure.

She bent over him, placing her mouth at the top of his scar in the center of his chest. His breaths were slow and even, and she felt each one as a caress against her lips. How different this second healing was, compared to the travail of the first. A pleasure, almost.

She clasped his shoulders, finding comfort in the firmness of skin and muscle. Her mouth traveled the curve of the scar, soothing it and smoothing it. He no longer felt hot to the touch, but warm and vibrant. A pleasure, indeed, touching him. Almost like making love.

Her breath caught. It was, indeed, what she was doing. She was loving him. Worshiping his body as she had once worshiped her husband. And how she had missed that bond. The closeness between man and woman. The companionship. The love.

She no longer felt any puckered welts on Darringford's skin. She had done her work. The scar was gone. But she did not sit up. She held him, her cheek pressed against his chest. How good this felt. How right.

An arm slid around her middle, held her close.

"Anna." His voice was soft but no longer raspy or weak. "Please stay."

One tear, then another, slid down her face. Yes, she would stay. For just a moment or two. Until he was asleep again.

Until she had the strength to let him go. And she must summon that strength before she fell completely under his spell.

"Wheatley?"

"Yes, ma'am."

"Do you think you can move his arm without waking him?"

"I'll try, ma'am."

When the valet gently raised Darringford's arm, she slid off the bed.

"He will sleep now, Wheatley. Several hours, I should think. Then he'll be right as a trivet."

She did not look at Darringford again but walked quickly from the room, down the stairs, out of Darringford House, and stepped into the carriage waiting to take her home.

Chapter 8

The Fire

Anna slept until Marthe roused her, reminding her that there would be an additional performance late that afternoon, the benefit for Maryann, a young actress whose sailor husband was crippled in a fall from the topmast during his last sea voyage.

Dressing quickly, Anna then dropped to her knees and pulled a small trunk out from under her bed. The trunk contained her entire collection of publications on vampires. She stared at them helplessly. She knew that neither the publications by dilettantes nor scholarly treatises, like Calmet's *Dissertation on the Vampires in Hungary,* contained the answers she sought. She flipped through several volumes anyway. It was better than stopping to think about the previous night. About Darringford. About the burning need to feel that closeness again.

"Anna."

She dropped the book, slammed the trunk shut. She had not heard Szeben come in.

"You know what I must do."

The implacable note in his voice chilled her, but she could not allow fear to invade her mind. She must be as strong as Szeben, as levelheaded.

She rose and faced him. He always looked pale, but never had he looked so haggard. The usually expressionless eyes seemed darker than ever with some emotion she could not fathom.

She said calmly, "I do not see that you must do anything at all, except to make arrangements to close the theater. Then we can move on. We haven't been to Russia since the coronation of the first Catherine. Is it not time to go back?"

"It is too late, Anna." And he was not referring to a return to Russia. "I warned you about placing us in danger. Last night, you sealed his fate."

Impossible not to be afraid, especially since Darringford was unsuspecting of danger. Even if she warned him, there was nothing he, a mere mortal, could do against Szeben.

She said, "We have no reason to think that he suspects you at all."

A short, sardonic bark of laughter was his only reply.

Undeterred, she continued, "His interest is in me alone, and he will not betray me."

"That is not the point." Something flamed in Szeben's eyes. He gripped her shoulders, pulling her against him. "He wants you, Anna. And I will brook no rival."

"You're wrong, Vladim!" She suffered his tight hold,

wanting only to make him see reason. "I grant you that Darringford is beset by some romantic notion about me. But it won't last. As soon as I am gone, he will—"

"Don't lie!" Szeben's voice was harsh, pained. "Even if you do believe what you're saying, it makes no difference. Only that you would prove yourself more naive than I thought possible. But you *must* know that Darringford will never give up. He will pursue you to the end of his days. And you're mine, Anna! Mine."

"No." Shaken by his unusual display of passion, she tried to pull away. "You are hurting me, Vladim. Please let go."

He released her shoulders but only to enfold her in his arms. "I watched you with Walter before the attack. And I envied him, Anna! You shared such tenderness, so much warmth and love. And I was . . . alone."

She no longer struggled against him. She could not. How well she understood his feelings. How often she had been consumed by longings such as he must have suffered when he saw her with her husband.

He said, "I was returning from Rumania, was still several leagues from Hermannstadt, when I saw the smoke and heard the clamor of battle. I hurried, but a short while later, all noise ceased. Only the smoke remained. I rode straight to the castle. I saw your husband and daughter, but there was nothing I could do. They were dead. I healed others, still clinging to life, while I searched for you. I did not know I would find you in town. And almost too late."

"I wish—"

But she did not say what she wished. She wasn't sure any longer that it would be true.

"I love you, Anna."

"Vladim—" She had been about to tell him that he did not mean it. That he could not possibly love her; he was beyond such human emotion. But the words would not form, not when she could so clearly see the truth in his face.

All she felt was pity.

"Vladim—"

"Don't speak."

Cupping her face in his hands, he bent his head and kissed her hungrily. She did not fend him off but stood stiff and unresponsive, torn by a welter of emotions. Pity again. Sadness. A flash of resentment that it was Szeben, not Darringford, who held her in his arms.

It could never be Darringford.

Szeben released her mouth. "Precisely, my Anna," he said hoarsely. "It can never be Darringford. But we can have so much together. We can make the years, the decades, the centuries bearable. Nay, we can make them pleasurable."

She knew he made sense. But she also knew she could never accept him as her husband. Her lover.

She felt the hurt she must inflict and could not bear to look at him. Putting her arms around him, she pressed her face against his chest. When she spoke again, her voice was muffled by his coat. "I am sorry, Vladim. So very sorry."

He stood quite still, then brusquely set her aside. He did not speak but cocked his head as if listening for something. At the same moment, she felt that stir inside her, that rush of warmth that told her Darringford was near.

Not now! Oh, please, not now, while Szeben was here.

Turning her back on Szeben, she rushed into the sitting room, then stood irresolute. A moment later, the knock on the door was answered by Marthe.

Darringford, carrying a stack of leather-bound volumes tied with string, stepped into the sitting room. Her heart raced. How well he looked. How strong. Indomitable.

How vulnerably mortal.

"Good afternoon, Anna." His smile warmed her heart. He flicked a casual look toward the open bedroom door and inclined his head. "Szeben."

"You've worn out your welcome, my lord." Szeben's voice was cold. "I will not have you pester Anna any longer."

"I appreciate your concern." Darringford was unperturbed. Setting his burden on the table, he said, "Unfortunately, I cannot oblige. Courtship, you see, requires frequent visitations."

Szeben's eyes slitted. Quickly, Anna stepped between him and Darringford. "I shall see you at the theater, Vladim. I shan't be late, I promise you."

Szeben's jaw tightened, but he left. From the door, he said, "I'll take Marthe. No doubt, Darringford will oblige and offer you a ride."

"But of course," Darringford said smoothly.

Anna did not look at him until she heard the outer door close behind Szeben and Marthe. Then she turned.

"You must not see me anymore, Darringford."

Again his smile melted her heart.

"What I must do is thank you. Those injuries have plagued me for nigh on a year. No physician could help me, and you have healed me with a kiss. I am very grateful, Anna. Thank you."

"You are welcome." She went to the credenza, where, side by side, sat the Darringford Ruby and the ring Walter had given her. It felt as if her heart was breaking, but she picked up the ruby and held it out to Darringford. "Please take it. I have no need of it any longer. And you will not need me anymore."

He took the ring, then her hand, and slid the ring onto her finger. "No matter what, it will always be yours, my dear."

"I cannot take it. It is the ring meant for the Darringford wives."

"And if I have my way, you will be a Darringford wife. And if not—" He raised her hand to his lips for a brief caress. "If not, then I shall have no need of it. I have an heir. Henry. And his son, my namesake, after him. They are welcome to everything I have, save for this ring. It is yours, Anna."

She wanted to reach out and touch him, the spot on his temple, his chest and side, where the scars had been. Wanted to feel the strength of his arms around her. Wanted to forget who and what she was and let him court her.

" 'Tis madness," she said. "If Szeben would not kill you, *I* would bring you nothing but sorrow. You have no notion—"

"But I do, Anna. I know you are immortal. I know you would once more lose a husband."

"Don't!" she cried. "Don't speak like that."

"I must. I want you to understand that I know exactly what I am doing. I know we cannot set up house in town and expect acceptance of your everlasting beauty and youth. But we can live anywhere we wish, move as often as necessary."

"As I do now."

He was silent for a moment, then said, "Or you can turn me into one of you."

She recoiled. "No! You don't know what you're asking. It is purgatory and eternal hell combined, existing the way we do."

"Anna—"

"No!" she said fiercely. "You know nothing at all about life with someone like me. Someone who is most comfortable in the dark of night, who will insist on thick curtains drawn to shut out the light of day. Could you bear a wife who will need the taste of blood for her well-being? Who, if she abstained too long, would need to be locked up at full moon or turn into a monster?"

"I would do better than bear such a wife, if the wife is you. And I'll gladly offer my own blood."

The quiet words were so unexpected, they rendered her speechless, made her want to cry and, at the same time, filled her with tenderness. Aching with the need to be in his arms, she drew back. "You're not afraid of . . . of me? What I might do? After all, I tried to attack you."

"And you certainly took me by surprise that first time." Face and tone were rueful, but his eyes held just a hint of a twinkle. "Had William not mentioned in his journals that you become wretchedly ill at the sight of blood, I might have been afraid. So you see, I am not such a brave heart after all. Merely a fellow prepared to take a slight risk."

His reasoning was so ridiculous, the twinkle in his eye so infectious, that she had to draw on her acting skills to scold him. "Be serious, Darringford! It is not a laughing matter, I'll have you know. And now I must fetch my hat and shawl." She turned toward the bed-room. "Will you take me to the theater? We give an additional performance today."

"Just tell me this, Anna. Do you believe in fate? Or, perhaps, destiny is a better term. I believe that if we make the right choices during the course of our lives, if we do not disregard the directions given us, we will reach our destiny."

"Directions? Are you referring to Marika's entry in the journal? 'It is Anna ye must court. My goode friend Anna. Ye will find the ringe. She will find herself.' "

"There is more. That is why I brought the journals. You must read them, Anna."

She heard the urgency in his voice. In fact, she felt it herself, almost as if an invisible force was pushing her toward the journals. But it could not be. Not now.

"We must leave."

Darringford had come in the carriage, so Anna suffered no discomfort from the sun that peeked now and again. But she had felt stronger anyway, ever since she'd healed Darringford.

The drive from Tavistock Street to the Venus Theatre just off Castle Street, in the outer reaches of Seven Dials, would be short. Hardly worth starting to question Darringford about the journals. But again, something pressed her on.

"Wheatley mentioned a soothsayer you found in Hungary. I did not understand. . . . She told you that no female child of your family would survive?"

"Until the woman I seek is returned to her mortal shape. Yes, Anna, that is what she said."

When he said no more, the tension in her mounted. "And is it true, then, about the female children?"

"My cousin Henry's firstborn, Jane, died of the whooping cough when she was eight. I had a sister who died in a fever epidemic. She, too, was eight years old. Anna, how old was your daughter when she was killed?"

Her reply was barely audible. "She was eight years old."

Darringford reached for her hand and held it. Grateful, she returned the gentle pressure of his fingers. If only she could have . . .

But she could not.

She said, "The excerpt from the journal you sent mentioned Marika taking her 'children' to the brook to gather forget-me-nots."

"Yes, Marika and William had two children. Henry. And Anna. Anna died. Marika had a premonition that her daughter was in danger, but she could do nothing to help the child."

Tears stung her eyes. A child named after her. And she had not known.

She blinked the tears away, looked out the carriage window. They were almost at the end of St. Martin's Lane. Just a few more minutes to cling to his hand.

"Anna, the woman I sought is you. And the gypsy said the female children of my family would not survive until the woman I sought was returned to her mortal shape."

"Her mortal shape." A trembling started deep inside her. "Does that mean . . . ?"

The carriage slowed. The coachman yelled, "Summat amiss, my lord! Fire, belike!"

Then they stopped. Anna became aware of shouting in the street, of people running. Darringford let down the window. Immediately, they could smell the smoke.

"I hate fires," said Anna. "I fear them. The marauders burnt the whole city and the castle. It was horrible."

"Castle Street looks impassable," said Darringford. "We had best turn back, if we can."

"No. I must get to the theater. If there's danger, I must help. If not, then we must have the benefit." She opened the carriage door and stepped down.

Darringford followed. "No one will attend with a fire nearby."

She snatched up her skirts and started to run. Darringford caught up. Placing an arm firmly around her waist, he forged a path through the ever-thickening crowd of shopkeepers, clerks, seamstresses from shops nearby, and idle curiosity seekers drawn from afar by the commotion. Without Darringford, she would never have made progress.

The smoke burned her eyes and throat. At times, it was so thick, Anna could scarcely see where they were going, but, at last, they reached the lane where the Venus Theatre was located.

The crowd grew quiet around them. In the stillness, one voice rang out. "Jump, lady! Jump!"

Anna blinked. The theater, the former stables which now housed the stage and auditorium, was engulfed in smoke and flames. More smoke was pouring from the attached posting inn, where the Green Room, storage, and dressing rooms were located. So far, the smoke there seemed contained on the ground floor.

She heard Darringford's voice, strangely hollow and unsteady. "Lydia. And Gareth."

Anna had already seen them. On the third floor of the inn, at the window to her own dressing room.

Pulling Anna with him, Darringford pushed closer to the building. "Why the devil doesn't she come down?

Anna, I must go in. What is the quickest way? Is there a back entrance?"

The crowd was noisy again, yelling and screaming as smoke billowed from an upper-story window of the inn. Anna had to shout to make herself heard. "Yes, but you'd be lost in the warren of old kitchens and pantries. Best use the main door. Be careful! To the right of the stairwell is the passage to the auditorium. The smoke and flames would travel that way from the theater."

He squeezed her hand, then bent swiftly and brushed her lips with the fleetest and sweetest of kisses.

And then he was gone, forging through the crowd that suddenly retreated to escape a shower of sparks and hot cinders from the collapsing stable roof. Anna was swept along by the crowd. She stumbled, but someone held her up. Then Marthe was beside her, dragging her away from the crowd, around to the side yard of the inn, where the well was located.

All the theater people were there, filling buckets, hoisting them from hand to hand into the main door. But she did not see Szeben.

Marthe handed her a bucket. "His lordship is tryin' ter get to the lady on the third floor, but the stairs have caught fire."

She looked at the building, the smoke, and fought the cowardly urge to turn and run. "I'll go in the back. Douse me, Marthe."

The older woman looked as if she would protest, but Anna's fierce look stopped her.

"Take yer hat off," Marthe ordered, removing the large kerchief from her neck.

Deftly, she bundled up Anna's hair, then tied the kerchief around it. A moment later, Anna was dripping wet from head to toe and running to the back of the old inn. With her soaked skirt, she could not move as quickly as she wished, but when she stepped through the back door, she saw at once that dry clothing might have spelled disaster.

The building itself was solid brick, but wooden beams, furnishings, and paneling inside were plentiful and tinder dry and would burst into flame with the tiniest spark. So far only smoke filled the kitchens, the stillrooms, and pantries, but Anna could hear an ominous crackle and the shouts of the men trying to douse the fire in the old public room, where the main staircase was.

Holding her shawl to mouth and nose, Anna darted through room after room until she reached the farthest pantry. Here, all but forgotten, except by Anna who preferred to leave the theater without passing through the Green Room, were the back stairs. Steep, narrow stone steps, safe enough in themselves, but sided by warped, ancient paneling. She was moving as fast as she could; but the smoke traveled faster, and by the time she reached the second story, she could not see through the thick, acrid clouds billowing up both stairways.

She heard cries, a woman's voice. "Help! For goodness's sake, please help us!"

Anna tried to answer but was seized by a fit of coughing. Why on earth did Lydia Rossiter not come out and try to save herself and the boy!

Her dressing room was the fourth door down the corridor, closer to the main stairs than the back stairs. Feeling her way, Anna moved on, her eyes tearing, and every breath an effort.

The cries for help were joined by a child's voice. "Mama! Put me down! Want to go, Mama!"

The fright in the child's voice tugged at Anna's heart.

Little Gareth, Darringford's namesake, placed in danger by his very foolish mama, who should not be at the theater in the first place.

At last she reached the fourth door. She flung it open, dashed inside, and shut it quickly to keep out the smoke. Some was seeping in beneath the door but drifted out the open window, where Lydia Rossiter stood with her squirming son in her arms. At Anna's entrance, she turned awkwardly, relief clear in her pale face.

"Come." Breathing deeply, Anna leaned against the door for a brief respite. "It's only smoke, you know. We can get through easily."

Lydia did not move. "Please take Gareth, I beg you. I fell. My foot . . . I think it's broken."

Chapter 9

The Sacrifice

Anna took the boy, probably no more than five or six years old, but sturdy. And he did not want to be carried. She set him down but held on to his hand.

"Lean on me," she told Lydia Rossiter. "I may not be tall, but I am quite strong."

Lydia tried to take a step but cried out in pain. "I cannot do it. Please take Gareth!"

"But I cannot leave you here."

A spark of the old Lydia from Darringford House emerged as she commanded, "You must! What good will it do if you stay?"

"You're quite correct, of course," Anna conceded. "But what on earth are you doing here in the first place? And with a child!"

Lydia's gaze fell. "I am sorry. I was foolish. Henry mentioned the afternoon performance, and I thought . . . I wanted . . . Oh, it does not matter now! I'll never forgive myself for placing Gareth in danger. But he was ill, and I have kept him close. Please, Miss von Hermannstadt, for my son's sake, go! Take him to safety!"

Anna wrapped her shawl around the child, despite his protest, then picked up the large water pitcher Marthe kept filled. "I'm sorry, young man, but you will have to suffer a wetting."

When the boy was drenched, she set the pitcher down beside Lydia. "Not much left, but you can wet your handkerchief and breathe through it if the smoke gets thicker. Darringford is trying to come up the main stairway. When he gets here, tell him to turn left and bring you down the back stairs."

Lydia nodded. She moved the shawl off Gareth's face, kissed him, then covered him again. "Be good, my son. Be brave."

Anna picked up the boy, perching him on her hip, the way she had done with her daughter. Her precious little Marika. Anna's arms tightened around the boy protectively.

Lydia gave her a slight push. "Go! And may God bless you and preserve you both."

Anna's throat was tight when she closed the door on Lydia. But Gareth must be saved. If only she had told Darringford about the back stairs. Or taken him herself. But she had not thought it necessary to enter the inn. Only when Marthe told her that the main staircase had caught fire. . . .

How long the corridor was. How heavy the boy. At least he was quiet and still.

The smoke seemed thicker, and she did not have the shawl to cover mouth and nose. And was it warmer? She could feel the clothes drying on her body.

"Anna!"

She almost stumbled.

"Vladim, where are you?"

"On the main stairs with Darringford. Our hero, who wants to save the woman and child."

"I have the boy."

"Then, I had best help you."

"Darringford needs you more. Lydia Rossiter has broken her foot."

There was no reply from Szeben. The silence was disquieting.

And it wasn't a true silence. She heard ominous crackling sounds. She had passed three doors. Should be at the stairs now. But she could not see them. Only smoke that burned her eyes and rasped in her throat.

Little Gareth whimpered, coughed. She stopped, pressed his face more firmly against her shoulder, then put a tentative foot forward. There was nothing. She stood at the top the stairs.

She felt for the banister, found it, and gripped it tightly. Step by step, she went down. She was drenched in sweat, but not for long. The heat was sucking every drop of moisture from her clothing, from her body, until she thought she would shrivel like a prune in the sun.

Suddenly, flames were there, licking at the paneling just in front of her. Heart pounding, she stopped. Did that mean the pantries and kitchens were unpassable?

"Fire, my Anna," Szeben said behind her.

To hear his voice should have been reassuring, but his words filled her with foreboding.

"Where are Darringford and Lydia Rossiter?" she asked.

"Not far behind. Anna, do you see the flames? You can do it now, what you have wished. You need no longer struggle through eternity. You can die by fire."

Her breath caught, causing another fit of coughing. Blindly, she took a step down, and another. Whatever she may have wished in the past, she did not for an instant contemplate it now.

"We can both die, Anna."

"No, Vladim! Help me save the boy!"

Flames shot up the paneling on either side of her. She snatched her hand off the banister as it, too, burst into flame. The heat singed her.

"Wait, Anna!"

But she did not stop. Something heavy and damp was draped around her shoulders. A man's coat. Szeben's coat. She pulled it over Gareth, who was squirming again and coughing.

"Hold still," she told him. "Just a moment longer. Then you can run and play again."

Would that her words came true. She could not believe them herself.

Then she heard Darringford's voice, and her spirits soared. "Szeben," he said, sounding breathless. "Have you found her?"

"She's safe."

Young Gareth had also heard Darringford's voice and started to wriggle and cry for his Uncle Gareth.

"Soon," Anna soothed him. "Soon you'll see your Uncle Gareth."

She had reached the bottom of the stairs. The

smoke seemed less here. She could see charred walls, the smoldering remains of what had once been shelves and cupboards. Overhead crackled large ceiling beams as the fire feasted on them and spat down glowing embers. The tiled floor was hot, burning her feet through the soles of her slippers. But they would make it to safety. She believed it now.

Near the doorway to the next pantry, Anna looked back and saw Szeben. A moment later, Darringford emerged from the stairwell. Slung over his shoulder, Darringford carried Lydia Rossiter coughing and gasping and covered with a damp blanket.

They would all be safe!

A sound like gunfire exploding above her made her look up at the ceiling. Szeben shoved her. She stumbled backward into the next room, keeping her balance with difficulty, just as Darringford with Lydia reached the spot where she had stood, and where a burning beam creaked and groaned overhead, then ripped free.

"Gareth!" she screamed.

He looked up, tried to veer, but his burden made him clumsy and slow. The beam caught his free shoulder and would have hit Lydia as well if Szeben had not caught it in his arms. Face contorting in pain and effort, he raised the burning beam.

"Go!" he shouted, and Darringford stumbled toward Anna.

His coat was charred across the shoulder and upper sleeve, but not burning. He put Lydia down, turned back to help Szeben. But there was nothing he could do.

Lydia moaned and averted her face. Anna could only clutch little Gareth to her breast and watch in mute horror at the impossibly huge flames bursting from the beam, catching Szeben's sleeves, the front of his coat, until he was engulfed.

"Go, Anna!" Szeben shouted. "Go!"

The mortar between bricks started to pop and crackle. Bricks spewed from the walls of the pantry. The heat was unbearable.

Darringford, his face white and drawn, picked up Lydia. He took Anna by the hand. "Come," he said gently. "We must go, or his sacrifice will have been for nothing."

Anna turned. She was numb. She had no tears. Or, if she did, they dried as soon as they welled into her eyes.

"God speed, my Anna."

"Thank you, Vladim. I am sorry . . . so sorry!"

"I will make it right for you, Anna, my love. Trust me. You can be happy now."

She lurched forward as something sharp hit her back. There was a pain, not unlike the pain when the Turkish marauder had knifed her in the back. But she could not stop now. Must get out with the child.

She was not aware of passing from one smoldering room to another, but she must have done so. When she noticed her surroundings again, she was outside the inn, at a safe distance. Marthe took the boy from her. Henry Rossiter was there to accept his wife from Darringford.

And then she was in Darringford's arms. His mouth covered hers, and his kiss was the most exquisite tonic she could ever wish for. Numbness and exhaustion dropped away as she clung to the man whose very presence had become as essential to her well-being as breathing.

"My dearest Anna." He cupped her face. "I was never more afraid than when Lydia told me that you were in the building. How could you do that to me!"

And he kissed her again, gifting her with a taste of

the love, the devotion, the passion that might be hers forever.

If she would let him.

When he set her free, a fire engine had at last arrived, a huge monster with three pumps, pulled by six horses. Men wearing the yellow hats and badges of the Sun Fire Company trained their hoses on the old posting inn. To no avail. Anna had not thought there was enough wood to sustain the flames that leaped and darted from every window. Again, there was the sound of an explosion.

The firemen dropped their hoses, shouting, "Back! Everyone back!" and started running.

His arm securely around her, Darringford drew her farther back. Her gaze remained fixed on the burning building. Slowly, very slowly, it collapsed. Burying Szeben.

Darringford's arm tightened around her. "I should, perhaps, wait for a more opportune moment. But, dash it, Anna! I cannot wait. Will you permit me to court you?"

She looked at him, his soot-stained face, hair disheveled, charred coat, and said wryly, "If I look half as disreputable as you do, and yet you still ask me, you must be serious, indeed."

"Then, what do you say?"

She drew a deep breath, smoke and soot and all. "Yes."

His kiss drew applause from passersby, men and women who had lost interest in staring at the ruins of an old building.

Darringford gave them a jaunty grin. "Thank you, ladies and gentlemen. Would you like us to oblige with an *encore?*"

A few of the theater troupe approached, Maryann and Marthe among them. Anna told them to see her in

Tavistock Street on the morrow to discuss what could be done, and to pass the word to others.

"What's that on your back, Miss Anna?" asked Marthe, tugging at Szeben's coat still slung around Anna's shoulders. "Gracious! If it ain't Mr. Szeben's little knife! It's stuck in the coat. But how did it get there?"

Darringford took the knife from Marthe. It was only about an inch and a half long, the handle inlaid with ivory, with two small but very efficient blades. One of the blades was open.

Anna remembered something sharp hitting her back when they left Szeben in the fire. But how could it possibly have been the small pocketknife?

"There's blood on the coat," said Marthe, already plucking it off Anna. "And blood on yer back! Miss Anna, you're hurt!"

"Nonsense." There could be no blood. She did not bleed. Any wound she might sustain would always heal itself in an instant.

"There is blood." Darringford's voice was not quite steady.

He pressed a finger against her back, the precise spot where the marauder's knife had delivered a perilous, deep cut. She had been unconscious, dying, when Szeben healed her. And not even a scar had shown.

Now Szeben's knife had drawn blood.

"I scarcely feel it." She craned her neck to look down her back. "A slight burning, that is all I feel."

"You'd hardly feel more from a toy knife like this." Clasping her shoulders, Darringford held her gaze. "Do you see what this means, Anna? Do you understand? You are bleeding!"

She started to shake and clutched at his coat for support. "But how is it possible?"

"What does it matter?"

"Szeben said he'd make it right for me," she whispered. "He must have known how—"

"How you could regain your mortal form? Perhaps he did. As did the old gypsy woman I met. She said fire can kill an immortal. Or, if all the signs and conditions are right, fire can transform."

"You knew and did not tell me?"

"How could I?" His grip tightened. "How could I ever have sent you into a fire when I did not know whether it would kill you or save you?"

"But—"

He silenced her with a kiss. "The only important thing is that now you truly have no reason to refuse me." His smile was quizzical. "Unless you take me in aversion."

"Never!" She was half laughing, half crying. "You may now court me to your heart's content. You may marry me, love me, and worship me when I grow old and frail."

"That I will." Once more, he caught her in his arms. "I love you, Anna."

She looked at him and with the greatest joy spoke the words she feared she would never have the right to say, and which now held quite a different meaning.

"And I love you, Gareth. I will love you for as long as I live, and through eternity."

THE COSSACK

Judith A. Lansdowne

Chapter 1

Whenever Nancy had stumbled and fallen, she had risen again—day after day, year after year, for ever so long. But this evening the little flower seller had slipped down into the gutter on her way to Covent Garden, and she could not find it in herself to rise again. Feverish, exhausted, she remained sprawled like a bundle of rags in Maiden Lane, her bunches of flowers scattered around her. She attempted to move once, but it was a feeble attempt as though the rags she wore were merely being ruffled by the stinking wind from the Thames. Like the wind, she emitted a long, low, sobbing sigh. The sigh became a weak gasp as she felt a shadow hovering above her. Nancy opened fear-filled eyes just as the soldier in his red-and-gold tunic touched one knee to the cobbles. The deep blue of his pantaloons met the muck of the street beside her with a distasteful squish.

"It is all right, dear one," the soldier said gently, quietly, touching his other knee to the cobbles as well. "Do not be afraid. I have come to do what I can for you."

His arms went around her. He sat back on his heels and lifted her effortlessly until she was sitting secure in his arms, her head resting against one of his broad shoulders. She peered wearily up at him. He had a strong jaw, lean cheeks, and eyes like clear country night skies—eyes filled with compassion, with empathy—as they gazed down into her own. Nancy could not think why he gazed into her eyes so. When she was young she had had beautiful eyes, and many a lad had delighted in them. But they were clouded with illness and poverty now. No man could wish to so much as look at them any longer. And yet, this soldier gazed into them deeply, intently, and he smiled a slow smile.

As his smile formed, the stars in his dark eyes began to dance, stirring something deep inside of the little flower seller, lifting her up, sweeping her into the tender nights of her youth. Moon-bright skies, spring-laden air, the peace of a country night wound like a precious cloak around her. "Wh-who are you?" she asked in wonder, her voice barely audible as it scraped from her throat.

"I am called Stauss," the soldier whispered, smoothing the dull blond hair from her brow with a touch like cool velvet. "I have come to cure you of your illness, Nancy. To bring you peace."

His voice spread over her like soothing balm. She did not question how he knew her name. She did not question how there could be any cure for her suffering. Moments ago she lay wretched and dying in the gutter in Maiden Lane. Now she floated carefree and filled with awe in the country nights of her youth.

"There is a grand house that awaits you, Nancy, a house filled with family and friends who yearn even now to welcome you home. I will see you safely there. Trust in me." The soldier leaned down and kissed her fevered lips as tenderly as any shy country lad might kiss a country lass. Nancy sighed at the sweetness of it. Then the soldier leaned farther still and touched his cool, gentle lips to her neck.

She gasped at first as his teeth pricked her, but almost at once the slight discomfort was forgotten. Her sense of joy and wonder increased. True spring breezes brushed the little flower seller's cheeks; nightingales sang above her; the scent of newly scythed hay tickled at her nose. Without hesitation, Nancy raised her arms and clasped the soldier fervently around his neck. She clung to him as she had never clung to any man, rejoicing in his embrace, in the glorious world to which his kiss, his warm, powerful body, the strong, steady beat of his heart carried her. All remembrance of Maiden Lane, her rags and wretchedness, fled. A grand, uncomplicated peace gathered her in. Serenity filled her mind, her heart, and then slipped into Nancy's very soul.

When her heart ceased to beat, the soldier halted his kiss. Slowly, sensuously, his tongue came out to lick at the blood that remained on her neck. He realized that some had sprayed onto the high-standing collar of his tunic, dimming the golden embroidery there. *And doubtless I smell precisely like the gutter I'm in,* he thought. *I shall need to return to the Pulteney and don a fresh uniform. Vlad will wish me at the devil when he sees this one, and I shall be late besides.*

He stood then, with Nancy in his arms, and carried the little flower seller through the mews to the shelter of a stable where, unnoticed by a sleeping stablehand, he laid her down in a bit of straw and covered her with a horse blanket.

Miss Aphrodite Coop backed awkwardly out from the space beneath Sir Merrill's enormous mahogany desk on her hands and knees. She hit her head twice and caught the toe of her slipper in one of the flounces on her gown, ripping the thing loose. In her rush to be out, up and away, she was oblivious to the fact that her hair was coming undone and she was scattering a multitude of hairpins across the Chinese red carpet. *I must tell Uncle Merrill at once,* was all she could think as her heart thumped against her ribs. *He must know and know as soon as possible.*

"I see you, Aphrodite!" announced a whispery little voice as Miss Coop dashed into the corridor. "I found you! I win! I win!"

"Yes, yes, you win, Lydia," Aphrodite said quietly, giving the child a pat on the head as she hurried past. "Now run up to Nurse at once, dearest. Hurry. Up the servants' staircase and all the way to the nursery without pause."

Aphrodite knew she ought to escort Sir Merrill's daughter up those stairs and into the nurse's arms. She was, after all, responsible for Lydia's having departed the nursery in the first place. But she could not spare the time to do it, and Lydia was generally a dependable little being who did precisely as she was told. Surely she would not disobey tonight, not when the house was filled with important guests, not when the Prince Regent and the Russian Tsar were present. Lydia knew quite as well as Aphrodite what a great deal it meant to Sir Merrill and Lady Merrill that the prince and Tsar Alexander had accepted their dinner invitation. No, the child would do nothing to disrupt the gathering.

Without further thought to Lydia, Aphrodite rushed along the corridor to the vestibule and the main staircase. Strands of her fine chestnut hair, set free by the fallen pins, puffed this way and that in the breeze she created as she ran. Her torn flounce flopped and floundered like a fish gasping its last. Her long white gloves sagged below her elbows, and tiny pieces of lint from Sir Merrill's carpet clung to the skirt of her pale gold gown.

Yet, even if she had taken note of her dishevelment, none of it would have mattered to her. Nothing mattered at the moment but the hideous conversation she had overheard in her guardian's office while playing hide-and-seek with Lydia.

Without so much as a pause in her stride, Aphrodite caught at the newel post with her left hand and spun herself from the checkered floor of the vestibule up onto the staircase and directly into the posterior of a gentleman who had paused on the third step to tug the sleeves of his military tunic into proper position.

"Oh!" Aphrodite gasped, at last taking note of her surroundings.

The soldier turned and gazed down at her with one raven's wing of an eyebrow lifted in silent question.

"I do beg your pardon," Aphrodite managed to say, though she was quite out of breath. "I have—I was—I did not take note of you until I turned up the staircase and—"

"You did not take note of me?" asked the soldier, his eyebrow rising even higher. "How can one not take note of a person as large as Stanislaus Nicolaivich Kuechera when he is on such a tiny staircase as this?"

"S-Stanislaus Nicolaivich—? Oh, I *do* beg your pardon," Aphrodite gasped. "You are one of the Russ—I mean to say—you are with the tsar."

The soldier above her bowed. His heels clicked together. A smile edged onto his face—edged so slowly that it compelled Aphrodite to watch it as it teased at his lush lower lip, tugged at the corners of his mouth, sauntered across the valleys of his cheeks and up the austere ridges of his cheekbones, then mounted into the black velvet depths of his eyes. There, it glistened and glimmered like moonlight from behind the sultry clouds of his slightly lowered lids.

"Are you all right, Miss Coop?" asked Sir Merrill's butler, who stood above the gentleman on the staircase. Hawkins had been escorting the soldier in the enormously impressive uniform to the saloon where Sir Merrill, Lady Merrill, and their guests had gathered after the dinner.

"Y-yes, Hawkins," Aphrodite responded. "I am fine. I was in a great rush and did not in the least expect that anyone would be—That is to say, dinner is long over and all the guests—"

"I arrive late," Kuechera replied in a rumbling sort of voice, his eyes gleaming with humor. "I am forever late in this England. There is so much to be—seen." His gaze lingered on her with such intensity that little goose bumps arose on Aphrodite's upper arms. The goose bumps served to draw her attention to her sagging gloves, and she pulled them back into place at once.

Hawkins coughed softly, and Aphrodite looked up to see the butler pantomime the straightening of his hair. "Oh," Aphrodite murmured, only now feeling the loose chestnut strands teasing at her cheeks and neck. "I expect I am a perfect sight."

"Indeed," Kuechera chuckled softly. "A *perfect* sight."

Two steps above the foreigner, Hawkins's right leg twitched madly as though he had the palsy in it. Aphrodite gazed down at her own legs and discovered her torn flounce. "You must go up and join the gathering, Mr., ah, my lor—ah . . ."

"Miss Coop, may I present Count Stanislaus Nicol-aivich Kuechera," Hawkins inserted rapidly, glancing at the name on the invitation card in his hand.

Aphrodite felt her cheeks burn brightly. "Count? My lord. You must go up and join the gathering, my lord. Do not linger on my behalf. Please, do not."

"No, no, Miss Coop," the soldier replied with a self-deprecating shake of his head. "Not my lord. I am not so high as all that. I am *gospodin*, merely. Sir. Sir is quite respectful enough. To be a count in my country is of no great consequence, you see. We are countless, we counts," he added with a mischievous smile. "Will you take my arm? May I escort you?"

"Oh! No, I cannot. I must—I thank you for your kind offer, but I am most disheveled and must repair to the ladies' room before I dare . . ."

"I will be delighted to wait while you undishevel yourself, Miss Coop."

What seemed to be tiny silver stars of glee fairly danced in Count Kuechera's eyes, and for the longest moment Aphrodite imagined she could not withdraw her gaze from his. But then she sighed softly at the power of her own imagination, glanced away from the count to a smiling Hawkins, and stepped up to place a hand on the arm the count offered her. "I will accompany you to the first floor divide, my lor—sir," she declared, "but then I must turn right and you left. Hawkins will guide you safely to the Sunset Saloon and the rest of your party. I assure you of it."

"You have got to hold still, Miss Coop, or I will never get this flounce properly repaired," the young maid declared. "You cannot go back to the party with it flopping about so. You know you cannot. Lady Merrill would have an apoplexy to see it. She is prickly as a hedgehog this evening, what with that foreign tsar person and the Prince Regent both guests in her house. Not calm and self-possessed, this Lady Merrill, not born to be the wife of a diplomat, she weren't."

"Yes. I realize how very nervous Lady Merrill is this evening, Aggie. I shall do nothing to increase her worries. Thank goodness Hawkins pointed out the state of my dress to me or I should have gone rushing into the saloon without the least thought, and poor Lady Merrill would have squeaked and fainted dead away."

"Or burst into tears," Agatha replied. "A person would suppose that such a noted diplomat as our Sir Merrill would choose a wife accustomed to the rigors of entertaining royalty and foreigners and such. The first Lady Merrill was most accustomed to it. But it is not so with this one."

"No. And yet, Uncle Merrill fell madly in love with her, Aggie, and she with him. And thank goodness for it, too, for he is so much happier now that he has her beside him, and she is beyond kind to Lydia. Enough sewing, Aggie. It is quite good enough. Let it be."

"Very well, miss. I expect it will hold. Now, if you will just sit down for a moment, Miss Coop, I will see to your hair."

"No, no, do not, Aggie," Aphrodite protested, settling down onto the little bench before the vanity. "I will see to my hair myself. There is something more important I require of you."

"Yes?"

"You must go to Hawkins and request that he tell Sir Merrill—very quietly and unobtrusively, mind—that I must speak with him in the winter parlor as soon as possible."

"Yes, miss. I shall be pleased to do so."

"Then, do it now, Aggie."

How foolish of me to think I could dash straight into the saloon, seize Uncle Merrill by the arm, and drag him from the room without causing poor Claire to swoon dead away at the legion of raised eyebrows such an action would produce, Aphrodite thought. *It will be much better to place Uncle Merrill's method of departure in his own hands. He will know how to extricate himself from the gathering without sending Claire's heart to pounding with terror. Likely as not, he will find a way to simply fade from sight and reappear just as quietly, and no one, including Claire, will realize he has gone at all.*

Kuechera noted his host's departure—a quiet departure designed to go unnoticed by anyone in the room—and took immediate advantage of it. With a charming smile and a gaze that filled Lady Merrill with the oddest confidence, he convinced her to accompany him through the French doors of the saloon and out onto the small balcony beyond. Unaccustomed to the sense of assurance that enveloped her in the count's presence, but rejoicing in it, Lady Merrill agreed. Once there, she allowed her hand to remain on his arm as they gazed off into the night. She stood close beside him, so very close that the scent of her wound its way seductively into Kuechera's brain, teasing him, despite her married state, daring him to draw her into his arms and kiss her as passionately as she deserved to be kissed. All he had heard of the English ladies was true. His impatient anticipation as he had approached the English shore had been justified. They were like innocent wild-flowers begging to be picked, these ladies of England. And Stanislaus Kuechera wished to pick them all.

Surely Sergio must feel some of what I feel when he is among them, Stauss thought. *As old as he is, as jaded as he claims to be, such beauty, such innocence, must call out to him. I know we are different, he and I, but we cannot be as different as all that.*

Images of his cousin Sergio flickered through Kuechera's mind as he listened to the pleasant drone of Lady Merrill's voice describing the celebrations scheduled to take place throughout London. And with the images came anxiety. They had sailed with Tsar Alexander on the HMS *Impregnable,* he and Sergio. And, until the night they had seen the cliffs of Dover shimmering in the moonlight, Kuechera had convinced himself that his cousin had been renewed at last. He had actually come to believe that Sergio, having agreed to accompany him to these foreign shores, had thus signified his intent to abandon his quest for the ancient tome that would teach him how to change himself into a mere mortal. But on that night, beneath the half-moon, a particular uneasiness had manifested itself in Sergio's manner; a craving beyond Kuechera's comprehension had peered from the unfathomable depths of his cousin's eyes.

"You and your women," Sergio had said with a grimace as he had leaned nonchalantly against the ship's rail. "I, on the other hand, have heard talk of a very special library."

The dratted volume was rumored to be in England! Utter devastation had wrapped itself around Kuechera's heart. But he had not let on. He had dared not disclose his feelings or Sergio would despise him. At thirty, Kuechera was far too old to wear his emotions on his sleeve like some puling infant. Instead, the young count had hinted to his cousin that perhaps if he were to marry, he would find new meaning to his continued existence. But no sooner had the words passed Kuechera's lips than the same cloak of devastation that had just descended on him wrapped itself around Sergio's proud form as well. "Marriage has always seemed an overly complicated problem with which to deal," his cousin had responded quietly, solemnly.

"You have grown most silent, Count Kuechera," Lady Merrill said, interrupting his thoughts. "Can it be that the night compels you to melancholy? It often does as much to me. Especially when the fog steals in and wraps London in its silent shroud as it does this evening. Our lights flicker so feebly against the darkness. Demons may stalk our streets undetected and unabated on such nights as these. All seems quite frightening and tinged with such hopelessness, does it not?"

"This is so? Melancholia consumes you?" Kuechera asked, glancing down in surprise. His gaze captured Lady Merrill's and held it. "Ah, I understand," he murmured after a few silent moments. "You are like the tiny mouse married to the lion, are you not? To have your own Prince Regent and the Russian Tsar and all the rest of us as guests in your house does not fill your heart with joy, but with fear."

"How do you—does it show so very much?" Lady Merrill asked. "Do they all see? Oh, I am such a failure. I cannot think how Merrill puts up with me."

"No, my lady, you are not a failure," Kuechera replied, placing a long, slim finger beneath her chin. "They do none of them see what I see. Only listen. They laugh; they bicker; conversation buzzes about the room.

Your guests are pleased with the evening with which you provide them. And I am the most pleased of all."

"How can you be? You have just arrived."

"And already I know of something I can do to please you. You are very beautiful, my lady," he added, his voice growing soft, intimate. "My heart beats a ragged rhythm in my breast simply because you honor me with your presence."

"Oh," whispered Claire.

"No, do not turn away," Kuechera whispered as she took a step back. He tugged her gently forward and with the tip of one well-manicured finger drew a line softly along her cheek.

Claire knew she ought to flee this foreign gentleman on the instant. He could not be aware how she thrilled at his touch.

"No, do not look over your shoulder at those doors, dear lady," Kuechera murmured. "I will do you no harm. I give you my word. Look at me."

Claire did look, and his eyes stirred the most potent desires in her breast; the very tone of his voice set her afire. She must separate herself from him and return to the saloon at once. And yet, she found she did not wish to part from him at all. As his strong arms went gently around her, she did not protest but chose instead to float in the starlit midnight of his eyes. When his lips touched hers, such a passionate dream encompassed her that she knew nothing but an urgent ache for him, for his touch, for his kiss.

"There, that's done," Aphrodite declared, studying herself in the looking glass. "Not a hair out of place. I shall prove quite acceptable to everyone. And once I have told Uncle Merrill what I overheard, I will feel a good deal more sociable, too. Oh, but I cannot believe anyone would think to do such a dastardly thing. And to think that whoever they are, they have come to this house as Uncle Merrill's invited guests!"

With a disgusted shake of her head at the thought that such men had taken advantage of her uncle's hospitality, Aphrodite rose, left the chamber, and made her way down the corridor to the winter parlor.

"Aphrodite? What is it? Are you not well?" her uncle queried, his face a mask of worry as she entered. "You did not injure yourself playing some childish game with Lydia? It was kind of you not to forget her in the midst of this gathering, but—"

"I am fine, Uncle Merrill."

"Something has happened to Lydia?"

"No, no. Lydia is quite safe."

"Thank goodness. I imagined one or the other of you had bumped your head or banged your knees or worse when Hawkins came to me. What is it that demands my presence in this parlor, then, when we have a swarm of notables in the saloon? Out with it, m'dear, and quickly, too, before Claire discovers I have gone and panic overwhelms her. You know how she is, Aphrodite. She has no confidence at all in her abilities."

"There are some gentlemen planning to assassinate Tsar Alexander, Uncle Merrill," Aphrodite said abruptly, her hands taking hold of her uncle's sleeve.

"Some gentlemen? Assassinate Tsar Alexander?" The amazement on Sir Merrill's face quite equalled the wonder in his tone.

"I knew you would wish to know at once."

"Aphrodite, wherever did you get such an idea as that?"

"I heard them speaking together in your office, Uncle."

"Never."

"Indeed, I did."

"Some of my guests departed the saloon, made their way to my private office, gathered 'round, and proposed a plan to assassinate the tsar as you looked on? I think not, my dear. Is it a game? I truly haven't time for games at the moment."

"They did not realize I was there, Uncle. Lydia and I were playing hide-and-seek. Well, I did not think for a moment that I would be missed, and I certainly did not expect any of our guests to be anywhere but in the saloon. At any rate, I hid under your desk, and just as I tucked myself thoroughly from view, some gentlemen entered the office and closed the door behind them. They began to say the oddest things. The upshot of it is that there is a most devious plot afoot to assassinate Tsar Alexander."

Sir Merrill stared silently at his elder sister's only child. He ran his fingers through his thinning blond hair. He placed his hands on his hips, removed them, replaced them, removed them again, and stuffed them into his pockets. "Aphrodite," he murmured. "What am I going to do with you? You grow more like your mother every day." He then removed his hands from his pockets, stepped forward, and gave his niece an awkward but well-intentioned hug. "I ought to give you a tremendous scold," he muttered as he set her free. "But I have never been able to do that. You are so very like Grace, and she was the kindest and most caring of all my sisters. But she did have the most wicked imagination and such a penchant for melodrama."

"I did not imagine it, Uncle Merrill. I heard every

word, I assure you. And I am not being in the least melodramatic. You can see plainly how calm and composed I am."

Thank goodness, Aphrodite thought, *that I fixed my hair and allowed Aggie to attend to my flounce and did not rush straight from his office into the saloon. Perhaps it was exceptional good luck that I ran into Count Kuechera.*

"You do not appear to be in the throes of some imagined drama," Sir Merrill conceded, "but such an announcement, Aphrodite. Surely such a thing cannot be. You have misunderstood their conversation. Who were these gentlemen?"

"Who?"

"Yes, who. There is no one in the house you have not met, I believe. Wait. There is one. Count Kuechera."

"I had the honor to meet the count as he arrived, Uncle Merrill, as I was on my way to send Hawkins for you."

"Well, then, he is not one of your conspirators, certainly. Not there, eh? Could not have been one of them."

"No."

"Who were the gentlemen, then? Can you give me their names?"

"No, Uncle. I did not actually see them. There were three men who spoke. I did think I had heard two of the voices before, but I cannot be certain to whom they belonged."

"Just so. You did not see them. You were under my desk. Tell me precisely what was said, Aphrodite."

"One said, in the most horrid voice, 'All is set. The time, the place, all most convenient for our intentions.' And another replied, 'Indeed. There is nothing or no one to stand in our way now.' And a third, 'It will write *fini* to the tsar's endlessly altering policies, I'll give you that. But we cannot remain away from the party any longer tonight. I only wished to know that all has been arranged.' "

"And?" asked Sir Merrill.

"And what, Uncle?"

"What else did they say?"

"Why, nothing. They departed as abruptly as they appeared."

Sir Merrill Heath stared at his niece with the most perplexed expression. "And from this conversation you leaped to the conclusion that Tsar Alexander is endangered?"

"They said all was set, that nothing would stand in their way. What else could it mean to 'write *fini* to the tsar's endlessly altering policies' than that they intend to assassinate him?"

"It could very well mean that someone has come up with a plausible bargain to be struck, or a treaty the tsar will readily sign and adhere to, or that Blücher has gained the influence over him that he has longed to have and will now prove a factor in steadying the tsar's resolve. It could mean any of those things and more, Aphrodite. But I certainly do not believe it means that the gentlemen you overheard are assassins. Do not worry about it, dearest. The language and machinations of governments and diplomats are foreign to young ladies, as well they should be. Come, let us return to our guests. And you are to enjoy yourself, Aphrodite. Drive all thoughts of this fiddle-faddle from your mind."

Lady Merrill felt somewhat discomposed as she reentered the saloon on Count Kuechera's arm—discomposed and a trifle weary—yet no longer nervous and highly excitable. She remembered gazing off into the night and the sense of melancholy it had caused her. She recalled the count speaking softly of melancholy. But the melancholia had not lingered, merely the vague memory of it, its last vestiges being slowly smothered beneath a growing fondness for Kuechera as he assisted her to a seat on the red velvet sofa.

Truly, with his face aglow in the lamplight like some shining alabaster statue, his sultry eyes and his black hair sweeping across his proud brow, this Count Stanislaus Kuechera must be the most gallant and handsome gentleman in all the world.

Where on earth is Aphrodite? Claire wondered. *I must introduce Aphrodite to his notice as soon as humanly possible. She and Sir Leslie are not likely to ever make a match of it, and every eligible miss in London will be after this Count Kuechera soon.*

Chapter 2

Miss Ellen Petersen regretted enormously that she had chosen to escape through the mews and dodge up Mill Street. Had it been daylight her choice would have proved most practical. But the sun had set hours ago, and Mill Street seethed with darkness. Her pulse beat heavily in her throat as she pressed herself against the soot-covered bricks of the side of Warbaesh's warehouse. She gulped, heard the thumping of her heart, attempted to force it back into its regular rhythm. She listened for the sound of his boot heels ringing on the cobbles behind her. Nothing. Perhaps she had escaped him. Perhaps she had lost him in the mews, and he had turned toward Boyle Street.

Oh, dear God, Miss Petersen thought, *please let him have turned toward Boyle Street. But even if he did turn toward Boyle Street, would I not still hear his boots? Would they not, even now, be echoing off in the distance? Where has he gone? Where?*

Cautiously, she stepped away from the bricks. In the distance to her right the lamps of Conduit Street glimmered. Once she gained that thoroughfare she would be safe. There was considerable traffic in Conduit Street day and night. Surely he would not think to attack in the presence of others. She had thought to bring her reticule, at least. She would hail a hackney cab and ride safely to the booking office where she would purchase a ticket on the mail to Mrs. Eleanor Pierce's School for Young Ladies in Twickenham. He would not think to follow her there, even if it was such a short distance from London. From Twickenham she would send word to—to—Miss Petersen gulped. To whom? To Bow Street? To the House of Lords? To the Prince Regent, himself? Whom *did* one tell? In whom did a poor young governess confide such a secret? *Mrs. Pierce will know,* she assured herself silently. *Mrs. Pierce knows everything.*

Miss Petersen gathered her courage around her and took a determined step toward Conduit Street. And another. And a third. No footsteps echoed her own. Relief rushed through her every vein. *He no longer follows,* she thought, rejoicing. *He is likely even now searching for me in completely the wrong place.* Buoyed by these thoughts, her steps grew less fear filled, and in a moment she was actually running up Mill Street, toward the lamps, toward the traffic, toward comfort and safety. Just as she rounded the corner into the larger thoroughfare, a hand reached out from the shadows, seized her by the elbow, and tugged her back into the darkness of Mill Street.

Miss Petersen screamed. The hand jerked her across the cobbles and swung her around, up against a broad chest where her face was pressed tightly against a ruby stickpin, the prongs of which cut deeply into her cheek. She attempted to scream again, and she was shoved back from the chest. A large hand smacked her across the face, cutting her other cheek with the ring on one of its fingers. Then two strong arms gathered her up against a very solid body, and one hand descended over her nose and mouth.

"Cease that obnoxious noise at once, Ellen," hissed a gruff, terrifying voice in her ear. "I shall kill you here and now if you scream again. Do place your trust in that, won't you?"

Miss Petersen's muffled reply was indecipherable. She could not speak. She could not *breathe*. Desperately she attempted to disengage herself from the hand that covered her mouth and nose, but her captor held her so tightly that she could not force his hand aside. Thinking she would surely smother, she twisted in his grasp, inhaled desperately as his hand came free, and then pounded her fists wildly against his chest, scratched at his face, and kicked at his legs in an attempt to escape him. Her wide-brimmed bonnet slipped from her head. The front of her pelisse tore open. The string that held her little reticule to her wrist snapped, and the tiny purse soared out of the alley into Conduit Street and whacked against the sensitive nose of one of a pair of blooded chestnuts in the traces of a landau just then passing along the thoroughfare.

Startled, its nose smarting, the horse reared in the traces. The second horse followed suit. The elderly driver cursed loudly and directed every bit of his attention to the pair. The lone passenger, who sat in the forward-facing seat of the carriage and had lowered both sides of the divided hood to enjoy the star-filled sky, sniffed at the air, then stood and stepped from the jolting vehicle as though it stood completely still. His dancing shoes touched the cobbles lightly, soundlessly. There was raw fear in the air. He could not only smell it, but feel it as well, crawling along his arms and up his spine. The hairs at the back of his neck prickled with it. He flowed around the corner into Mill Street just as Miss Petersen's captor shoved her, face first, against the bricks of the corner building. The dastard was so tall, so broad, that his body hid her completely from view. He tore the remainder of her pelisse from her. His fingers scrabbled at the high collar of her dress, ripped it downward across her back as his knee and one arm continued to press her mercilessly against the wall.

Ellen Petersen screamed again and again and again. She fought to escape him, struggled to get out from beneath him. "No!" she screamed as she felt the back of her dress torn from her. "No! Please!"

Chester Nuberly laughed and spun her around to face him. "No?" he chuckled. "Please? No what, m'dear? Don't have my way with you? Don't kill you? But I desire the first and I must do the last." He cocked his right arm back and smashed his fist into her pretty Cupid's bow lips. Then he pulled his fist back and prepared to hit her again. But he did not hit her again. He could not. From behind him, something strong closed over his ready fist, froze it in place, then crushed it. As though Nuberly's fingers and hand were made of chalk, something ground them into powder. Nuberly screamed as loudly as Miss Petersen had screamed.

Her face a mask of horror, Ellen shuddered visibly as Nuberly's arm was then twisted behind his back. She gasped at the snap of it. She blanched as Chester Nuberly shot forward, propelled through the air into the rough bricks of the building across from her with a negligent toss, like a piece of rubbish into a bin. Nuberly slumped to the cobbles, whimpering in pain.

"*Gospodin,*" an elderly voice cried. "What goes forward?" Miss Petersen watched, dazed, as a slightly bent, silver-haired little man hurried into the alleyway.

The gentleman who had rescued her shrugged out of a dark cloak, stepped forward, and wrapped it around the shaking governess. "Fear not, my lady," he said, his voice soft, gentle. "This fiend will harm you never again. You have my word on it. Vlad, escort this lady to our carriage. I will follow in but a moment more."

Sir Leslie Hedington's eyebrows wiggled somewhat like agitated caterpillars, which made Aphrodite smile up at him despite the seriousness of their conversation.

"I daresay you misunderstood them, Miss Coop," he said after a moment of grave thought. He gave the hand she had placed on his sleeve as they promenaded along the edge of the dance floor a gentle pat. "Such a thing could not happen. Not here in England." Hedington gazed down into Aphrodite's determined blue eyes and thought how truly beautiful they were and how truly telling. He could always discover how Aphrodite was going to respond to something he said by the simple expedient of gazing down into those eyes and observing the emotions they inevitably displayed. Of course, he had been courting Miss Coop for five long years, in Season and out, so he ought well be able to tell from her glance what odd little twists were occurring in her mind and precisely what words would spill from between those marvelous lips. If Sir Leslie and Miss Coop were not soul mates or lovers, they were nonetheless exceptionally well acquainted.

"I did not misunderstand," Aphrodite protested in an exasperated hiss. "That is precisely what Uncle Merrill thinks, but it is not so."

"It is," Sir Leslie responded. "I realize that you *believe* you heard some sort of conspiracy going forward, but that's merely because you are prone to—to—"

"To what? I am prone to what, Sir Leslie?"

"Fits of drama."

"I am not!"

"Yes, you are." Sir Leslie smiled at her, hoping to soften the blow. "You know you are, Aphrodite, and so does almost everyone in London. Do you not recall the day that you rode neck-or-nothing to Lady Anne Harbock's rescue in Rotten Row when she required no rescuing at all?"

"Well, but anyone might have concluded from the manner in which she rode that her horse was—"

"And then there was the evening that you rushed from the Gatelys' ballroom in tears," Sir Leslie interrupted, "because you imagined that Black Jack Armenton had—"

"This is not the same thing at all," Aphrodite protested, her cheeks burning with embarrassment.

"I beg your pardon, my dear. Truly I do. But it is precisely the same thing. I am one of your most ardent admirers. You know that I am. But you are prone to—to—leaping before you look—and leaping most dramatically, too."

Aphrodite opened her fan and began to make use of it to cool not only her cheeks but her simmering temper as well. "I admit I have been mistaken in the past," she managed to say after a long moment. "I am the first to admit that I have a tendency to——"

"Make mountains out of molehills?"

"Very well, if that is the manner in which you prefer to think of it."

"It is not the manner in which I prefer to think of it, my dear Aphrodite. It is precisely what you do."

"Yes, well, but I am not doing it at the moment."

"You never think you're doing it at the moment you're doing it, m'dear. It's one of the things about you that terrifies me, and one of the things that endears you to me as well. Life with you, Aphrodite, will never be peaceful, I fear. And yet, I cannot imagine my life without you."

"Leslie, do not."

"Do not what?"

"Do not propose to me again. This is not the moment for it. Oh," she added, looking toward the ballroom doorway.

"Oh?" Sir Leslie followed her gaze. "Who is he?"

"Count Stanislaus Kuechera. He attended Uncle Merrill's dinner last evening. That is to say, he arrived a good deal too late for dinner, but——"

"So that's the man." Sir Leslie studied the tall, lithe figure posed on the threshold with some consideration.

"That's the man who?" Aphrodite asked.

"Eh? What?"

"Why do you say 'so that's the man' and in such a voice, too?"

"Because I have heard of Count Kuechera. He is a Cossack, m'dear—the fiercest of all soldiers. Napoleon marched into Russia with six hundred thousand men, and a mere eleven thousand of them survived the experience. Some people will tell you it was the Russian winter that decimated the legions of that French upstart, but it was not. It was Kuechera and his bands of Cossacks."

"Count Kuechera commanded all the Cossacks?"

"Not in name, Aphrodite, but in actuality. No one could prevent him following and attacking the retreating French. And because he persisted, all of the Cossacks persisted, taking their lead from him regardless of rank. What a mind-chilling thing it must have been to feel the ground shudder beneath your feet from the pounding of horses' hooves and peer up through the lowering dusk to see such men as Kuechera ride down on you with sabres high, intending to send you to your Maker."

Aphrodite's eyes grew large as she imagined it.

"We shall need to be certain that that one is not close by," the gentleman with the fine brown moustache observed in a hushed voice, his gaze fixed on Kuechera as Lord and Lady Cossington welcomed the count quite properly to their ball. "Be the devil to pay if he is anywhere near us when we do the thing."

"Balderdash! If he's near enough to pose a problem, we shall take him down as well," replied the gentleman in the diamond studs with considerable bravado. "Besides, I have yet to see Kuechera actually accompany Tsar Alexander anywhere. He turns up eventually, of course. Always late, that one. Apparently, the heroic Count Kuechera has no thought to devote himself exclusively to the tsar now that they have arrived in England. Much too busy

with the ladies. Drawn to our English roses like a bee to
the buds, he is. And they to him. One glance from those
black eyes, the merest hint of his smile, and our women
all but swoon before him. Look there. Even as I speak
the new Lady Merrill is bound in his direction. She accompanied him out onto the balcony last evening, and
he returned her to the saloon speechless, dazed, and
smiling. Sat her down upon her own sofa, he did, while
she gazed up at him as though she had taken leave of
her senses."

"Great heavens, did Sir Merrill take note of it?"
asked the gentleman with the moustache.

"Never. Gone off somewhere when it all came
about."

"Yes, well, perhaps the Cossack will not prove a problem, but we have another. I think we were overheard
last evening."

A most amazed pair of blue eyes focused intently on
the gentleman with the moustache. "Never! There was
no one anywhere about to overhear us."

"I think, perhaps, there was. A female."

"A female? What on earth makes you think—"

"Hairpins."

"Hairpins?" The gentleman with the diamond studs
gazed at his companion, his blue eyes sparkling with
laughter. "How the devil could hairpins make you think—"

"It's not a jest," the other replied. "I had cause to return to Sir Merrill's office before I departed last evening,
and there were hairpins scattered about on the carpeting—a little trail of hairpins which I followed."

"And where did they lead?"

"They led under Sir Merrill's desk. More likely, you
understand, the trail began under Sir Merrill's desk

and led to the corridor as she loped away. You could hide an entire battalion under Sir Merrill's desk, you know, and no one would take the least note of it."

"Devil! Now what do we do?"

"I expect we shall need to consult with Nuberly. Even if some little serving girl hid from us because she feared to be caught in Sir Merrill's office at such an hour, even if she overheard every word we said, she could not have understood. We have been most cautious throughout, and we were exceptionally so last evening."

"Still, it would be most beneficial to discover who the woman was and what she thought she heard," the gentleman with the diamond studs said quietly. "I've a footman with yearnings toward one of Sir Merrill's maids. I shall send him on an errand to Sir Merrill's establishment first thing tomorrow. If the little wench who overheard has confided her escapade in anyone, James's gossipy maid will know of it. She passes all the gossip on to James with the utmost pleasure, too. He will return home bursting with the news and pass it on to Dimity. And Dimity will think it his duty to inform me that James is gossiping again and report all to me."

"And then we'll tell Nuberly." The gentleman with the mustache nodded. "Good idea. Nuberly will know what to do. Where the deuce is Nuberly?" he added. "He ought to have been here an hour ago."

As the gentlemen ceased their conversation and gazed once again toward the ballroom entrance, they noted Lady Merrill adjusting the set of a black velvet riband about her neck as she made her way to Count Kuechera's side.

It is quite old-fashioned to wear such a riband as this, Claire thought, _even though I have pinned my new cameo to it. But it was the only thing in my jewelry box wide enough to_ *cover the blemishes. I cannot think from where they came; but I am certainly not going to display them to the world, and especially I am not going to display them at Anne's little ball. She would tease me mercilessly did she take note of them. She would likely spread it about that Merrill had taken a bite of me. I hope Merrill did not take a bite of me.* Lady Merrill smiled shyly to herself. *I hope I would remember if he had.*

With a last little tug at the riband, Claire came to a halt before Count Kuechera and smiled up at him. "I am being most forward," she announced, her eyes sparkling with good humor, "but I do not care in the least. I wish you to come and make the acquaintance of my husband's niece, sir."

Kuechera returned her smile with an easy grace. "Then, certainly I cannot refuse."

Despite the fact that the wrinkled little servant had passed a bedwarmer between the sheets and provided Miss Petersen with two extra blankets, Ellen shivered uncontrollably in the bed. Where the tall soldier in his elegant tunic and his odd trousers had discovered the high-necked, flannel nightgown for her to don, she could not guess. How he had got her out of her own torn clothing and into the gown, she could not quite remember. What she did remember—and therefore realized that all of this night must be nothing more than a fevered dream—was that the soldier had lifted her from his carriage in strong arms, and with her head resting on his shoulder, he had risen straight up through the air to a small balcony outside the window of this very chamber. He had waited patiently, murmuring encouragement to her, until his man had opened the window and bid them enter.

Which certainly could not have happened, Ellen thought. *And so none of this evening could have happened either. I did not panic, put on my pelisse, seize my hat and reticule, and run from the house. Nor did that horrid Mr. Nuberly follow me and attack me in Mill Street. I am even now in my own little bed in the chamber beside little Janet's. I am ill but I am safe. In a short time, I shall awaken from this fever dream and return to my position as Janet's governess and never think of any of it again.*

Except, she knew perfectly well that she would think of Mr. Chester Nuberly again. And she would be certain never to let herself be alone in his company—in the library, in the garden, not even in the schoolroom. Never. Fever dream or not, Mr. Chester Nuberly had frightened her from the first moment he had taken up residence in Mrs. Bennett's house, and she would be even more careful of him now than she had been in the past.

There was a slight scratching at her door, and then it was pushed open, and the bent, silver-haired servant appeared with a glass filled with liquid in his hand and another blanket over his arm. "You are petrified, little one," he said in a wavering old voice with a quaint accent. "You must drink a bit of medicine, and I will tuck this blanket around you, and then you will sleep."

"I am d-dreaming you, aren't I?" Ellen asked, as he lay the blanket at the foot of the bed and helped her to sit up against the pillows so she might sip at the liquid. "I am ill, and you are n-not the manservant to some strong, foreign soldier at all, but a physician come to make me well."

"Just so," agreed the old man, his dark eyes sparkling behind his wrinkles. "Drink a bit more, child. We must drive the shock of your dreams from you and help you to sleep peacefully."

"And you are a Scot; that's why your words sound so odd," Miss Petersen continued. "And Mr. Nuberly has gone off to Lady Cossington's ball just as he intended, has he not?"

"Hours ago," the man assured her.

"And when I wake, there will be much to do. Janet heartily wishes to view some of the celebrations, and I h-have promised to take her to Green Park tomorrow to view the Castle of Discord."

"And so shall you do." The elderly man nodded, tipping a bit more of the liquid between Ellen's lips. "You shall do whatever you wish once you are well again. The master will see to it. Good is my master. Kind, young, caring, honorable."

Ellen thought his response somewhat odd for a physician, but she could not quite grasp what it was she found odd about it because the more of the liquid she drank, the more her thoughts seemed to jumble and fade. In little more than five minutes, the shivering left her, and she sighed.

Vladimir Ryzinsky set the laudanum mixture aside and removed two of the pillows from behind the young woman's back, easing her down once again between the sheets. He was careful to see that enough pillows remained to give her adequate support, that the blankets were tucked carefully in around her, and that the small coal fire continued to sputter and warm the chamber. He would see to the horrid abrasions on her face now that she was truly asleep. It was nasty what the Englishman had done to her soft, smooth skin. And the man had pushed her against bricks, the master had said. Ryzinsky must pick the tiny bits of cinder brick from out of the wounds to keep them from festering before he spread the healing salve over them. Even so, there would be scars. Many of them.

For such an appealing face to be damaged in such a distasteful way is most offensive, Vlad thought to himself as he set about his task. *The master will not allow it. Tonight he will search for his cousin to aid this poor woman. He does not say this to me, but I know. The master cares for these English as he cares for his own people. His heart is large and his intentions, noble.* "He comes of the finest stock," Vlad murmured softly. "How could he be anything else but noble? And if all goes well, he will discover in this England what his papa wishes him to discover. I am certain of it."

Aphrodite could not understand why Sir Leslie did not go away. She glared at him. She tapped her dancing slipper restlessly. She even went so far as to place her arm through Count Kuechera's arm and urge the count to stroll with her around the edges of the dance floor. But even such audaciousness as that proved to be of no avail. Sir Leslie simply ignored what he knew to be her strongest feelings and fell into step with them at the count's other side.

"Leslie," Miss Coop hissed, peering around Kuechera as she drew both gentlemen to a halt at the far wall, "please go ask someone to dance!"

"Who?" queried Sir Leslie, his hands clasped behind his back, his head tilted a bit forward in order to see around Kuechera himself.

"I do not give a fig. Ask Miss Layton or Daphne Quinn or one of the upstairs maids. Ask anyone."

"Ask me. I will dance with you," Kuechera offered, and then he chuckled at the look of astonishment on Sir Leslie's face. "No. I forget," Kuechera said, rescinding the offer. "In this England gentlemen dance with ladies only. They do not dance with other gentlemen. It is not so in my country."

"Gentlemen dance with gentlemen in Russia?" Aphrodite asked.

"In Russia, yes. And in my country as well."

"You are not Russian, sir?"

"No, Miss Coop, not Russian. I was born in the most beautiful mountains on the face of the earth—the Carpathians."

"Near Romania," Sir Leslie offered with a knowing nod. "I will show you on a globe, Aphrodite, where he means."

Kuechera laughed quietly. "You know, do you, Sir Leslie? And here I believed my homeland so insignificant that such a nation as the mighty England would never have heard of it. Transylvania, Miss Coop," he added, with a cock of his raven's wing of an eyebrow. "It is on your globe, Sir Leslie? My Transylvania?"

"Indeed, it is." Sir Leslie's gaze abruptly discovered the silver stars winking in Kuechera's eyes, and without the least thought, he tumbled down into the bottomless depths from which they had arisen. His smile slackened; his heart grew large and floated upward to pound in his ears; his insides shuddered. His lips parted, but no sound emerged from between them.

"Sir Leslie?" Aphrodite could not believe the utterly lunatic expression that had just spread across the gentleman's face. "Leslie, are you not well?" she asked quietly, reaching around Kuechera to give the bottom of Sir Leslie's coat a hearty tug.

"Eh? What?" responded Sir Leslie, tearing his gaze from Kuechera's. "What did you want, m'dear?"

"I want you to go dance with someone and leave the c—I mean, Sir ah—"

"Stanislaus," inserted Kuechera easily.

"And leave Sir Stanislaus to me."

"Go, Sir Leslie," Kuechera said. "You wish to speak about the war, and we will do so before my visit is over. I give you my word. But I will speak with this young woman now."

Sir Leslie nodded, bowed from the waist, and set off toward the opposite side of the dance floor.

"I cannot think what got into him," Aphrodite apologized. "Sir Leslie is generally the most polite person. He would never think to fix himself to us like sealing wax if he were in his right mind."

"Sir Leslie is in love with you, I think," Kuechera offered, taking her arm and urging her to turn right rather than left, thus avoiding three rather large mirrors that appeared to be lying in wait for him. He had no wish to deal with mirrors and frivolous explanations tonight. His mind was already occupied with the young woman who occupied his bed at the Pulteney.

"No, he is not in love with me," Aphrodite replied after considerable thought on the subject. "He should like to be, but he is actually not."

"I see."

"Do you? I should not think any gentleman would understand what I just said. Gentleman are generally simpletons when it comes to such things."

"In my country, Miss Coop," Kuechera said, flashing the most boyish and irresistible smile directly at her. "In my country are many men who would like to be in love with a particular woman but are not. To our great misfortune, we most often call the men husbands and the women wives."

Miss Coop did not smile, but scowled instead.

Kuechera stared at her with something approaching wonder. It was beyond his experience that a woman would not smile back at him once he had bestowed his own charming smile on her, and completely beyond his understanding that rather than laugh politely at his little jest, Miss Coop should frown. Perhaps she did not quite understand. "It was intended as a jest, merely, Miss Coop," he said. "You need not look so serious."

"Oh! I do beg your pardon. I was not at all listening. I was thinking of something else entirely. I wish you will escort me out onto the balcony, Count Kuechera. There is something I should like to discuss with you. Something quite serious."

Chapter 3

Kuechera arrived back in his rooms at the Pulteney shortly before dawn. He was unusually upset with himself. He had not intended to linger at the Cossingtons' ball for longer than it would take him to discover if his cousin Sergio was present. He had known in a matter of moments that Sergio was not there and had been about to turn and leave the place when Lady Merrill had approached him with a stunning smile and a subtle, defiant look in her eyes. The tiny seed of self-confidence he had planted the previous evening had obviously taken root, and he had not been able to resist nourishing the tender shoot that was just then putting forth; so he had agreed to accompany her to

Miss Aphrodite Coop's side. Once there, he had lingered much longer than intended.

At first he had remained merely to be polite. A few minutes, a bit of conversation with Miss Coop and her gentleman friend, and then he would go to search the streets of London for his cousin. But once Miss Coop had ordered Sir Leslie away and led Kuechera out to the balcony, his search for Sergio had been postponed. Her tale of a conspiracy to assassinate Tsar Alexander had startled him. Equally as startling had been Miss Coop's apparent ability to resist his powers. His every move to coerce her, to dominate her, to bend her to his desires, had been thwarted. Even more mystifying, when he had fastened his determined gaze on her that final time, the warmth of her own brown eyes had nearly melted him into a puddle at her feet.

How can this be? he wondered, tugging at the buttons of his tunic, freeing his neck from the stranglehold his high-standing collar had taken on it. *Am I ill? Do I suffer some strange malady because of the great transgression I committed this night before I brought Miss Petersen to safety? Is my lack of power over Miss Coop a consequence of my own sin? She is merely a mortal woman after all, and not even a woman of the intelligentsia—not even a woman of the mind.*

"However," he murmured, his hands on his hips, staring off into space, "she has assuredly become a woman of *my* mind."

A vision of Miss Coop on the staircase at her uncle's house—strands of chestnut hair flitting around her face, her gloves drooping, her flounce hanging from her gown like a dead flounder from a fisherman's line—arose at once before him and made him smile despite his puzzlement. This was followed by memories of their encounter this evening—the sweet, fresh scent of her, the husky whisper of her voice, the silken touch of her gloved fingers on his hand returned to haunt him.

Enough, he thought, giving himself a slight shake. *Surely it is in payment for my lack of discipline and will fade with time.* He made his way silently to his bedchamber, opened the door, and gazed inside. Miss Petersen was fast asleep.

He crossed the carpeting to her bedside and stared down at her. Her name was Ellen Petersen. That much he had learned from her thoughts before he had departed for the Cossingtons' ball, but little more. Her mind had been a rat's nest of hysteria. Kuechera's brow creased with worry as he studied her. Vlad had done well to calm her, to dose her with the laudanum and apply the salve to the cuts and abrasions on her face. She had been badly bruised on other portions of her delicate young body as well. Those bruises would ache deeply for a time, but they would heal properly. It was her face that worried him. It must have been quite a pretty face, but it was not now, nor would it ever be again without his cousin Sergio's help. The salve would prevent further damage, but . . .

"Do not fear, dear one," he whispered as Miss Petersen stirred in her sleep. "I did not find Sergio this night, but I will seek him again soon. He will touch you with his mind, and the wounds that threaten your beauty will heal and fade. I cannot do such a thing, but Sergio has this power."

Kuechera lowered himself to the edge of the mattress. *Sergio will heal you,* he thought, smoothing the fair hair from Miss Petersen's brow. *He has a heart as large as the universe, my cousin. He thinks no one knows this. But I know this. I have always known it.*

"How can Sergio wish to destroy himself?" Kuechera murmured. "In him are combined all the best qualities of vampire and mortal. He is both blessed and a blessing beyond measure. How can Sergio come so coldly to this England in search of a way to shed his vampire nature and become wholly mortal? Why does he wish to die? Will I wish to die when I have lived three hundred years instead of thirty?"

"*Gospodin?*"

Vladimir Ryzinsky's quiet voice surprised Kuechera. Where had his senses gone that he had not known far in advance of his servant's approach? Could this, too, be a consequence of his allowing his anger to rule him this evening? Of his stubborn display of hatred for the man who had attacked Miss Petersen? He would ask Sergio when he found him. Sergio would know.

"What is it, Vlad?" he asked quietly, rising from the edge of the bed and turning to face the old man.

"I have moved your things to my little bedchamber, *gospodin*. You will dwell there until this lady is well. I have drawn the curtains tight, and there is a fire on the hearth."

"I did not find Sergio, but I will. You are to wake me if the day dawns cloudy enough to be out in it, or if the clouds come later. Sergio plans to leave London for the countryside. I shall not take the chance of missing him entirely."

Aphrodite rejoiced in her good fortune as she turned down her lamp and climbed into bed. Stauss had believed her. He had listened to her every word, had not once interrupted her tale or suggested that she had misinterpreted the meaning of the words she had overheard. No, nor had he wiggled his eyebrows at her or called her a featherbrain.

"Well, that is not at all fair," she murmured, hugging one of her pillows to her. "Leslie did not call me a feather-brain, nor did Uncle Merrill. But they thought it," she added with a pout. "Stauss did not so much as think it. I am certain of that. He would have turned away from me directly, did he think me some peagoose, my head stuffed with feathers. Assuredly, he would not have agreed to meet with me tomorrow evening at the Jerseys' rout to discuss how to discover who these assassins are and how to foil their despicable plot. I am so thankful Leslie told me just who Stauss was and how courageously he fought for the tsar or I should never have thought to confide in the man."

Stauss? she thought then. *Whenever did Count Kuechera give me leave to call him by such a name as Stauss? I expect in his family it may be a name of endearment, for it sounds like a shortening of his given name, but I cannot think he ever once gave me leave to use it. I cannot remember him even so much as mentioning it.*

But he must have done, she told herself silently, as she tucked the pillow behind her head and stared up at the ceiling. *Certainly, I did not conceive of such an appellation on my own. But I like it. I like it very well.* "It suits him," she said aloud. "It is strong, proud, forthright."

Forthright? she wondered. *Why did I add that? He is a roundaboutationist if he is anything. All the while we conversed, those remarkable eyes of his peered at me in the most sultry manner, as if I were some foreign delicacy and he intent on tasting me. But did he say anything at all straight to that point? No. Not a word. And was he not constantly smiling that charming smile of his because he wished to make my heart beat ever so much faster? And when he spoke, did he not plan for the tone of his voice to send the most delicious tremors through me? And he succeeded, too. Yet he did not once speak up as any forthright gentleman would do. He did never so much as say, "Miss Coop, I find your company enchanting, and I should like very much to come to know you better."*

But then Aphrodite heard in her mind the grim, determined words of Stanislaus Kuechera as he described what he would do to the men who threatened the tsar's life, and she knew instantly why she had called him forthright. Merely the memory of those words, that tone, set her teeth to chattering.

Sergio! Wait!

Sergio Dimitro Alexander Kuechera heard the command in his mind as if it had been shouted aloud. He halted in midstride and glanced back over his shoulder to see his cousin Stauss hurrying toward him. It stunned Sergio to see his cousin out in the afternoon. Stauss, unlike himself, could not bear the sunlight. It did not merely bother Stauss's eyes; it assaulted them, almost blinding him. It sapped his strength and his power enormously and sometimes befuddled his mind. This afternoon, clouds hung heavy in the skies over London, but even so, something must be seriously wrong for Stauss to chance a sudden ray of sunlight breaking through.

"What is it, cousin?" he asked as Stauss drew up beside him. "What has happened? You have not been— that is to say, no one has discovered that—"

"I came to seek your aid, Sergio."

"Indeed. What else would bring you out in the middle of an afternoon? Tell me what has happened, and I will see you well out of it. I give you my word."

Stauss smiled. It was, as always, a virtually irresistible smile, and it tugged, as it was meant to do, at Sergio's heart. "It is not for me, the help I require of you. It is for a particular lady, Sergio."

"A lady?"

"Yes, the lady lying in my bedchamber. Miss Petersen, she is called."

Sergio's eyes narrowed suspiciously.

"No, it is not what you think, cousin. I have not so much as nibbled on the lady's ear. Vlad was driving me to a particular ball when one of the horses reared in the traces. At the same moment a great stink of fear rose up all around. I followed it into an alleyway where I discovered the lady being brutalized by some ruffian. He intended to ravish her, I think, when he had finished beating her senseless."

"You stopped it."

"Certainly. I—after I did, I—you must come to the Pulteney and help the lady, Sergio. She requires you. You will see how it is with her if you will come."

"Of course I will come." Sergio stepped off the pavement on the instant and hailed a passing hackney. "To the Pulteney," he commanded the driver as he climbed inside.

"In Picadilly," Stauss added, as he followed his cousin into the coach. "I begin to enjoy saying the silly words these English name things," he added as he settled down beside Sergio. "Picadilly is one of my favorites."

"Stauss, what set you to stuttering when you told me about this lady? Something happened you did not say."

Stauss nodded, his eyes not quite meeting his cousin's. "I was furious," he said quietly. "I—I—"

"You are stuttering again."

"Because I am ashamed. I was so enraged by what that man had done that I transgressed the Decrees, Sergio."

"How?"

"I took his evil head in my hands and twisted it until it faced backward like a devil's."

"Well, you ought not to have done that."

"No. But I did not care. And I—"

"You did more?" Sergio interrupted, his dark eyes widening.

"I squandered him."

"Stauss!"

"I did not taste of his blood. I would not drink of something so repugnant to me."

Sergio stared at him, shook his head slowly from side to side. "Rage is one thing; squandering a mortal is another. You are very lucky, Bearcub, that this is England and not Transylvania. Such things might lead to a great upheaval in the villages of our homeland."

"But not here?"

"No one will know what to think of them here. The specter of a rogue vampire will not be the first thought to enter any of these enormously civilized minds. I shouldn't think it will make a bit of difference with the English. But do not do it again."

"No. Never. But something has happened because of it, Sergio. I attempted to bend a certain young woman to my will, and I could not. And when Vlad entered my chamber, I was not aware of him until he spoke. I thought because I had transgressed—"

"That's odd," Sergio replied, thinking of the woman he had met in the bookshop earlier. A woman who had set him to doubting his own powers. "But I doubt it has to do with the Decrees. Breaking the Decrees sets us at risk among the mortals. That risk is a tremendous consequence, but the only one as far as I know."

"Then, why did Miss Coop not fall under my spell?"

"I cannot imagine," murmured Sergio. "Something odd has happened to me, as well. Perhaps it's the English air?"

The gentleman who had attended the Cossingtons' party in diamond studs the evening before was this afternoon wearing the most unique catskin vest. He was seated in his library, a newspaper spread out on the tabletop before him, a cup of coffee cooling beside his right elbow. He whistled a low whistle as he perused the newsprint. "Most incredible bad luck," he declared. "No wonder Nuberly did not turn up at the Cossingtons' last evening. He was just then quite busy being beaten to death by a gang of footpads."

"Yes, well, it doesn't say precisely that, old fellow," replied his visitor, fingering his short brown moustache as he paced the length of the room. " 'Killed by a person or persons unknown,' is what it says."

"Yes, but we know what that means when it's in the *Times*. Most conservative newspaper when it comes to describing such things, the *Times*. Only wait until the penny presses get hold of it, and then you will read the real story."

"I don't wish to read the real story," replied the gentleman with the moustache. "What I wish to know is what we're going to do now, without Nuberly."

"I expect we shall have to proceed with just the two of us. You are not saying that you want to call a halt to it? You cannot be saying that, old boy? There are villas in Genoa and Venice await us. Enough monies to live out the rest of our lives like royalty if we succeed with the plan. And now, we shall split Nuberly's share between us as well."

"I—n-no, I don't mean to call a halt to it. But does it not seem strange to you that Nuberly should stick his spoon in the wall less than twenty-four hours after we were overheard in Sir Merrill's office?"

The man in the catskin vest sat back in his chair and grinned. "You think someone from Sir Merrill's establishment went roving about Mill Street after dark with the express purpose of killing Nuberly?"

"N-no. It is merely that—Nuberly's death is not the only misfortune that occurred in Mrs. Bennett's household last evening."

"What else happened?"

"It's there in the paper. In the very next column."

"I don't care to read it. Tell me," said the man in the catskin vest, lifting his neglected cup of coffee to his lips and taking a sip.

"Apparently, her daughter's governess disappeared."

"What? The pretty Miss Petersen? Last evening?"

"Yes. Thing is, the watchman discovered Miss Petersen's reticule lying on the cobbles in Conduit Street and went nosing about the area to see if the lady who lost it was lying injured nearby. Noticed the door to Warbaesh's warehouse hanging off its hinges. Raised his lantern and peered inside. That's where he discovered Nuberly."

"Nothing stolen from her reticule, eh?"

"No. Had money in it, and her handkerchief and so forth. Watchman discovered Nuberly's money still in his pocket. Discovered his card case as well. Knew Mrs. Bennett had a nephew visiting by that name. Went to tell her the sad news. It was she who recognized the reticule as Miss Petersen's."

"Likely the gang of ruffians dragged Miss Petersen off to taste of her delights," the man in the catskin vest observed. "Delicious-looking little thing, Miss Petersen.

Still, other than making our work a bit more difficult, I fail to see why any of this ought to make us alter our plan. We haven't time to formulate a new one, you know. It's all or nothing."

"It is merely that extraordinary things such as these always happen in threes," the man with the moustache replied, ceasing to pace before the library table and staring down at his comrade. "I mean to say, there is Miss Petersen's disappearance and Nuberly's death. You can be certain that a third unexpected and devastating event even now hangs heavy over our heads."

"Well now, suppose I tell you that the person who overheard us at Sir Merrill's was not a serving girl, but Sir Merrill's niece. Might that not be the third in your trio of extraordinary happenings?"

"Aphrodite?"

"So says my footman's little maid, Aggie. She told James that Miss Coop came dashing into the ladies' room, her flounce torn and the pins fallen from her hair."

"Aphrodite will have told Sir Merrill everything she heard."

"Which was nothing substantial, thank goodness. I doubt if Sir Merrill will make heads or tails of it."

"Doesn't matter. He will not have believed her," sighed the gentleman with the moustache thankfully. "She has cried wolf too often in her life."

"Are you certain?"

"Positive. Sir Leslie will not believe her either. And chances are, Aphrodite did not understand the significance of what we said herself. She is not the brightest candle in the chandelier."

"I shouldn't like to be forced to—eliminate—Miss Coop," the man in the catskin vest murmured.

"We cannot. Not possibly," replied the other.

"No, no, I can understand how you would balk at that, Manning. Still, we ought to attempt to keep track of her, just in case she should speak to someone who might take her seriously. I don't recall her being on anyone's arm but Sir Leslie's last evening, do you?"

"No."

"No. Just so. But if she did make something of our conversation, and if she should appear inclined to confide it in someone who is unaware of her—propensity to exaggerate—someone in a position to pose us a problem—well, we shall be obliged to prevent her from doing so, don't you know."

The Kuechera cousins crossed the lobby of the Pulteney Hotel in matched strides and marched up the staircase, shoulder to shoulder, to the third floor. Down the corridor to the very rear of the building, Stauss and Sergio matched each other step for step. The door to Stauss's set of rooms was opened to them before they knocked. Vladimir Ryzinsky smiled up at them, his old eyes bright. "I have given her more of the medicine, *gospodin*. She sleeps soundly. Good afternoon, Master Sergio. I am blessed to see you again."

Sergio smiled. He did not do so often. Not such a true smile as he smiled that moment. "You certainly are," he responded. "It means that you are still alive, eh, Vlad?"

"Just so, Master Sergio."

The servant escorted them to the bedchamber where Miss Ellen Petersen lay and then quietly bowed himself out of their way, disappearing back along the corridor toward the sitting room.

Sergio paused on the threshold for a moment, then crossed the chamber to Miss Petersen's bedside. Stauss followed part of the way, stopping at the foot of the bed as Sergio moved to the head of it. The elder of the two gazed down at the sleeping woman and then looked up at his cousin. "The man who did this to such a delicate, pretty little innocent, Stauss, I would squander this man myself."

Sergio looked down at Miss Petersen once more, and he touched her first with his mind, then with a long, lean, perfectly manicured index finger. He stroked her cheeks, her brow, her chin. He touched the tip of her nose and smiled a most bemused smile. "There will be no scars now, little cousin," he said then, glancing up.

"I thank you," Stauss replied. "Miss Petersen would thank you as well if she knew. What the devil was all that touching her with your finger about? I have never seen you do such a thing before."

"Nothing. I was merely thinking as I looked at her what a pretty young lady she was and will be again. Almost as pretty as a young lady I met today in the bookshop. Almost, but not quite."

Stauss's heart gave a tiny leap of hope. His cousin had seen a pretty lady, and he had wished to touch her, to stroke her, and likely to kiss her lips. Sergio did not say that, but it was clear enough to Stauss. Perhaps this lady would provide the reason for Sergio to forsake his quest for true mortality. But he dare not mention it. He would not say a word to Sergio about it. He would merely cling stoically to the bit of hope provided him.

"There is nothing else you require of me, Stauss? I shall be leaving London in a few days and do not plan to return until the moon is full again."

"Nothing," Stauss declared with a slow smile. "There is some plot afoot to assassinate the tsar, but I shan't require anyone's aid to foil that."

"Cocky little bear cub," Sergio observed.

"Not at all. Well, perhaps a bit. If there is anything I can do to return this particular favor, Sergio," Stauss said, "you will merely mention it and it is done."

"As a matter of fact, little cousin," Sergio replied, crossing the carpet to where Stauss stood and putting an arm around Stauss's shoulders. "There is a favor you can do for me."

"Speak it."

"Provide me an entree to Lady Jersey's rout this evening."

Aphrodite knew why she had been fidgeting about the entire day, unable to settle in one place for more than a quarter hour. And she knew perfectly well why she had changed her gown four times before deciding upon the one she wore now. It was because Count Kuechera had promised to meet with her at the rout this evening and discuss with her plans to catch the men she had overheard in her uncle's office. At least, she told herself that was the reason. It could have nothing at all to do with an opportunity to gaze into his mysteriously compelling eyes again, or to contemplate his very tempting lips. And it certainly had nothing to do with his thick, dark hair, or his proud alabaster brow, or the soft, seductive rumble of his voice.

"Is she never coming?" Aphrodite asked impatiently at the foot of the staircase, her arm tucked through her uncle's.

And then Lady Merrill appeared on the landing above them, and Aphrodite noticed at once. Sir Merrill's arm stiffened in surprise. Obviously, he noticed as well. Lady Merrill fairly floated down the steps to them in a cloud of ruby silk, her fair hair piled high atop her head and threaded through with gemstones all the colors of the rainbow. Around her neck was a red velvet riband which held a diamond brooch close at her throat. Lady Merrill's eyes glittered with anticipation, her lips curved upward in the most beguiling smile.

"This is not my Claire," Sir Merrill said, extending his free hand to help her down the last of the steps. "What have you done, lady, with my wife?"

"Oh, I have stuffed her in a trunk in the attic," Lady Merrill replied flippantly. "Belongs in the attic, little mouse."

"Truly, Claire, you are exceptionally beautiful this evening," Lord Merrill said, once the three of them had entered the coach and were on their way to the Jerseys'. "It is not merely your gown or your jewels or your hair—"

"No, it is none of them," Claire interrupted. "It is something much more important. It is a gift given me by a gentleman friend."

"What? Who?" Sir Merrill asked, scowling abruptly.

"Merrill, do not even think to be jealous. You haven't the least cause. I do not even know if the gentleman is aware he has given me this gift, but it began to grow in me right after we spoke together."

"Claire, what the deuce are you saying?" Sir Merrill asked, perturbed. "Who is this fellow? Ought I to call him out?"

Lady Merrill laughed quietly and squeezed her husband's arm. "It was the Cossack, Count Kuechera. And no, I do not believe you have reason to call him out. He merely escorted me onto our balcony the evening of our dinner party, and we spoke together. It all seems very cloudy and dreamlike now, when I attempt to recall it. I cannot so much as remember where he stood, where I stood, how our conversation began or ended. But I do know that the little mouse who was afraid of everything and everyone, the one who ought never to have married a very famous diplomat, began to change that very evening. I could feel the fear fading all day yesterday, too. And last evening at the Cossingtons', it was replaced by a certain, tender confidence. And tonight, tonight I fear no one and nothing, not even Sally Jersey. I am filled with confidence in myself, Merrill. I cannot begin to tell you how wonderful such a feeling is to one who has never experienced it. It is a glorious thing."

"Then, I won't shoot him dead," Sir Merrill replied, kissing her cheek. "Will I, Aphrodite? I'll shake his hand instead. Though, how a foreigner managed to fill you with confidence when neither Aphrodite nor I could do it in all these months—"

"I cannot think how," Lady Merrill said. "But there is something about that man. Something—mystical."

Aphrodite found the crowd milling about the Jerseys' saloon daunting. *However am I going to find Stauss in such a squeeze as this?* she wondered. *Why, Uncle Merrill and Claire were merely three steps ahead of me a moment ago, and now they have disappeared completely. I expect they slipped between these two groups here. Yes, there's Uncle Merrill stopping to speak with the group surrounding General Blücher. But where on earth has Claire gone? Oh, just there, beside Mrs. Barrister. Well, I expect neither of them will take it into their heads to worry about me in such a throng as this. There is barely room to breathe much less do anything the least bit scandalous. Not that I have actually done anything scandalous,* she thought with just a touch of longing.

Carefully avoiding shifting feet and rising elbows, barely squeaking between this group and that, stepping sideways and stopping to stand on her toes from time to time in an attempt to see Stauss's tall form among the guests, Aphrodite made her way slowly from the front of the room to the rear, and was gratified to discover that at the very rear of the saloon bits of space existed which were actually unoccupied by constantly shifting bodies. She was even more gratified to discover Stauss, resting his shoulders against the rear wall, his arms crossed over his chest, awaiting her. She took four quick steps in his direction before she noted that Stauss was not wearing his uniform. She paused. The gentleman was not Count Kuechera at all. He had the same dark hair and proud alabaster brow, but his eyes were more deep-set, his cheekbones not quite as prominent. He appeared to be more substantial as well, and older. Aphrodite assumed at once that Count Kuechera and this gentleman were related in some way, for the overall resemblance was quite amazing, but the subtle differences were apparent as well. Without so much as a glance in Aphrodite's direction, the gentleman stepped away from the wall and walked to his right, toward a group of potted palms. He laughed. A rather cynical sound, Aphrodite thought, and obviously intended for no one but himself, though the sound drew several sets of eyes in his direction.

Her thoughts returned to her quest for Stauss. Aphrodite turned in the opposite direction of that the gentleman had taken and discovered, of all things, an empty ladder-backed chair. She hurried to it and moved it a bit until its back touched the wall. She stood staring down at it, pondering.

I truly ought not, she told herself. *It is most extraordinary. But it will take me hours to find him if I must work my way through all these people.* Aphrodite looked carefully around her. No one was paying her the least attention. No eyes glanced in her direction. Quickly she lifted the skirt of her gown and stepped up onto the chair seat. She wobbled a bit at first but found her balance quickly and turned to look out over the crowd. There he was. Near to the front of the room, very close to the windows. Stauss. Smiling that extraordinarily seductive smile that was his alone. Surrounded by a gaggle of giggling, blushing, hopeful young ladies.

"Incorrigible flirt," Aphrodite murmured angrily. And then, as she climbed from her perch, she could not think why she was angry. Count Kuechera was an eligible gentleman, after all. Of course the eligible young ladies would be dropping their handkerchiefs at his feet. But once she appeared before him, he would cease his nonsense, escort her to some quiet place—perhaps behind one or another of the potted palms—and they would thoroughly discuss the plot against the tsar and what they would do about it.

Chapter 4

Aphrodite tossed and turned in the darkness, punching at her pillows and mumbling every forbidden word she knew. The words were not great in number, but repeated over and over, they sufficed. How could she have been so stupid as to think the handsome count had taken her seriously at the Cossingtons' ball? He had not believed a word of her tale of the pending assassination of the tsar. The entire episode had been nothing more than an evening's flirt for that monster. And now what was she to do?

She had approached Kuechera amongst his bevy of admirers at the Jerseys', and he had turned to her and in the coolest voice said, "How do you do, Miss Coop. How pleasant to see you again." Then he had turned back to the gaggle of chirping young women around him and ignored her completely. If Sir Leslie had not come along and taken her up at just that moment, she would have felt such a fool.

I did feel a fool, she thought. *I feel a fool now. A perfect peabrain. How dare the man? Count or no count, how dare he lead me on at the Cossingtons'? How dare he pretend to take my every word seriously and promise to meet me at the Jerseys' to discuss further what can be done, and then ignore me in favor of—of—Lady June Baesch and Laura Collins and Gabrielle Smith-Hyer and all the rest of them?* She swiped angrily at the tears of humiliation dribbling down her hot cheeks and said the most forbidden words she knew. "Damn!" she exclaimed in an angry whisper. "Blast and damn and devil it!" A paltry vocabulary of curses, but nevertheless effective.

Aphrodite was so upset with herself that she did not at first notice the foglike cloud gathering outside her window—the window where she had sat peering out at the night for the longest time, berating herself for her foolishness. She had opened the window curtains and forgotten to draw them closed. She had opened the window as well, and she had not set it down properly into its sill. And now the cloudlike fog slipped through the minute space that remained. Had she not at that moment sat up, turned up her lamp, and taken one of her pillows into her hand to toss it at the unoffending window seat, she might never have noticed at all.

But she saw it, shimmering like something alive in the glow of her lamp, and she stared wide-eyed at it. Abruptly forgotten were her tears and curses as more and more of the cloud entered her chamber, seeming to boil now, bubbling in through the tiny space, splattering down toward the carpet below the window seat, and at the same time rising upward until the window itself disappeared from view. Aphrodite heard but could not see the window clank shut and the curtains slither along their rods until they touched one another.

She thought to ring for help but discovered fear had frozen her limbs. She attempted to scream, but her throat, her lips, her tongue, would not obey her. For a moment she was certain her heart had ceased to beat and her lungs to pump air. All her senses scurried down into some deep, dark hollow in her brain.

I am asleep, she thought. *This is some wretched nightmare.* She watched in silent horror as the bubbling, boiling, foglike cloud began to form itself into the shape of a man.

For the first time in his life, Stauss did not know precisely what to do. She sat there in her bed, her prim little nightdress bunched around her, her lips parted, her eyes wide with terror. He had located her window by scent and had assumed, since no light shone from it and because it was so very late, that Aphrodite had fallen asleep. Obviously, she had not. That was the problem with shape shifting into something as amorphous as a cloud. It got you through very tight spaces admirably, but you couldn't actually see what was around you until you shifted back again.

It did occur to him that it made not the least difference what he did or said now. At least Aphrodite was not screaming, so the household would not be aroused, and he could erase all memory of his sudden and unconventional appearance in her bedchamber from her mind. At least, he was fairly certain he could erase it. It worked with every other mortal. But then, he had thought he could step into Aphrodite's mind and bend her to his will, too, and that hadn't worked at all.

"Don't be frightened, Aphrodite," he whispered as his form began to solidify. "I have not come to harm you." The whisper had a definite hiss to it, and though he thought nothing of it at first—generally one needed solid lips to whisper properly, and his were not quite solid as yet—he had second thoughts immediately as he saw Aphrodite dive down and pull the bedclothes over her head.

Chagrined at himself and at last returned to his original form, Stauss stepped across the carpeting, sat on the edge of the bed, and gently patted what he assumed to be Aphrodite's head. "Come out, Miss Coop, please," he urged quietly. "It is I, Stanislaus Nicolaivich Kuechera."

The pile of bedclothes shivered in response.

"Please, Miss Coop. I apologize for frightening you. Truly, I do. I thought you were asleep."

The bedclothes moved a bit without shivering, and Aphrodite's voice squeaked, "This is a nightmare, is it not?" from the end of the bedclothes that Stauss was not patting.

"Very well. If you will have it so. I am a nightmare," he replied, clasping his hands in his lap. "You are fast asleep and dreaming, Miss Coop. What does it matter, therefore, if you come out from beneath the quilt and speak to me? Nightmares do nothing more than disappear with the dawn."

"Th-that's true," Aphrodite acknowledged.

"Indeed, it is, and it is merely an hour or so until dawn."

Aphrodite thought it over for a moment, then righted herself, tossing the bedclothes from her. Her eyes met his on the instant. She drank deeply of them, and her heart began to stutter in her breast. "How— how did you—I saw—I thought I would—you are not human!" she exclaimed in a hushed whisper.

Kuechera shook his head slowly from side to side.

"What are you, then?"

"A vampire, Miss Coop."

"A what?"

"A vampire. Surely you have heard of vampires?"

"Well, of course I have heard of vampires," Aphrodite replied. "They do not exist. You cannot be one of them."

Stauss smiled his slow, charming smile.

Something deep inside of Aphrodite flashed brightly and began to glow with the most delicious warmth. Her cheeks flushed a very alluring pink. The tip of her tongue came out to lick sensuously at her lower lip.

"How truly beautiful and intriguing you are," Kuechera said in a low, husky growl. "Aphrodite. May I call you Aphrodite?" he asked, reaching out to stroke her cheek with the tip of one long, lean finger which he then touched first to his lips and then to hers, sending a series of spine-tingling shivers up and down Aphrodite's back.

"N-no, you may not call me Aphrodite," she replied breathlessly.

"Why not?"

"Because you are in my black books."

"I thought I might be," he murmured, leaning toward her and, with both hands, straightening her ruffled nightcap, carefully whisking the loose strands of hair from her cheeks and tucking them slowly, gently beneath it.

"Oh, do cease touching me!" Aphrodite exclaimed in a hushed whisper, pushing his hands away. "I did never give you permission to touch me. I cannot think clearly when you are touching me! What was I saying? I know. I was saying there are no such things as vampires."

"There are more things exist between heaven and hell, Miss Coop, than any mortal mind can imagine."

"And you are one of those things?"

"Yes. I am, as I said, a vampire."

"I ought to scream for help, then."

"No, you ought not."

"Yes, indeed, I ought. If you are truly a vampire, you've come to drink my blood and carry my soul to Hades."

"I have not! I would not think to drink your blood without you give me leave to do it. And though I should like to carry you away and keep you somewhere safe forever, I have not the least power over your soul. And I have never been to Hades, so I would not know how to carry you or your soul there at any rate."

"Why are you here, then?"

"I have come to apologize for the manner in which I treated you at the Jerseys' rout. I wish to explain."

"Why?"

Is that not just the question? Stauss thought. *Why? Why can I not bear this woman to think ill of me, not even for the space of one night? Why did I come here like a perfect lunatic, not caring spit for my own safety? Why do I, even now, confess my true nature to this mere mortal woman when I cannot so much as trust that I can make her forget all?*

"I do not know why," he said softly, rising from the edge of her bed and beginning to pace the chamber with his hands clasped behind his back. "It is—there is—my response to you is incomprehensible to me, Miss Coop. *You* are incomprehensible to me. All I truly know is that the look on your face this evening when I greeted you so cooly pierced my heart. The proud manner in which you raised your chin and walked off on your Sir Leslie's arm tied knots in my stomach. Likely tied knots in my soul as well, it hurt so deeply. I knew at once what you thought. I knew that you believed I had not taken you seriously from the first. I know that even now you think you were utterly stupid to confide in me. You think I was secretly laughing at you that evening on the balcony and saw you as nothing but a bit of entertainment. None of that is true."

"It is not?" she asked as his pacing led him to her chamber door.

"No. It is not," he replied, turning, meeting her gaze with his own, then glancing down to inspect the carpet at his feet. "I had good reason to make it appear so, but it is not so."

"What good reason?" Aphrodite could not think why the answer to this question seemed so much more important to her than the fact that there was a lunatic who imagined himself to be a vampire standing in her bedchamber, but it did. It seemed of the utmost importance.

"You were in danger," Kuechera replied, lifting his gaze from the carpeting, staring into her eyes. "You are yet in danger, I believe. These men know that you overheard them. They must know, for two men kept watch on you the entire time you were at the Jerseys', noting to whom you spoke and on whose arm you wandered about. Had I claimed you as I wished to do, they may have guessed that you had understood their secret conversation perfectly and intended to confide in me."

"You know who they are?" Aphrodite asked excitedly.

"No."

"But you just said—"

"The moment you entered the room, their apprehension rose to the surface of my mind, and it boiled there the entire evening."

"You were nowhere near when I entered the room. You have no idea at all when I arrived."

"I know to the instant when you stepped across the threshold," he replied as he stepped closer to her bed. "I felt your presence at once. And then, I felt them. Two of them." He studied her upturned face with the greatest intensity. "Their attention never wandered from you, Aphrodite. It followed you to the rear of the chamber. It followed you forward as you came to my side. That is why I greeted you as a stranger and then ignored your presence. So they would not suspect you had already confided in me or intended to do so."

"Well," Aphrodite said, her eyes gazing deeply into his. "Well," she said again, rising to her knees and taking his incredibly serious face between her hands. "Well, then you are—forgiven." Her hands moved from his cheeks to the back of his neck as she leaned close and kissed him tenderly, her lips barely touching his and then parting from them quickly.

"Am I truly forgiven, or did you say that because I willed you to say it?" Kuechera asked, touching his lips wonderingly with the tip of his index finger. "D-did you truly intend to kiss me, or did I somehow will you to kiss me?"

"Will me?" Aphrodite positively scowled. "I daresay, Count Kuechera, that neither you nor any man can *will* me to say anything I have not already determined to say. And if you cannot tell when a woman kisses you because she intends to kiss you, then where is your brain, Stauss?"

"I merely wondered because—Stauss? You call me Stauss?"

"It seems correct, somehow, to call you Stauss. I thought you had mentioned it to me. Is that not what others call you?"

"Only my family."

"Oh, now vampires have families?"

Aphrodite smiled at him in the most disconcerting manner. It set the Carpathian winds roaring in his ears, the heat of the great fires of Castle Kuechera flaring across his cheeks. His palms itched. His teeth ached. His mind melted into mush.

"You are not truly a vampire, are you?" Aphrodite asked, taking his strong, lean hands into hers, holding his gaze with her own, smiling, oh, so innocently up at him. "What I thought I saw—the cloud boiling beneath my window, the curtains closing themselves, the window lurching shut—all that was trickery of some sort, was it not? You climbed up my trellis and hid yourself until I was so weary I would not realize the trick, and only then did you enter my chamber. Is this not so? You came to apologize. You came to explain. You could not wait until the morning to warn me that I might be in danger. And so, you thought of this most unusual way to overcome my scruples."

Yes, he thought, his fingers entwining themselves

with hers. *Say yes, you lunatic. She will think you a fool if you agree with her, but no worse than a fool. Say yes.*

"No," he said. "I came as you saw me come. I am a vampire."

"You did not drink of her blood, *gospodin?*" Vladimir Ryzinsky sat down beside his young master on the flowered sofa in their sitting room at the Pulteney and put an arm around Stauss's sagging shoulders.

"No. Not once," Stauss responded, his hands dangling between his knees as he stared at the carpet between his feet. "I tasted of her lips only. I could not take her blood, Vlad. It seemed indecent to do so. Only had she offered it would I have sipped from that precious fountain. Ah, what a fool I become when I am near her. My mind deserts me. Am I truly mad? Do I have some secret wish to shed my life as Sergio wishes to shed his? That cannot be. And yet, I *told* her I was a vampire. I betrayed myself to a mortal, Vlad. And I insisted that she believe me."

"Did she believe you?"

"I don't think so."

"How did you exit the chamber, *gospodin?*"

"She opened her window for me, and I climbed down the trellis so as not to frighten her again."

Vladimir Ryzinsky smiled. "Poor boy," he murmured. "Poor, poor boy. You have discovered what your father hoped you might discover, young master."

"Lunacy?"

"Love."

Stauss looked up, stared at the man, his fine dark eyes wide with wonder and yet tinged with fear. "Do you think this can be, Vlad? That I love Miss Coop?"

"It can be." The old man nodded gravely.

"Do you think she loves me?"

"I cannot say. Mortals do not come to love as abruptly and irrevocably as vampires, *gospodin*. Especially mortal women. Most slip bit by bit into it as if it is a cool, murky pool and they yearning to swim in its waters, but hesitant because they cannot see what lies at the bottom."

Aphrodite lingered at her window for almost ten minutes after he had disappeared into the night. Her lips felt swollen. Her cheeks glowed. Her nightcap had disappeared, and her thick chestnut-colored tresses were in wild disarray. Her pulse throbbed in her throat even now, and she ached deep inside. Ached for him. For Stauss. Ached for Stauss to take her once again into his strong arms, to kiss her once more.

At last, she drew the curtains closed and turned from the window. She floated to her bed, her feet barely touching the floor, turned down her lamp, and tugged the bedclothes up around her. *What was I thinking?* she wondered. *I allowed a gentleman I barely know into my bedchamber, and I in my nightgown! I did not cry out for Uncle Merrill. I did not box Stauss's ears and send him running. I did not so much as point out that if we were found together, he would be honor bound to marry me. Instead, I allowed him to kiss me. More than once. Many more times than once.*

"I have never been kissed so thoroughly in all my life," she whispered into the darkness. "His lips as cool and sweet as cherries on mine, his tongue tickling at my lips, teasing them apart. His heart pounding and pounding and pounding along with my own as though they would both burst from our bodies and join together into one. And I could feel my soul fluttering madly, struggling to be free so it might fly to him and live with him forever. Great heavens, if he is not a vampire, he ought to be."

She closed her eyes then and sighed. *Of course he is not a vampire,* she thought. *Of all the things to do, to attempt to make me believe he is such a horrid, devilish thing as that. But perhaps the young women of his country find the idea of such creatures romantic, and that is why he—No. How could anyone find such creatures romantic? And yet he persisted in it for a goodly long time. But he could not hold to it at the last,* she thought with a smile. *When it came time that he absolutely must be gone, he climbed down the trellis just like any other man.*

Miss Petersen awoke a mere four hours after Count Kuechera had retired to his bed. She yawned and stretched luxuriously, enjoying the subtle flex of her muscles. A sense of health and well-being encompassed her from top to toe, and she was bursting with energy and anticipation. She tossed the bedclothes aside and dangled her legs over the side of the bed, wiggling her bare toes. And then she noticed the carpet. "What is this?" she murmured, staring at the deep green sea in which scarlet roses floated. Miss Petersen had never seen such a carpet as this in her entire life. Certainly, one did not lie on the floor of her little chamber off the schoolroom at Mrs. Bennett's. Her senses jolted into full wakefulness. She divined, simply by the feel of the mattress on the edge of which she sat, that the bed was not her bed at Mrs. Bennett's either. With an encroaching sense of confusion, Miss Petersen gazed at the bedchamber in which she had awakened. A lump began to form in her throat and another in her stomach. "Where am I?" she whispered. "What is this place? What has happened to me? Why, this is not even one of my own nightgowns. And my knitted slippers are nowhere to be seen."

Barefooted, Miss Petersen left the bed and stepped across the thick carpeting to the window. She pulled the curtains aside and looked out on a fine summer day. A small balcony existed outside this particular window. The wall of the Dashfords' establishment was nowhere to be seen. She turned and, noting a most extravagantly carved armoire, hurried to it and opened its doors. To her amazement, three perfectly sensible gowns were stored there. Gowns quite as practical and well-made as she would have selected herself—had they been hers. But they were not hers. She had never seen one of them before. She tugged out the drawers one by one to discover underclothes, stockings, gloves, more nightgowns, and lined up in the very bottom drawer, a number of pairs of slippers that looked to be just her size.

A slight scratching at the door disturbed her, and she turned toward it in somewhat of a panic. *What ought I to do?* she wondered. As if in answer, her hands closed the drawers and the armoire doors, and her feet carried her quickly back to the bed, into which she climbed, tugging the bedclothes over her and sitting back against a plethora of pillows. *A plethora of pillows,* she thought. *Why did I not notice all these pillows?*

"Come in," she called, when the scratching came again and her heart had settled down to a mere thudding in her chest. And then her fine gray eyes grew quite large as a short, elderly man in a suit of clothes that appeared, somehow, not precisely English, stepped into her chamber balancing a tray with a cup and a covered dish upon it. He looked familiar. This man looked very familiar.

"You are well again," Vladimir Ryzinsky said with a smile as he carried the tray to the table beside Miss Petersen's bed.

"Y-yes," Miss Petersen replied, attempting to recall being ill. "I am quite well, thank you."

"You must not fear, Miss Petersen. You do not remember all that happened, but you are safe here, I assure you." Vlad placed the cup in her hand and uncovered the dish.

Why, it's hot chocolate, Miss Petersen observed, staring down into the cup and inhaling the enticing aroma. *And there on the side table is a breakfast of eggs and buttered toast.* "Wh-where am I?" Miss Petersen asked.

"You are in the Pulteney Hotel in Picadilly," replied Vladimir Ryzinsky as if he were quite accustomed to young women awaking in rooms they had never before seen. "You are the honored guest of my master, Count Stanislaus Nicolaivich Kuechera, whose rooms these are."

"C-Count Kuechera?"

"There is no reason to grow pale, Miss Petersen," Vlad said most amiably. "You have done nothing to cause you shame. You have been ill. Nothing more."

"But, I d-do not remember."

"You will," replied Ryzinsky with assurity. "You will remember in bits and pieces. In fits and starts. Not all, but enough. And then, my master will be pleased to do your bidding."

"To d-do my bidding?"

"Whatever you wish to do, Miss Petersen, once you recall what has happened, my master will help you to do it. And do you require anything—anything at all—in the meanwhile, you must simply request it of me. There is a necessity immediately through that door—and it flushes," added Vlad, who had been thoroughly amazed by the Pulteney's indoor flush toilets from the very first—an amazement he shared with the Duchess of Oldenburg, herself. "There are gowns I purchased for you in the armoire, and other womanly things as well. A brush, comb, and hairpins there, on that chest. Oh, and there is a looking glass under the bed."

"Under the bed? A looking glass?"

"It is as tall as you, Miss Petersen, and heavy. I would have hidden it away in a drawer else. My master is not fond of the things," Ryzinsky explained. "He avoids them like the plague, and so I hid it away. But young women put them to use often, do they not? When you wish it, you must come and fetch me, and I will get it out for you. Do eat your breakfast now, Miss Petersen, and do not fret. You are safe in my master's care."

Safe? wondered Miss Petersen as the little man exited the chamber. *Had I need of protection? Why? From whom? I cannot think why I should grow ill at Mrs. Bennett's house and awake recovered in a set of rooms belonging to a count, of all things, in the Pulteney Hotel in Picadilly.*

Miss Petersen sipped at the hot chocolate which proved to be absolutely delicious. She took a bite of toast and then a bit of poached egg. Truly, she had never in her life been served breakfast in bed. *I feel quite decadent,* she thought with a smile on her perfect Cupid's bow lips. When she had finished the small meal, she arose again and accomplished her morning ablutions, dressed herself in the new clothing, donned one pair of kid slippers which fit quite as if they had been made for her, and wandered from her bedchamber in search of the

ancient servant. She had attempted to move the looking glass from under the bed herself so that she might
arrange her hair before it, but she had been unable to
do so. *How the count's servant will do so, I cannot imagine,*
she thought, turning to her right. *He is so old and not at
all strong-looking. Perhaps there is a younger servant also in
attendance, though the old man did say it was he who put the
looking glass away.*

*Why should a gentleman be so offended by a looking glass
that he demands it taken from his sight?* she wondered then.
*Perhaps there is something wrong with this Count Kuechera.
Perhaps he was injured in the war and cannot bear to see himself as he now is. Or perhaps he is most ugly and detests the
sight of himself. Well, it does not matter in the least. Whatever
the reason—if he is deformed or scarred or ugly as a hump-
backed bear—he has been most kind to me, and therefore, I will
perceive him to be handsome regardless.*

It was just as she stepped into the sitting room that
the sound of her own voice screaming and a vision of
Mr. Chester Nuberly's wolfish face sneering down at her
rushed into her mind and gave her such a jolt that she
came near to falling and stopped herself from doing so
only by seizing the edge of a heavy hunt table and holding on for dear life. Her breath caught in her throat.
Her heart beat as though she had run across the green
at school without stopping, and her pulses throbbed at
her temples. For a full minute she stood frozen, fearing
to move, and then her heartbeat slowed, the vision
faded, and she could breathe again. "Oh," she whispered. "Oh."

Chapter 5

Aphrodite, with the taste of Stauss's kisses lingering on her lips and questions of his intentions and her own wandering about her mind, drove with Sir Leslie to Hyde Park the following afternoon. They would have ridden in considerable silence, but Lydia was seated across from them in the landau and prattled away enthusiastically about what she thought twelve thousand troops all gathered in one place would look like. It would be the most extraordinary thing to watch the King of Prussia, the Prince Regent, Tsar Alexander, the Duke of York, General Blücher, General Lord Beresford, and General Hill riding together on their great warhorses reviewing twelve thousand troops. Lydia had been looking forward to this particular day of the Grand Jubilee in celebration of the victory over Napoleon and in honor of the one hundred years of Hanoverian rule for weeks and weeks. Not merely because of the gathering of dignitaries and troops, but also because this very evening upon the Serpentine, at precisely eight o'clock, there was to be a reenactment of the Battle of Trafalgar.

"I am to accompany Papa and Claire to the battle on the Serpentine tonight," she proclaimed with a gleam of childish triumph in her eyes as Sir Leslie lifted her down from the carriage. "You are going to escort Aphrodite, are you not?"

"If she will honor me with the privilege," Sir Leslie responded, taking Lydia's right hand into his own. Aphrodite at once took hold of the child's left hand, thus effectively separating herself from Sir Leslie while appearing to do nothing of the sort. The park was filled with people. Sellers of cakes and pies, tavern keepers, and purveyors of an enormous variety of refreshments, intent on providing for the public, had erected temporary stalls, booths, even pavilions. There were puppet shows, acrobats, musicians, even swings and roundabouts to be seen and enjoyed. It would appear most acceptable for Aphrodite and Sir Leslie both to keep hold of Lydia in such a maze of humanity as Hyde Park had become.

"I daresay if we take up positions on that knoll near the footpath, we shall be able to see them reviewing the troops quite nicely," Sir Leslie observed. "Can you walk as far as that, Miss Heath?"

"Of course I can," Lydia replied. "Are you not ever going to speak to Aphrodite again?"

"What? Well, certainly. It is merely that at the moment I have nothing to say."

"Oh."

"It also appears that your cousin is thinking deep thoughts, Miss Heath, and I hesitate to disturb her unless I have something of interest to impart." Sir Leslie sent a smile at Aphrodite over Lydia's head, but Aphrodite did not take note of it.

She is off in some world of her own, Sir Leslie thought, *and wants very much not to be disturbed at the moment—at least, not to be disturbed by me. It serves me right. I was cruel to dismiss her tale of assassins in the manner I did. As we wandered about at the Jerseys' last evening, she did not once mention that particular episode. Avoided it. Chattered on like a magpie about anything and everything but that. What a dunce I am. I hurt her terribly by my refusal to take her seriously. But she is so very imaginative and has such a flair for drama, and her interpretation of everything is colored by both.*

I thought she would outgrow the propensity, but she shows no sign of doing so.

Perhaps Aphrodite is correct to persist in refusing my proposals, he thought sadly. *Perhaps I am not the gentleman to make her a suitable husband. She requires someone who will not continually chide her for her excesses in these things which are, after all, her very nature. There is some special talent required to live with a woman like Aphrodite. Should we marry, I would likely destroy the very enthusiasm I so enjoy by stomping awkwardly on all her dreams and bursting each and every one of her balloons.*

They reached the top of the knoll and discovered a space among the gathering crowd. Sir Leslie placed on the grass the blanket he had carried beneath one arm, and the three of them sat down quite comfortably to await the spectacle. And a spectacle it was, filling Aphrodite with patriotism, pride, and immense thankfulness in her heart that such men as these had chosen to stand for her and for her family and friends against the threat of the upstart Napoleon. Twelve thousand strong, they lined up before her. Men who had fought and would fight again should it prove necessary in order to purchase peace for the world.

"And to purchase it at *such* a price," she said softly, remembering those who had given limbs and lives to the cause of her own safety.

"Eh? What?" asked Sir Leslie over Lydia's head.

"I was thinking how brave they are. How much so many men have sacrificed for us."

"Indeed," Sir Leslie replied, his own heart thoroughly involved. "How I wish I could have joined up."

"You could not have done," Aphrodite said, moving her hand behind Lydia's back to take hold of Sir Leslie's. "Your duty was to remain in England and see that supplies and monies reached our soldiers as they must. What would those on the battlefield have done without you and the others? If people knew all the crises with which you have dealt and all the crises you have averted, they would think you quite as worthy of their honor and praise."

"Don't wish honor and praise," murmured Sir Leslie gruffly. "Not at all. Merely hope this is the end of it. Hope this glorious peace we celebrate is a lasting one. Do you see the gentleman on that enormous chestnut, Miss Coop? The one immediately to the Russian Tsar's right? Count Platoff. Another of the Cossacks. His men have joined in the ranks with our own. You can pick them out by their uniforms. There are not so very many of them, but they are most apparent. Perhaps Count Kuechera is among them, eh?"

Aphrodite breathed a mental sigh of relief. She had been worried if this might be the time and the place designated by the assassins. She had pondered how the Russian Tsar could be protected in such a large public assembly. And she had been amazed not to see Stauss very near his endangered commander. But Stauss was likely very near, indeed, somewhere amongst the soldiers, and the gentleman directly beside the tsar was a Cossack. Surely Stauss had passed word to all the Cossacks to be awake to the possibility of an assassination attempt. Surely he had, for none of the announcements, though they listed all the others present, had mentioned Count Platoff would appear among the dignitaries.

The sun was lowering in the sky, and Miss Petersen was joined in conversation with Vladimir Ryzinsky, both of them nibbling at strawberry tarts and sipping tea. "I have no wish to return to Mrs. Bennett's house. None at all, Mr. Ryzinsky," she said. "My intention was to book passage to Twickenham, to return to Mrs. Pierce's School for Young Ladies. I taught there until I obtained my present position. They will give me shelter, I think, until I can obtain another. Only—only I lost my reticule that horrid night, and now I have not the funds to purchase a seat on the mail. Oh, I wish I had not remembered that night! Never mind. Never mind. I ought to remember it. It will make me more cautious. I will never take a position in a household where any single gentleman resides. Never again."

"It is not only single gentlemen who prove to be evil," Vlad pointed out quietly. "He might have been a married gentleman, or a woman with evil in her heart."

"Yes, that's so. But what am I to do? I must support myself. I cannot depend on Mrs. Pierce's generosity forever. She does not actually need another teacher. And a governess is all I am suited to be. Oh, dear," she added. "I cannot depend on Mrs. Pierce's generosity at all, can I? I no longer have the money to book passage to Twickenham."

"My master will see that you have whatever monies you require, Miss Petersen."

"It was he who rescued me. Why do I not so much as remember his face? I remember Mr. Nuberly's face well enough. I remember his plans for me, and I remember what he said about your tsar, Mr. Ryzinski, as well, but I do not—no, never mind. You need not remind me that I cannot expect to remember all in one great lump. Your master, however, has done enough for me, and I shall not—"

"He will see you have whatever monies you require," Vladimir repeated. "He is a rich gentleman, my master.

His family fortunes do nothing but increase century upon century. He will not allow you to venture from here penniless, nor deliver you back to this Mrs. Bennett if you do not wish to return to her."

"He is a kind gentleman, your master."

"Oh, extremely kind," answered a voice at Miss Petersen's shoulder. "Is that not so, Vlad?"

Startled, Ellen turned and looked up at once. It was all she could do to keep her jaw from dropping open. Tall, broad-shouldered, rumpled as though he had just arisen from sleep and therefore boyish and vulnerable-looking, his was the most seductive face, the most astonishing form, she had ever seen. How could such a man as this detest looking glasses? Were he an English gentleman, he would likely spend hours before one simply admiring himself as he dressed.

Miss Petersen pulled her thoughts together and said, "I am sorry, sir, not to have greeted you properly. I did not see you enter the room."

"You were deep in conversation with Vlad, Miss Petersen. I am pleased to see you looking so well. May I join you?"

"Indeed," Miss Petersen replied, unable to take her gaze from Kuechera as he made his way around to the front of the sofa on which she sat and took a chair beside Vladimir Ryzinsky and across from her. It was extremely odd. His servant did not rise, did not so much as ask if the gentleman required anything of him. Nor did this gentleman signify by so much as the lift of an eyebrow that he recognized any breach of etiquette in his servant joining him and his guest in polite conversation.

Of course, I am a servant myself, Miss Petersen thought. *The breach of etiquette is actually on the gentleman's side, to*

*take his ease with such as us. Perhaps, in his country, this is
acceptable.*

"You are my guest, not a servant, Miss Petersen," the
gentleman said, as though he had read her thoughts.
"And Vlad is more grandfather to me than anything
else. You are a teacher of young ladies?"

"Yes. How did you—oh, you overheard us, of course."

"Of course." Stauss nodded. "There is to be a spectacle on the Serpentine in Hyde Park this evening, Miss
Petersen. I wonder, will you accompany me there?"

"Oh, the reenactment of the Battle of Trafalgar! Is it
truly the twentieth of June already?"

"Indeed. And there is someone I wish to meet in the
park this evening. Someone I wish you to meet as well."

How Stauss had located them in the dimming twilight and in such a crowd, Aphrodite could not imagine,
but there he stood before them with a slight, fair-haired
young woman on his arm.

"May Miss Petersen and I join you, Sir Leslie, Miss
Coop?" Kuechera asked. "It is an extraordinary congre-
gation of onlookers, is it not? All to watch some little
boats paddling about on a river." He smiled, and Aphrodite's heart stuttered a bit. "Do Sir Merrill and the
lovely Lady Merrill not attend?" he continued. "Oh, I
beg your pardon, of course they do, and the little cousin
you spoke of as well," he answered his own question,
gazing in precisely the direction in which Sir Merrill
had only minutes ago led his wife and daughter a bit
closer to the Serpentine.

Aphrodite stared in the same direction for a moment, but even with the lights of the flambeaux, she was
certain she could not have identified her uncle, Claire,

and Lydia if she had not known perfectly well that they were there.

"I should like to present to you, Miss Coop and Sir Leslie, Miss Ellen Petersen," Kuechera said then, his eyes laughing into Aphrodite's as though he was hearing her every thought, including the one that had just arisen concerning the young woman on his arm. "Miss Petersen is former governess to a Miss Janet Bennett."

"Governess to Miss Janet Bennett?" Sir Leslie queried. "Great heavens! Do you realize that you have disappeared, Miss Petersen? It was in all the papers. You disappeared, and your employer's nephew was discovered dead in Warbaesh's warehouse."

"D-dead?" Miss Petersen stuttered.

Kuechera patted her hand as it rested on his arm, and the frown of horror that had flickered onto her face flickered away again. "Let us speak of pleasant things," he said quietly, gazing into Sir Leslie's eyes. "Let us forget such atrocities as we read in newspapers for this one evening."

"Y-yes. Yes, indeed," Sir Leslie replied.

"Miss Petersen? Should you like to have a closer look before the spectacle begins?" Kuechera asked. "Sir Leslie would be pleased to escort you, would you not, Sir Leslie?"

"I—y-yes. Come, Miss Petersen, allow me."

"Just so, and I shall see to Miss Coop until you return," Kuechera assured Sir Leslie's departing back.

"How did you do that?" Aphrodite asked, her hands on her hips, staring at him. "Why did Sir Leslie not tell you to escort Miss Petersen yourself?"

Kuechera smiled. "The tsar was safe today, yes?"

"Oh! Yes! I was so very worried when I did not see you; but then Count Platoff was beside him, and there were Cossacks ranged among the other soldiers."

"Just so. You are not offended that I confided in Platoff? He is a fine soldier and loyal to Alexander, and he has a distinct advantage in the daylight."

Aphrodite found the final phrase confusing. "An advantage in the daylight?" she asked.

"Yes. I, on the other hand, have the distinct advantage after sunset."

"You are not going to attempt to convince me that you are a vampire again, are you, Stauss?"

"No. I am merely going to attempt to get you to speak to your uncle about Miss Petersen. There is the little girl-child lives with you, yes? And she has not a governess?"

"Well, no, she hasn't one as yet, but—you wish Uncle Merrill to hire Miss Petersen, who disappeared from Mrs. Bennett's establishment without so much as a 'by your leave' and whose name has been bandied about in the newspapers?"

"Come walk with me for a bit, Aphrodite," Kuechera said, placing an arm familiarly around her waist and drawing her against him in such a fashion that Aphrodite wanted nothing more than to cling to him and taste the sweetness of his proud lips once again. "Not just now," he murmured, chucking her playfully beneath her chin, his eyes intimating that he knew precisely what she wished to do. "First, let me tell you the tale of Miss Petersen and how she came to disappear."

As the replicas of the ships that had fought at Trafalgar were maneuvered on a small lake formed by the Serpentine—the French ships at last bursting into flames and sinking beneath the waters to the tune of England's National Anthem—Aphrodite found herself worrying a good deal more about where Stauss had gone than ap-

plauding the magnificence of the spectacle. He had returned her to Sir Leslie's care, greeted Sir Merrill, Lady
Merrill, and Lydia as they returned from their closer
look at the little boats, and gone off into the night.
Aphrodite attempted to dismiss his absence from her
mind and focus her thoughts instead on Miss Petersen,
whose story had filled her heart with sympathy and to
whom, she was determined, her uncle would offer the
position of Lydia's governess before they left the park.

I will simply take Uncle Merrill aside, she thought, *and
say that Miss Petersen was given a slip on the shoulder by a
most unpleasant gentleman in Mrs. Bennett's household. He
will understand that she cannot possibly return there. Then I
will point out that Lydia is quite old enough to require a governess and suggest that we invite Miss Petersen home with us
this very evening. Once Uncle Merrill understands that she
has nowhere to go and suffers because she would not surrender
to a man's improper petitions, he will not quaver to offer her
the position and his protection.*

*In merely the time it has taken to refight the Battle of Trafal-
gar, Miss Petersen has captivated Lydia and Claire,* Aphrodite
observed with a smile. *To take her safely home with us is to ac-
complish little. To cease thinking about Stauss, however, is proving near impossible. How could the man kiss me so hungrily, so
passionately, before he returned me here and then depart my side
so quickly? No sooner did he make his bows to Uncle Merrill,
Claire, and Lydia, than he was spouting some nonsense about
an appointment and disappeared. He does not believe that I am
going to allow him in through my window again tonight to pro-
fess more apologies, I hope, because I am not.*

At the rear of the largest of the temporary pavilions,
which housed an extension of the White Horse Tavern,

grew an ancient oak. On the lowest of the oak's branches, Stanislaus Nicolaivich Kuechera sat swinging his legs in the darkness, debating whether to return to Aphrodite's side or not. In the time it had taken the English to re-fight the Battle of Trafalgar, he had dined at the tables of Lady June Baesch, Miss Laura Collins, and Miss Gabrielle Smith-Hyer. One by one he had lured them out from beneath the noses of their escorts and into the shadows where he had tasted each velvety, enticingly throbbing throat. They would not recall it, of course. Nor would their escorts so much as remember his presence among them. But what he had taken from the three of them would not truly sustain him through another twenty-four hours.

I ought to have drunk more deeply, he thought. *But I could not. It seemed wrong to drink too deeply. It seemed—a betrayal of Aphrodite. I expect it is, too, taking such pleasure in arousing the passions of her friends and supping on them. I expect I shall be forced to hunt amidst the—*

Kuechera ceased to swing his legs. He sniffed at the air. He listened closely—listened to sounds below the noise of the crowd that milled about beyond the pavilion, below the strains of England's National Anthem and the cheers and applause rising up from near the Serpentine. Softly through the grass they came, cautious footsteps, hurried whispers, and with them, the smell of certain death. With hungry eyes aglow, Kuechera watched in silence as two men carried a third around the side of the pavilion.

"Ye ought not 'ave hit him with no stone, Tom," whispered one man. "Only see what ye've done. He ain't goin' ta see the mornin'. An' fer what? A few pound notes an' a glass stickpin."

"I didn't mean ta hit 'im so hard," the second man whispered back. "I only meant ta tap 'im like."

"Ye done tapped 'im, all right," replied the first as they laid the man they carried down on the grass, very close to the building. "Ye done tapped the bloke right inta eternity."

They stared around them for a moment, nervously squinting into the darkness. Then, with a long look at each other, they ran off in the direction of the east gate as fast as they could.

Kuechera swung lightly to the ground, crossed to the man they had left behind, knelt down beside him, and lifted him gently to a sitting position. Pain-filled, terror-stricken eyes met his own as the man's head lolled back against Kuechera's arm, soaking his uniform with blood. "D-dying," the man stuttered dazedly.

"Yes, this is so."

"H-help me."

"Do not speak. It is too great an effort," the Cossack whispered. "I hear all that you long to say without your words. I and The One who created you know that you have stumbled and fallen. We understand your guilt, your sorrow. I forgive you, Gregory, in the name of all you have offended and so, too, will the Merciful One forgive you."

Slowly the soldier bent over the man whose eyes even now clouded with death. He bit swiftly, the sting of his sharp, elongated canines unfelt by the dying mortal in his arms. The fear that rocked the mortal's soul erupted into the Cossack with his lifeblood—the fear of death, the strongest of all mortal passions, the most exquisite of all food.

"Who are you? What are you?" whispered a small, frightened voice just behind Kuechera.

He set the now peaceful corpse aside and, rising, turned.

"We were going to the carriage, and I stepped off the path to—I thought I saw you. I came to—who are you? What are you?" Aphrodite asked again, her hands fisted and pressed to her lips. Her eyes wide with disbelief and loathing.

I can disappear now, Stauss thought. *Muddle her mind. Make her forget me and believe she found only a dead man here.* But he did not wish to do so. It was then he was certain Vlad was correct. He loved this woman, this mortal woman, and because of it he wished neither to control her nor lie to her.

He took a step forward. Aphrodite took a step back.

"You killed that man," she said.

"No. I shared in his death, Aphrodite. It is not the same."

"How is it not the same?" Aphrodite's question was a breathless gasp.

"He would have died with me or without me, Aphrodite. For mortal men, it is far better to die in my arms than alone."

"You drank his bl-blood."

"I did. And with it his fear. I drained away his terror and gave him peace in its stead."

"N-no."

"I attempted to tell you, Aphrodite, but you would not believe me. I am a vampire. I am born of vampires. I am an angel of death, born of angels of death. It is my duty to give peace, to banish suffering, to digest the fear of all mortals who die within my reach. This I do and have done in villages, in cities, on battlefields under smoke-clogged skies."

Tears streamed unimpeded from Aphrodite's eyes.

This could not be. It was a horrid dream. She was at home, in bed. She would wake soon. This man whose kiss she craved, whose arms she wished to keep forever around her, this Cossack whom she knew beyond doubt that she loved—as early as this morning she had known she loved him—he could not be a vampire. How could there truly be vampires? And how could she, how could anyone, love such a creature?

Kuechera stepped toward her again, and she did not step back; so he took her stiff, frightened little body in his arms and with one long finger dashed the tears from her cheeks. Keeping his arms around her, he drew her away from the pavilion, up toward the path from which she had wandered and where, even now, he could hear Sir Merrill's and Sir Leslie's and even Miss Petersen's voices calling her name, though she could not hear them as yet.

"I am not some vile creature," he whispered in her ear. "I am a creation of the One who created mortal man and all things in the heavens, on the earth, and below the earth. I have honor, duty, and pride. I have a mind, a heart, a soul, and a will that is in my own keeping. And I love you, Aphrodite. I will not lie to you now or ever, *because* I love you. The members of your party are frightened at your long absence. They are searching for you. Go to them. Betray me if you must. But know that I have done nothing wrong here. Nothing cruel. Nothing to offend the One or the nature He bestowed upon me."

He kissed her then, in the darkness just off the path, kissed her until her stiffness wilted, her tears ceased, and her hands, fisted against his chest, unfisted and clung tentatively to him. Then he freed her from the circle of his arms, stepped into shadows deeper than those in which she stood, and disappeared from her sight.

Chapter 6

Aphrodite discovered that she could not betray him. Instead, she threw herself feverishly into the social whirl that was the Celebration of the Glorious Peace and the Centennial of Hanoverian Rule. She would not betray him, but she would drive him from her mind—and from her heart. But he seemed to follow her everywhere. He did never attend the dinners, but always he arrived later in the evening. She decidedly ignored him, choosing instead to wander on Sir Leslie's arm or the arms of other gentlemen at the routs, at the balls, at any and all of the gatherings she attended. But he persisted. He was among the seventeen hundred people at White's Ball at Burlington House. He attended the small rout at Lady Wagenall's, an unofficial and rather rowdy welcome for the Duke of Wellington on his return to England. He even made an appearance at the Service of General Thanksgiving for the Allied Victory held in St. Paul's Cathedral, though he remained standing in the very rear of the chamber and appeared to Aphrodite, when she glanced back at him, pale, weary, and actually quite ill. Her heart longed to comfort him, her hand to caress his pale, feverish brow, but she would not allow herself to do either.

He sent her flowers day after day, small bouquets of violets, Johnny-jump-ups, roses, and once, an odd little plant whose leaves closed when one approached it. Miss Petersen informed Aphrodite that the plant was called a heartbreaker and would produce the loveliest pink flowers which, legend had it, were droplets of blood from the broken heart of the Fate, Atropos. Aphrodite's heart cried at the thought of it.

But she would not surrender to what she could not bear to imagine. She was adamant about driving thoughts and images of Stanislaus Nicolaivich Kuechera from her, so intent on it that she did not at first notice Miss Petersen's increasing presence beyond the schoolroom in Sir Merrill's household, or Sir Leslie's mounting interest in that young woman. It was not until one afternoon as she stared from one of the windows—attempting to exorcise a handsome, austere, noble face from her mind—and saw Sir Leslie, Miss Petersen, and little Lydia happily cavorting about the bit of green just beyond the kitchen garden that it occurred to her how often she had seen Sir Leslie of late and yet, how little she had conversed with him, or taken his arm. She studied him closely. "He is much attracted to Ellen," she whispered in amazement, "and she to him." It pleased her.

Ellen is gently bred, she thought, observing as the governess took Sir Leslie's arm. *She has no penchant for drama. Her imagination does not run wild, and she is both kind and beautiful. She will make him a lovely and proper wife. I, on the other hand, shall marry no man.*

Despite her intentions, her thoughts turned again in the direction of the Cossack. *Why did Stauss not wipe the memory of what I saw from my mind?* she wondered. *He said he could. Why did he not? How easily I could have loved him had I never seen him in the shadows, bending over that dying man, drinking—no, I will not dwell on it. I wish to be-*

lieve he is not that vile creature. Perhaps he did bring the man peace as he claimed. Perhaps he is, in a manner of speaking, an angel of death? And yet, what woman in her right mind could love and marry an angel of death? Still, he looked very much like an ordinary man at the rear of the cathedral yesterday. He looked like a gentleman who has fallen ill but will not admit as much. Do vampires grow ill?

And then she remembered. She had spoken at one of the receptions to Count Platoff. Dark, tall, and lean with a broad brow and a fierce countenance, Count Platoff had proved kind and attentive, and he had not looked at her oddly when at last she had gathered her courage and asked if in his country people believed in vampires.

"Ah," he had replied, "you are *Kuechera's* Miss Coop. Yes, Miss Coop, in my country the people of the villages and the mountains believe in vampires, and they will tell you so. The people of the cities, of education and science, believe as well, but they will not tell you so."

"You are an educated man," Aphrodite had replied.

"But also a child of the mountains, raised to respect the Rulers of Darkness, the Lords of the Night."

"The Rulers of Darkness," Aphrodite whispered now. "The Lords of the Night. Sunlight is poison to them, Count Platoff said. And yet Stauss c-came," she stuttered. "He came in sunlight to St. Paul's. Why? Why did he do such a thing?"

But Aphrodite knew the answer. Her heart came near to breaking because of it. "He came because I was there," she murmured, tears mounting to her eyes. "He came because I told him long before that I would attend."

* * *

Stauss could not keep his mind on anything but Aphrodite. Each time he stepped into a saloon or a ballroom or even a parlor, her scent, as clean and fresh and enticing as the mountains in spring, spoke to him, lured him into dreams of a life with her beside him. It was apparent to him that she had not spoken to anyone of his heritage. Sir Merrill, Sir Leslie, Lady Merrill, all treated him as they had, going so far as to thank him for introducing Miss Petersen into their household, suggesting that he come to pay a morning call, commenting on the beautiful flowers and his kindness in sending them to Aphrodite, who had fallen into an odd melancholy of late.

An odd melancholy. The words gave him hope. He followed her from place to place. Discovered from others which celebrations she would attend and attended the same. He had gone so far as to attend at the cathedral, which he ought not have done. But he could not help himself that day. He could not help himself now. Nor could he think what else to do but to keep his face and his form before her.

Vladimir Ryzinsky could not tell him what to do either, though he asked the man. Vlad was a mortal, a very old and wise mortal. The servant had blanched to hear that Aphrodite had discovered Stauss at a dying man's throat, but he had said merely that young vampires in love sometimes grew careless.

"Mortal women have come to love vampires at times. Your cousin Sergio's mother was mortal," Vlad pointed out encouragingly. "I did not know her, but I know she was mortal and that she loved Master Sergio's father for all of her life. You know this yourself, *gospodin.*"

"Did—did Sergio's father die when she did?" Stauss asked hesitantly.

"No. Why do you ask such a thing?"

"Because Sergio searches even now for a way to shed his vampire nature and face a quicker death as a mortal, and I wondered if his father, having loved a mortal, wished to die with her, and that is why Sergio—"

"Sergio's father died only the year before you were born, *gospodin*, in a fire in a theater in Vienna. He was a Kuechera to the end—fine, noble, certain of his duty, and proud of his honor. He loved life always, but he remained there, in the theater, to do what he could among the panicked mortals. He saved many lives and ushered many others to their Creator in peace despite the terror of what occurred around them. Those who saw and survived still speak of his bravery with reverence."

Vlad's words settled in Stauss's heart. They would be remembered, but they were not of much use in the present situation. Aphrodite would not so much as approach him. And if he took one step in her direction, she would seize the arm of the closest gentleman and encourage the man to lead her away.

I am a fool, Stauss thought at last, returning weak and nearly blind from his excursion into the sunlight merely to stand at the back of the chamber in St. Paul's Cathedral and feel Aphrodite's presence. *There are mortal women who can accept and love vampires, but the woman I love is not one of them.*

Late in July, he forced himself to accept what must be truth and began an attempt to drive all thought of Aphrodite from his mind, to drive all hope of her from his heart. He relit his charming smile, assumed all the qualities of seduction born in him, and cut a mad swath through London's *ton*. "I will sip the nectar of the buds of London at my will," he told himself, "and in that

sweet liquid I will drown all my longing for the English
rose I cannot have."

New ladies' fashions appeared instantaneously in
the drawing rooms and ballrooms of the *ton*. Dresses
with high-standing collars appeared. Velvet ribands with
jeweled pins adorned young ladies' throats. Fichues,
silken scarves, multiple strings of pearls, and wide-banded
gold necklaces decorated velvety young throats. All of
them concealed the oddest little blemishes that had
come from nowhere and faded with time.

Stauss came to a halt on the staircase of the Pulteney
Hotel and stared. He was bound for a soiree at Lady
Darlington's, and as usual, he was late. But the gentleman climbing the staircase toward him drove all thought
of the entertainment from his mind. "Sergio?" Stauss
said softly. And again, "Sergio!" clasping his stalwart cousin
in a welcome bear hug. "You have been gone from London forever. I thought never to see you again."

"But I must look in on you from time to time, little
cousin, to see how you do," Sergio replied. "Is your Miss
Petersen with you still?"

"No. Gone. To a position as governess in a much
finer household than the one she left."

"Just so. And are you enjoying the ladies of London
as you ought, Bearcub?"

Stauss took his cousin's arm and led him back down
the stairs and into the public room, where he ordered
ale and they settled into a private booth far from curious ears. He thought to tell Sergio about Aphrodite,
about the ache in his heart, the emptiness he could not
seem to fill, but he found he could not. Sergio was smiling. Sergio expected to hear of adventures, of lovely

women and nights of reveling. Stauss would not deny him. He described the celebrations, the dignitaries, the sweet and compliant young ladies who had succumbed willingly, harmlessly, to his allure. He assured Sergio of his safety, of his happiness. He smiled and smiled and hid his pain deep in his heart.

"And you, Sergio," Stauss asked, when he could think of no more stories to tell. "Have you found these writings for which you search? Are they in this special library?"

"I am close," Sergio said. "That for which I search is there. I can feel it. Almost taste it."

"And you will follow their instructions and be lost to us." The ache Stauss carried in his heart increased twofold. Not only would he never share his life with his beloved Aphrodite, but his cousin Sergio, whom he loved and admired, wished to leave him forever, too. Stauss shook his head sadly. "Sergio—" he began, but then the ache in his heart closed his throat so no more words could tumble out.

"Stauss, I have a new reason for using it," Sergio said. "You once asked if I had ever wed, and I believe I said it was too much nuisance. But now I have found the woman I would take to wife, and I do not feel free to do so. I cannot go to her as I am. I will not. She must not know the torture of growing old while I do not. And I do not wish to lose her and be forced to live when she ages and dies. I must do this thing."

Love. Sergio loves a mortal woman, too! Stauss stared at his cousin's face which shone with excitement. He said something in reply. He did not know what. Something congratulatory. Something inane. Something Sergio would expect to hear. But his mind raced. If Sergio did find this recipe for mortal life, would it work on a vampire born of the union of two vampires or would it work only for those like Sergio, whose nature was already half mortal? If he could become mortal, would Aphrodite then accept him, love him, become his wife?

It was the first of August, and the guests who had gathered for dinner at Sir Merrill's were just then speaking together in the drawing room until they were called to their coaches. They intended to form a happy caravan on the way to St. James's Park. This very day was the anniversary of the Battle of the Nile, and Lord Nelson's brilliant strategies and great daring were to be commemorated by a representation of that battle on the canal. Then they intended to drive on to Green Park for the illumination of the Temple of Concorde.

In her bedchamber a floor above the guests, Aphrodite helped Miss Petersen to don the cloak which matched the hat and gown she had had altered for the young woman. "There is nothing to fear, Ellen," she said, urging Miss Petersen toward the staircase. "Sir Leslie looks forward to having you on his arm, and Uncle Merrill and Claire will be as pleased as punch to have you with us."

"But I am a mere governess," Ellen protested as they descended the steps. "What will your guests think?"

"We do none of us care," Aphrodite proclaimed.

And then they were at the first floor and making their way toward the drawing room. Miss Petersen hesitated on the threshold, stepped back, and dodged to the side of the doorway, taking Aphrodite with her.

"What is it? Ellen?"

"I cannot go in there."

"Whyever not?"

"Because he will recognize me on the instant."

"Who?"

"The gentleman with his arm resting along the mantel."

Aphrodite peeked around the corner into the drawing room. "Arthur?" she asked.

"I do not know his name. He has a brown moustache."

"His name is Arthur Manning."

"You *know* him?"

"I cannot avoid knowing him. He happens to be my cousin. He has been absent from town for a bit or his presence here would not surprise you. He runs tame in this establishment whenever he is in London."

Miss Petersen peeked around the door frame over Aphrodite's shoulder. "And the gentleman with the blue waistcoat just now approaching him, is he one of your cousins as well?"

"No, that's Mr. Jeremy Bent of the Kentish Bents. He and Arthur have been chums forever."

"I must get word to Count Kuechera at once," Ellen hissed, dodging back out of sight and tugging Aphrodite with her. "He must know their names."

Aphrodite could not believe her ears. "Stauss? I mean, Count Kuechera? Why should he care to know Arthur's and Jeremy's names? Do not shudder like a schoolgirl, Ellen. Tell me."

"Because Mr. Chester Nuberly did not merely give me a slip on the shoulder as the count told you."

"He did not?"

"No. I pleaded with him not to tell all of the truth. Mr. Chester Nuberly did importune me, but he also attempted to ravish me and kill me."

Aphrodite paled at the thought.

"Count Kuechera saved my life. I cannot seem to re-call much of it, but that matters not at all. Chester Nuberly wanted to kill me because he bragged to me when he was in his cups that he and his friends would have a fortune soon and that he would not then even look at such poor fare as me. I would read all about it in the papers, he said. I must simply watch for a headline about the Russian Tsar's untimely demise."

"Oh!" Aphrodite gasped.

"I waited until I thought he had fallen into a stupor, and then I ran off. He chased after me and attacked me. When I came to myself at last, in the care of Count Kuechera's servant, I confided in him the threat to the tsar. Mr. Ryzinsky assured me that the count and his men were already aware of the threat, but that they would appreciate any hint I could give as to the identity of Mr. Nuberly's friends. His friends were often at the house. I described them, but I never did know their names. I know them now. Arthur Manning and Jeremy Bent. We must send word at once. Aphrodite, if they have been absent from London and returned only this evening, is it not likely that this is the evening they intend to do the deed?"

Vladimir Ryzinsky accepted the sealed note from the groom's hand and carried it into his master's bed chamber. "A communication from Miss Coop," he said.

"It is?" Stauss, his eyes abruptly aglow, took the bit of paper at once.

"And Miss Petersen," Vlad added.

"Oh. From them both." Stauss set the note aside and returned to fastening the collar of his uniform.

"The Englishman who delivered it said it was urgent,

gospodin," Vlad persisted, taking the note from the table and returning it to Stauss's hand.

"Urgent?" This raised one of Kuechera's eyebrows a bit. He broke the seal and stared down at the hastily written message. "Damnation," he muttered. "Vlad, you must carry a message to Platoff for me, eh? He must persuade the tsar to bypass the nonsense in St. James's Park this evening and go directly on to the illumination of the Temple of Concorde."

"Tonight is the night, *gospodin?* The ladies have discovered something?"

"The names of the would-be assassins and their whereabouts." Kuechera donned the dark, billowing cloud of his cloak as he stalked from the chamber. "You will find Platoff upstairs in the tsar's rooms. They await me even now. I was to make one of their party this evening. I will meet them at the illumination. Likely, I will be late in arriving."

Twilight lingered in the sky as Kuechera made his way from the Pulteney, took the reins of one of the horses awaiting the tsar's party, and tossed the boy holding them a coin. *There are merely three men involved in the attempt,* Stauss thought. *Both Aphrodite and Miss Petersen said as much. One of them I have already eliminated. I will see to these two, and Tsar Alexander will go merrily off to the talks in Vienna never once suspecting that his life was threatened.*

The Chinese pagoda in St. James's Park, erected especially for the Peace Celebrations, stood seven stories high and was lighted with gas lamps. It was the most amazing folly. Aphrodite, standing beside Miss Petersen and Sir Leslie on the little yellow bridge that crossed the canal, would have been content to contemplate the structure for a goodly long time if her mind were not boiling with thoughts of Mr. Arthur Manning, Mr. Jeremy Bent, and Stauss. The shadows were lengthening quickly now. Her cousin and Mr. Bent had already descended from the bridge on the other side of the canal and were strolling toward the pagoda, and Stauss was nowhere in sight.

He is coming as quickly as he can, Aphrodite assured herself. *There is a good deal of traffic on the streets, and the park overflows with people. He must thread his way through all of it, all the way from the Pulteney Hotel. If he was at the Pulteney when the message arrived. Perhaps Stirling is chasing him all over London attempting to deliver our note.*

Aphrodite glanced at the people around her. The row boats which would represent the ships present at the Battle of the Nile were pulling out to take their positions on the canal. Everyone's attention focused on them, even Sir Leslie's and Sir Merrill's. Only Ellen glanced worriedly in Aphrodite's direction. Aphrodite stepped closer to the governess. "We shan't know where they've gone or what they propose to do if we lose sight of them," she whispered in Miss Petersen's ear.

"Precisely what I was thinking," Ellen whispered back. "But we told Count Kuechera that we would meet him here, on this bridge."

"And so you shall, and tell him in which direction I have gone."

"Aphrodite, you cannot."

"I must. I intend merely to keep them in my sight, Ellen. I will not confront them. You will be able to see me more easily than Arthur and Jeremy. The white of my shawl will be visible for a goodly long way." And then Aphrodite took a step back, a step to the right, shuffled around Lord and Lady Cossington, and disappeared into the crowd to reappear moments later at the base of the bridge, strolling in the direction of the pagoda, a mere six yards behind Mr. Manning and Mr. Bent.

Kuechera abandoned his mount in the care of a slim boy at the foot of the bridge. Long, determined strides carried him through the crowd. The young women had assured him he would find them near the middle of this structure. His eyesight aided by the lowering darkness, his mind sorting rapidly through a random maze of mortal thoughts, his ears searching for the sound of Aphrodite's or Miss Petersen's voice, he discovered Ellen at once, but Aphrodite was not beside her. The miniature Battle of the Nile had already begun. He drew not even Sir Leslie's attention as he touched Miss Petersen's arm. She turned to him at once.

"Thank heaven you have come. I have just now lost sight of Miss Coop."

"Lost sight of Miss Coop?" Kuechera's heart stuttered in his breast.

"The men walked off along the canal, and the shadows were lengthening and—"

"Where is Aphrodite, Miss Petersen?" Kuechera prodded impatiently.

"She followed them around to the rear of the pagoda. She promised me she would not allow herself to be seen," Miss Petersen added, "that she would not confront them."

Kuechera's boot heels echoed in Miss Petersen's ears even before she had completed the words she hoped would reassure him of Aphrodite's safety. Fearful and hopeful at one and the same time, she watched his tall, well-muscled form progress ruthlessly and rapidly through the crowd until, very near the far end of the bridge, she saw him pause, gather his cape around him, and disappear, to be replaced by a bit of fog rising from nowhere and floating off in the direction of the pagoda. Ellen Petersen's gasp was covered by a roar and cheers from the crowd for one of the strategies displayed by the boats on the canal below.

Aphrodite stood at a door in the rear of the pagoda, her ear pressed to the slight space between it and its frame. She did not so much as notice the cloud's rapid, silent approach until it descended beside her. "They are inside," she whispered, assuming Kuechera's presence even before he solidified, not so much as shivering at the manner in which he arrived. "They are arguing. Arthur does not wish to continue, but Mr. Bent says he must because one man cannot succeed while two can. Their intention is not to strike here, as we thought, Stauss, but at Green Park, at the illumination later this evening."

"Arthur? You know this man so well as to call him—"

"He is my cousin," Aphrodite interrupted, her gaze sad, apologetic, turning upward to meet Kuechera's. "He has never been the most moral of men. But to think that he would consider—but he has changed his mind, and Mr. Bent—"

Aphrodite's words were interrupted by a crashing inside the pagoda, the ringing of boots on iron stairs, a shout, another crash, a great deal of clanging, a pistol shot, a whooshing of air, and a scream. Kuechera flung the door wide. High up in the structure a gas lamp exploded, then a second, then lower down a third and a fourth. A man screamed again. A second man shouted. Aphrodite looked up and screamed herself. Jeremy

Bent, awash in flame, was tottering on the stairs. Arthur Manning was attempting, amidst a rapidly spreading conflagration, to shrug out of his jacket and make his way down to Bent.

"Stauss!" Aphrodite cried, somewhere between a sob and a gasp. "Stauss!"

Kuechera was gone. In the blink of an eye he was in the center of the pagoda at the base of the circular staircase. Moments more and he was midway to the men, seeming to fly upward through the smoke and the flames. But the greedy fire grew as quickly as Stauss moved. By the time he reached the men, the top five stories of the seven were engaged.

Outside the pagoda cries of alarm arose. Inside, Aphrodite held her ground. With her shawl covering her mouth and nose, she squinted upward through the dense smoke, praying in her heart that Stauss would reach the men in time, that somehow he could save them. And then, the vampire was swirling his cloak around Bent, smothering flames, lifting him up with one arm, lifting Arthur Manning into the air with the other, and leaping from the staircase just as it came free from its moorings and whipsawed wildly above Aphrodite's head. In another moment Stauss was beside her, one man under each arm, urging her toward the door.

The smoke outside was nearly as dense as that inside the pagoda. Through a bevy of men hastily assembling to douse the fire with water from the canal, Stauss urged Aphrodite onward, farther from the structure, farther from the smoke, until at last he lowered Jeremy Bent and Arthur Manning to the ground. People gathered around them. Shouts for help on their behalf filled the air. Manning wheezed and coughed and closed himself up into the fetal position. A step or two away from him, Bent lay with terror-filled eyes wide, staring up at a horrified, helpless Aphrodite as she knelt beside him.

"H-help me," he begged through burnt lips that barely moved in a face turned black as coal. "Oh, G-God, I—" He screamed then—a sound more like a gurgle deep inside of him. But Aphrodite knew it was a scream from the look in his eyes. Her hands fisted and went to her mouth to keep from screaming along with him. She had never witnessed such agony, such terror, such despair as shone up at her that moment.

And then Stauss was kneeling beside her, taking her by both elbows and urging her to stand above him. "Take off your shawl and hold it around us as best you can," he said. "Do it now, Aphrodite. Now!"

Amongst the crowd that pushed and shoved on its way to help with the fire, amidst the curious who paused to see what could be done for Manning, Aphrodite spread her shawl as far as her arms would reach and watched, tears flowing, as the vampire leaned down over Jeremy Bent. She heard whispered words she could not quite comprehend. She saw Stauss take the man up into his arms and lower his head to Bent's throat. Over the vampire's shoulder, she watched the terror fade from Jeremy Bent's eyes and peace rise to replace it. Just as she dropped her shawl and reached out to touch Stauss, Jeremy Bent tumbled from the vampire's arms, and Stauss collapsed atop him.

Sergio Kuechera sat on the edge of his cousin's bed and waited patiently for Stauss's eyes to open. "You know I am here, little cousin," he said at last. "If you will not look at me, at least do me the courtesy to acknowledge my presence. I should hate to think that poor old Vladimir Ryzinsky drove alone through the slums of London by the light of the full moon to find me, all to no purpose. Or that I have postponed my return to the country simply to be ignored."

"Go away, Sergio," Stauss mumbled. "I do not want you here."

"Why not?"

"Because I cannot bear for you to watch me die when all the while it has been your dearest wish to do it, not mine."

"You will not die if we use our powers together, Stauss. You have managed to come very close to burning yourself to death, but you're not dead yet. What happened, Bearcub? Surely you did not forget that fire can kill you? You have known from childhood that you are supposed to run away from fires, not leap into them."

"I know, but one of the men was—was—"

"Was what?" asked Sergio, his mind already touching Stauss with its healing power. "What was he?"

"Aphrodite's cousin." Stauss's eyes blinked open at last. "I could not save him."

"Odd. I heard you did an excellent job of saving him. And that he, unlike you, is making a strong push to survive."

"He is? He was not the man I—"

"No, not the man from whom you drank. But you did your duty by that gentleman as well, Stauss. You know you did. I have never thought what it must be like to be responsible to drain the fear of death from mortal souls. My father knew, but not I. He would have been proud of you, little cousin. Your father and mother will both be proud of you."

"But n-not Aphrodite. Do you know—about Aphrodite?"

"Yes."

"Sh-she saw me drink once in the shadows. She would not speak to me or come near me afterward. And when at last she called to me, I—I drank before her again. The man was dying in the utmost terror and agony. I could do nothing else. It is why I was born. It is what I am. I can find blood and passion enough to fill my needs anywhere, but I cannot decline to—I love Aphrodite, Sergio. I love her with all my heart."

"I know you do. Vlad has informed me of it, you see. It is not merely a passing fancy, he says."

"N-no, not a fancy. I even thought if you—if you were to find the—the secret—perhaps I could change myself into a mortal. But I cannot. It would be a betrayal of all I am. I am proud of all I am, Sergio. I cannot despise my nature. And because I cannot, I shall never know the love of the dearest lady in the world. N-not even for a sh-short time. Cease attempting to heal me. It will not work because I am not going to add my powers to yours. I may as well be dead as live without Aphrodite."

"Of all the melodramatic nonsense I have ever heard," said Aphrodite, quite hoarsely, at a nod from Sergio.

She had been standing at the other side of the bed. Silent. Listening. Her eyes filled with tears. Her heart overflowed with love. He was burned so badly, he had not even sensed her presence. But his cousin could help him. Stauss must accept that help and help himself as well if he was to be saved.

Stanislaus Nicolaivich Kuechera was a creature beyond Aphrodite's imagination—beautiful, compassionate, proud, heroic. He had risked his life for two men who, in their greed, had made themselves his enemies. He had saved Arthur Manning's life. And he had saved Jeremy Bent as well. She had seen the terror in Jeremy's eyes and the peace that had replaced it.

Aphrodite had attempted, once Stauss had been carried to the Pulteney and Vladimir Ryzinsky had gone to find Sergio, to recall and understand the words she had heard him whisper to Jeremy Bent before he had taken the poor man's blood. And, at last, in the chill of the early morning, she had heard them repeated clearly in her mind.

"I forgive you, and He who created all will forgive you," Stauss had whispered. "I bring you but a taste of the mercy that awaits you beyond."

"Of all the melodramatic nonsense I have ever heard," Aphrodite said again, choking back her tears. "How are you going to marry me if you die, may I ask?"

"Aphrodite?"

"I rather think it is, yes." Sergio smiled.

"You are the most contrary creature," Aphrodite accused, gazing down at the pale face on the pillows that turned to seek her gaze. "You follow me about like a puppy dog for weeks and weeks, bury my uncle's house in vases of flowers, even come out into the sunlight for no reason but to stare at my back, and when at last, you prove to me, without even attempting to do so, how extraordinarily wonderful you truly are, you take it into your head to die. Well, you can just knock it back out of your head, Count Stanislaus Nicolaivich Kuechera. If you do not, I will knock it out of your head for you."

Aphrodite sat on the edge of the bed beside him and kissed him soundly, then more soundly still, nibbling at his lips, teasing him with her tongue, at last burying herself against his neck and biting him tenderly there. She clung to him for a long time, and when at last she sat up again, the great dark eyes that met hers had little silver stars shining in them where there had been none before.

"Wh-who taught you that?" Stauss asked, taking her hand possessively in his.

"Your cousin, Sergio. It is what vampires do, no? If I am to be the wife of a vampire, I must learn to do it correctly. *All* of it. Of course, if you would rather die than teach me the correct manner in which to—"

"I love you, Aphrodite Coop," Stauss said quietly, the stars in his eyes multiplying, shining more brightly. "Do you truly think you can love me?"

"I do love you. Even when I could not bear to think of what you were and what you did and told myself I despised you, I loved you. But now I do not love you in spite of what you are, Stauss. I love you because of what you are—because of who and what you are. Why, I do believe you are thinking of getting well," she added, bending forward to kiss the tip of his nose. "Yes, indeed. Becoming determined upon it." Aphrodite glanced at Sergio.

Sergio nodded. "As long as the bearcub and I have the same goal in mind, Miss Coop," he said, ruffling the crisp, sizzled tips of his cousin's hair, "I expect you must plan for a trip to Castle Kuechera to meet his mama and papa."

"They will love you, too," Stauss assured her. "You may depend on that. They will not oppose having a mortal in the family. We have already had a mortal in the family once. But I do not think you ought to tell your uncle and Lady Merrill that I am a vampire. Not at first."

"No," Aphrodite agreed, raising his hand to her lips and nibbling at his fingertips. "No, I rather think I will wait a while before I do that—perhaps when they come to visit at the birth of your heir."

Note

To discover the intriguing story of Stauss's cousin, Sergio, read Jeanne Savery's "Dark Seduction."

DARK SEDUCTION

Jeanne Savery

Sergio balanced easily against the gently heaving deck of the H.M.S. *Impregnable* and stared at the approaching cliffs. In the moonlight they were a milky glow along the horizon. He watched and wondered how he could have forgotten how beautiful they could be.

The vaguest hint of a scent drifted across his nostrils, and he stilled, his preternatural senses warning him of another's presence. Then, recognizing it, he relaxed, turned, and leaned back.

"So, cousin," said Sergio, "it has been a long and uncomfortable journey."

Count Stanislaus Kuechera smiled, heavy lids drooping over deep-set dark eyes. "Yes, at long last we arrive. I have heard wonderful tales of London and of English women. Now I shall discover for myself if the tales are true."

Sergio grimaced. "You and your women. I, on the other hand, have heard talk of a special library. With any luck at all, there I will find what I need."

"You and your research," Stauss observed with equanimity, his voice a soft, pleasant rumble. "What, Sergio, will you do if this manuscript exists? What if the answer you seek lies there? Will you truly deny your heritage and choose the short, benighted life of a mortal man?"

"I am over three hundred years old, Stauss. There is little I have not done and less I have not seen. One grows bored." Sergio laughed, a light sound floating away on the night air. "You do not believe me? Wait until you reach your first century and, one day, you look in a mirror and no longer see smooth cheeks and firm chin, but sagging jowls and wrinkles. I am tired of it."

"Ah, that is it, is it? You cannot bear to see yourself as an ancient? But that is a minor problem and one for which you ought to give thanks."

Sergio felt a frown start and smoothed his forehead with long fingers, wiping away any evidence of confusion. One had, after all, a reputation for omniscience, did one not? Still . . . why?

"Why?"

"Because when I gaze into a looking glass, dear cousin, I do not see myself as young or old. I do not see myself at all, and neither does anyone else."

Stauss's eyes glowed with laughter. The corners of his proud, pouting lips tilted sensuously upward. The bright, chiseled points of his canine teeth sparked a bit in the moonlight. Sergio, drawn by that smile, smiled with his cousin.

"At least," continued Stauss, "others see you in mirrors as clearly as if you stood before them, and you look young to them. I, on the other hand, do not appear in the blasted things at all. It is the silver backing keeps us purebreds from being seen, or so m'father says. Unfortunately, in all the best households, mirrors hang throughout entire establishments. How would you like to deal with that potential for disaster each day of your life?"

"It is true." Sergio nodded. "We are not all alike."

He studied his young cousin. Not surprisingly, the blustery wind had rearranged Stauss's raven-black hair, tumbling it from a semblance of order into a jumble of curls that cascaded down over his brow, whispered around his ears, and doubtless, tickled the back of his neck. He stood there, smiling that irresistible smile.

A smiling devil, thought Sergio. *No wonder women deny him nothing. . . . But however different we may be, there are likenesses,* his thoughts continued. *Our skin remains alabaster even when long out in the weather, and our features are similar, although I believe his lashes are longer, my eyes still more deep-set. We are bred to ooze sensuality—but Stauss! He exudes it to a degree to which even I am drawn.* Sergio chuckled at that thought.

"Of necessity," he said, speaking his last thoughts aloud, "we draw others to us, but, in you, the centuries have improved the breed. Ah, but so many centuries!"

"Still, Sergio, there must be much you have not done or seen," Stauss said quietly. "Even in three hundred years, you cannot have traveled everywhere. Besides, Father has commented upon how people and places and things change."

"I have lived more places than I wish. To move is, after all, the only way for us when those around us grow old and we do not and their suspicions are aroused. If there is anywhere of interest that I have not been"— Sergio shrugged—"then perhaps someone will tell me about it and I will feel an urge to see for myself." He frowned. "But no. I would be done with the need to hunt the innocent, even temporarily weakening others in order to continue as I am."

"Ah, and that is the part that bothers you the most. The innocents. But I love the innocents. And what is it to them, really, if I sip at a bit of their nectar? They will not miss the little I take. And, they are such delicious buds. Do you not find one or two of them always call out to you in the most pressing manner? In a way that—"

Sergio shook his head, a look of sadness enveloping him.

For a moment his cousin was silent. And then, with only a hint of urgency, Stauss asked, "Sergio, you never wed. Would you die, then, without carrying on your line?"

Sergio very nearly laughed at Stauss's change of tactics in his continuing effort to convince Sergio he must not hunt out the cure, not go through the change that would make him fully human.

"Marriage has always seemed an overly complicated problem with which to deal. There are too few natural-born female vampires, Stauss. Think of your mother. How do you think she would feel if she had not been born to the life, if she grew old while her husband did not?"

"She loves my father with all her heart and all her soul. Were she human instead of vampire, she would love him the same, I think."

"Not so loud!" Sergio glanced both ways, but there was no one near.

"Devil take it, Serge. Do you think me a complete idiot? Do you imagine I would speak so freely should the merest scent of a human twitch at my nostrils or the sound of a breath other than our own touch my ears?" asked Stanislaus softly, dangerously. "I am no fool, cousin, nor ever likely to be one."

"Unruffle your feathers," Sergio replied, his tone sour. "I have kept my skin whole by constant awareness and a lack of trust in others. Do not jump down my throat for who and what I am."

"And I have kept my skin whole by trusting my every instinct. Who and what you are is not quite the same as who and what I am." Stanislaus looked at his fingers, studying the perfect nails. "Tell me, Sergio, did my mother send you after me to see that I do nothing foolhardy in this foreign land?"

Sergio stared hard at his cousin. Then he barked a laugh. "Have you suspected such a thing? You, who survived a miserable war with nary a scratch? You keep a cool head in dangerous situations, Stauss. If I were the sort to hand out warnings, the only thing I would say would be that for us, all situations are dangerous." He pushed away from the rail. "I must see that Hans has my boxes ready. Will you be put up with Tsar Alexander's entourage?"

"Yes. I take shelter with him at an inn called the Pulteney. In Picadilly, wherever that may be. The English have the oddest names for things. I saved the tsar's royal neck more than once, and it was I and my Cossacks hounded the French from the Russian front—minus a few hundred thousand of their horde. He means to keep me near him."

Sergio grimaced. "Until he changes his ever-changing mind!" They both chuckled at the truth of that. "I will find rooms somewhere. London will have grown a great deal from when I was there before, so many years ago. Nevertheless, it cannot be so large that we will not run across each other." He looked up at the taller man. "If we do not meet again before we dock and go our separate ways, take care, little cousin."

"You, too," Stauss replied. "And if you should discover this library you seek," he added, reaching out to stroke Sergio's cheek, slowly, tenderly, with the tip of his index finger. "If it should hold the answer you would find, promise me something. Promise that you will consider all things—not merely the bad, but the good of what we are, what we have, and what we do for mortalkind—*before* you take advantage of that answer. We are separated, you and I, by centuries and by choices that were not ours to make, but my heart weeps even now at the mere thought that I may never see your indecipherable, self-contained, oh, so beloved face again."

Miss Tabitha Jerome clutched the heavy volume to her chest with one arm and attempted to cover an overly wide yawn.

Why, she wondered, *does anyone rouse themselves so early in the day? Why did I?* But she knew. She had managed to fall back to sleep after the maid finished creeping around her room doing morning chores. But then, far too soon, a loud roll of thunder had jerked her upright in bed. Once her eyes were opened wide, she could not make herself drop back into sleep.

Now, just as she reached the end of the tall shelves, her mouth gaped still wider, and involuntarily, her eyes closed. Her raised fist clenched, her jaw almost cracking with the yawn's intensity.

The side of her fist pressed against starched linen. Tabitha stilled.

Someone sneezed.

A subtle scent assaulted Tabitha's nose. It was like nothing she had ever before encountered, a spicy scent with undertones of—of she did not know what. She scrunched her eyes more tightly shut as the seductive aroma twisted down inside her, curled around, grasped some part of her to which she had rarely, perhaps never, paid attention.

Her eyes remained tightly shut as she studied the feeling. It was similar, but not exactly like those rare occasions in her twenty-eight years when she had encountered a man who drew her attention in ways a young woman should never admit to being drawn. But, if not that, then what was it? She drew in a deep breath and once again felt that odd twisty, squeezy stirring within her.

Tabitha did not want to open her eyes. Did not want to see the man who did this to her senses. She was certain she would find herself disappointed, and this was something so basic, something so . . .

She could not explain it, but she did not want it to end, wanted desperately to continue the . . . the . . . She was not sure what it was.

Almost, she would describe what was happening to her as a fundamental change in her being! She shook her head at the ridiculous notion, brushing her bonnet's curly feather, had she known it, across the man's face.

Sergio Kuechera sneezed again. He felt his eyes narrow in amusement, his lips curl slightly in an upward direction. He stared down at the wildly waving feather curling over the top of a truly frivolous little bonnet. It brushed his nose again . . . and again. He sneezed for the third time.

Sergio held his head back and away from the pink-dyed plume. Very slowly he lifted his hands. Very lightly he touched the woman at shoulder height. Very carefully, he held her steady as he stepped back. He took great care in all of that because somewhere deep inside where he rarely allowed himself to look he was distracted by a sudden and irrevocable recognition of . . . of . . . his other self?

Nonsense. He chastised himself for a fool. *Absolute nonsense.*

Perhaps, but now he was not so close, he caught a glimpse under the narrow brim and found himself staring. Wild curls peeked out from the feather-trimmed hat. Dark hair with a life of its own, the waves and curls hiding her features from him. Dark lashes lay against pale cheeks. . . .

But if his vision was next to useless, his other senses screamed at him. His nose told him she was all woman, just the sort he, at his cousin's age, had searched out when a need for blood was upon him.

And yet she was not quite the same.

Her soft body and her scent roused something inside him beyond the need his kind felt more often than he cared to admit. Roused something quite different. Ah yes! That scent. It was hers alone, intensely personal, a womanly scent that called to a part of him he had thought long dead.

Tabitha looked up.

Sergio's gaze locked with hers . . . an oval face, a strong chin, eyes the color of . . . What were they the color of? He drowned in their depths before he could decide. . . .

"I'm drowning," she whispered, her breath unbearably hard to draw in, force out—but she could not save herself by turning away.

Sergio watched her eyes widen and their color, a silvery blue gleam, intensify to something still nearer true silver.

Silver?

A shiver ran up his spine, and he blinked, breaking the connection between them. Silver, for good reason, was not a vampire's favorite color! His fingers, barely touching her shoulders, steadied her as he took yet another step back.

"My pardon and it please you," he murmured, fighting the temptation to once again capture those incredible eyes with the power of his own. It could be done so easily—but to do so was to snare himself as well. Reluctant to find himself trapped a second time, he stared over her head. But those eyes. . . . They drew him. . . .

Tabitha shook herself slightly and clutched her book more firmly. "Sir!" she said, recalling that some response was required. "It was my fault entirely." She blinked rapidly, easing herself a step back from the overpowering masculinity confronting her. She had never before encountered a man who, or so it seemed, was constructed entirely from energy, made of power, designed to overcome any and all odds. Not in the manner this man was.

"Ah no! It is never the lady's fault." Sergio wondered at the flirtatious sound of that. "It is never the lady's fault," he repeated, in a softly lilting tone. *What is this? I never flirt.*

"One more proof, if such is needed," said Tabitha a trifle mournfully, "that I am no lady." She shrugged, although it was not much of one. Such movement was difficult when both arms were hugging an overly large book to one's chest.

A deep, surprised-sounding chuckle rewarded her sally. "If not a lady, then what are you?"

That overly definite little chin rose. "A bluestocking, sir. Terribly, terribly blue. The pride of my tutor, the despair of my mother, the laughingstock of all who know me." She raised her eyes to his, and catching him unaware, once again they found themselves entangled in a mutual gaze that said everything . . .

. . . and nothing.

Sergio cleared his throat. "May I carry that exceedingly heavy book to the counter? A blue lady cannot be so very unlike other ladies when it comes to heavy objects, is it not so?"

Sergio lifted the book away, effortlessly overcoming her attempt to retain her hold on it. He glanced at the title. "Lycanthropy?" His dark brows rose, forming sharply defined, inverted vees above deep-set eyes so dark they appeared black to the woman watching him. "The study of shape-shifters? Specifically werewolves? My dear young woman, surely you do not mean to purchase this."

He stared at her. Her heavy lids took on a hooded look, the long lashes hiding their silvered expression, and despite the knowledge he should not, he regretted he could not see them.

"It is not for myself, of course."

"Oh, of course," he said a touch derisively.

Tabitha wished she still held the book. She felt—unprotected—without it. "You do not believe me?" she asked.

"Did not you yourself admit to being a blue lady?"

She nodded. "Yes, and it is *true,* you know." She spoke earnestly as if wishing to be entirely fair. "But *this* is not my particular interest. I have been delving into volumes relating to quite another occult phenomenon."

"Then, this book is a gift for a fellow scholar?" An emotion of some sort eeled its way around inside him. Sergio, unfamiliar with the sensation, studied it.

Jealousy, he thought in amazed outrage. *A touch of jealousy, roused by nothing more than the knowledge that this unknown woman would give gifts to another? But such emotion is utterly absurd.*

. . . and was, for that reason, dismissed.

"No, no," she interrupted his thoughts. "I merely do

an errand for a friend since, fortuitously, I had my own purchases to make."

"For someone you know well?"

She nodded. "My tutor."

"Your tutor." Sergio tipped his head. "May I ask the name of a tutor who would ask a young woman, however blue, to purchase for him a heavy book about werewolves?"

"Mr. Sidney Munson. He is a scholar of some note in his own particular field, but I doubt you would have heard of him."

Munson? But of course I have heard of him. What vampire has not?

"Munson is your . . . tutor." Sergio was shocked to discover the jealousy had not, after all, been dismissed, but, now he had a name, was roused quite fiercely against this Sidney Munson, who had written a number of essays of importance to the peripatetic but close-knit world of the vampire.

"You, perhaps, think me too old for a tutor?"

"One is never too old to learn," said Sergio absently. It occurred to him he was far too interested for anyone's good—including his own, *especially* his own—in the curly-haired young woman before him. "And," he said, recovering himself, "you, madam, are not at all old."

"Oh, yes I am," she averred. "Too old to be unmarried. A mere spinster destined to lead apes in hell. I am my mother's only failure."

Sergio shook his head at that, but turned without responding and walked toward the round counter. Inside the circle it formed were several of Hatchard's young clerks, all of whom were busy—or pretended they were. He stared at the back of one man's head, a moment's intense look. The fellow jerked as if pulled by a string, looked all around, turned, and then hurried toward where Sergio and Tabitha stood.

"This lady would purchase this volume," said Sergio. "You will see it is immediately transported wherever she wishes it taken, so that she need not carry it home herself. And any others she may buy as well," he added as an afterthought.

Tabitha blinked. She cast one quick, curious glance toward the man at her side and then looked down, demure as any proper young miss could be.

Very soon the transaction was completed, and Tabitha offered her hand to her new acquaintance. "Thank you. I much appreciate your assistance. Women, unless young and beautiful, are too often made to wait for service, especially when a more important customer of the male persuasion requires attention. May I know the name of my benefactor?"

He bowed, remembering to click his heels as his cousin did effortlessly and without thought. "Sergio Dimitro Alexander Kuechera, at your service."

She nodded. "You are with the tsar's party."

"In the sense that I traveled with it, yes, but I am not one of our tsar's entourage. Will you not return the favor of a name?" he asked, speaking softly.

Those wonderful eyes widened. "But, sir, I cannot."

"Cannot?" His lids drooped, and for half a moment, he considered forcing her to his will. So easily done. So very easy to gently insert into her mind the need to respond as he wished her to. . . .

"We," she said primly, "have not been properly introduced." Those silvery eyes twinkled and, for the moment, were very nearly a proper blue. Once again her gaze tangled his into a knot. "If," she added, sounding reluctant, "you were to attend Lady Jersey's rout tonight, surely someone will be kind to us and do the deed?"

"Lady Jersey." He bowed, wondering if he had somehow influenced her even when he had decided he would not. "Perhaps it can be arranged."

My cousin is certain to have obtained a ticket of invitation, he thought as he watched the woman walk away. When she disappeared back between the pair of shelves from which she had originally emerged, he frowned ever so slightly.

Stanislaus would have the invitation, yes, but if he, Sergio, had any sense at all, he would go nowhere near either his cousin or the Jerseys' town house. He had no time for this sort of lighthearted nonsense, the gay flirtation, the stolen moment of light passion, the intricate movements involved in the dance of love, at which his cousin excelled and which he unabashedly enjoyed.

Unlike Stauss, he had work to do, and it was time he got down to it. Sergio recalled the lady's eyes. That thing inside him that he did not recognize jabbed at him, heated his blood, and was difficult to thrust aside.

No time, he insisted, *for the courtiers' games of love I played so enthusiastically in the past. . . .*

But then jealousy toward the tutor who was allowed to spend hours with the unknown woman reared up into consciousness. After a moment it, too, was thrust aside. Even so, he cast a glance toward the bookshelves between which she had disappeared.

What sort of volume, he wondered, *does the blue lady look for now?*

Preoccupied with his thoughts, Sergio stopped short, staring blindly at a young man who, insecure in his youth and inexperience, wondered if he had tied his cravat awkwardly or had spilled his morning egg on it.

Curiosity? thought Sergio. *I allow curiosity to replace desire and jealousy?*

Sergio snorted at his own emotions, the derisory feeling strong enough to allow him to turn toward the newspapers spread out for the use of the bookstore's patrons. The youth, convinced there must be egg on his cravat, instantly returned to his rooms, certain he was in deep disgrace.

Hidden by the shelves, Tabitha forced her heart to slow. Never had she reacted to a man as she had to Mr. Kuechera. Mister? She did not even know that for a certainty. A frown creased her brow. Had she not read in the *Times* that there was a count of that name in Tsar Alexander's entourage? Good heavens! Had she bantered words with a Russian aristocrat? Her mother would never believe it. Not, of course, that her mother would ever know, since she would never tell her. Tabitha frowned, remembering he had said he was *not* with the tsar. . . .

Even if he is not a noble, he is a man. So how, she wondered, *did my tongue work so smoothly when it never does so. Not with tonnish men?*

And those eyes. She had never seen such eyes . . . the depth, the power. Dark and flecked with gold. Had he mesmerized her? Nonsense. The greatest mesmerist to ever visit England had attempted to hypnotize her and found it impossible.

No, it was something far more basic, far more easily understood—and far more incredible! The man had affected her senses to the point she had forgotten everything that was ever drilled into her concerning one's public behavior! And, moreover, how one behaved with

a stranger, a man to whom one had not been introduced!

*I treated the gentleman with all the ease and familiarity
with which I treat my tutor of many years.*

Not that she had ever felt for Sidney Munson anything approaching what she felt for this gentleman.
Her mind turned in circles as her eyes scanned the
shelves. Finding a volume in her subject, she plucked it
down.

Latin. Tabitha wished her Latin were more fluent
because she was unlikely to find anything in English in
the subject of her current interest. There might, however, be something in German or French. The next
book she checked was also written in Latin.

She sighed. It did not make any difference, really. After
all, she would not be studying tonight in any case. . . .
Tabitha stilled, her head lifting sharply, which set the
fluffy pink feather to bouncing wildly. Her eyes widened.

Did I promise that man I would be at Lady Jersey's tonight?
she asked herself as, without thinking, she reached for
still a third volume. Automatically, she checked and recognized the language. Latin, of course.

Giving up all thought of concentrating on a proper
search, Tabitha stacked the three volumes, picked them
up, and returned to the counter where it took her very
nearly a full five minutes to achieve what the foreign
gentleman had managed with merely a look. And that
to the back of the clerk's head.

Most interesting, thought Tabitha, recalling every moment of that scene. *Really, such control of another is something quite out of the ordinary.*

And that memory almost managed to put a cloak
over the other sort of memory. The unwarranted belief
in the man's strength when he had barely touched her.

That intense look in his deep black, gold-flecked eyes. The thick, healthy-looking hair that formed a vee on his forehead before flowing back to where, overly long, it was tied by a narrow ribbon, scarcely more black than the hair.

Yes, her curiosity concerning his method of calling the clerk almost wiped out that other sort of memory. *Almost.*

Locating his cousin was more of a problem than Sergio had expected. In the end, Stauss found him. Sergio, allowing Hans to give him a final brush before he left for the Jersey's soiree, gave a moment's thought to the news that a plot against the tsar existed. He smiled a very slightly wicked smile at how Stauss and the others would deal with that little problem.

He had his own problems. His eyes narrowed. The silver-eyed witch was only one. Far more important was finding the information for which he had searched for decades.

But not tonight. Tonight he would once again see his little witch and, perhaps, discover he was wrong and that he had not, at his advanced years, fallen in love with what, if one were centuries old, was a mere child!

Tabitha had the headache. Even her usually oblivious mother had drawn her attention from the crowd moving languidly around the Jersey's salon long enough to notice her daughter suffered from the headache. Which meant her mother had been exceedingly curious as to why Tabitha had insisted on attending just the sort of tonnish event she most abhorred.

Tabitha had talked very fast and, for once, thanked the heavens that her mother did not find her daughter of such interest that she cared that the explanation was both involved and quite obviously made up as she went along.

Tabitha glanced to where, finally, her mother was once again fully occupied by several cronies—all busily tearing apart Tsar Alexander's morals and, perhaps with a touch of jealousy, the morals of the women His Excellency's eye had already, in the short time he had been in London, lit upon.

Staying close to the wall, moving slowly, easing herself behind groups of talking men and women, Tabitha made slow progress toward a certain door situated behind a clump of potted palms.

Tabitha had noticed the half-hidden door when they entered the saloon after going through the receiving line. She had made a note of it, reminding herself that having a means of retreat was always an excellent notion. Especially when one had no interest whatsoever in doing the polite to people who were only interested in bowing and scraping to as many important people as they could each evening.

While waiting for a particular group of gossips to shift, Tabitha tapped her foot in a most unacceptable manner. This time her movements were blocked by the backs of a group of men discussing—with a touch of jealousy—the tsar's ability to cut a swath through London's women.

Tabitha sighed. Calling on what patience she could find, she turned her eyes elsewhere. For a moment she thought she had caught sight of Sergio Kuechera and felt a sudden spurt of jealousy—until she realized the man she watched flirting with several giggling girls was *not* the man she had met earlier that day. Very like, but not the same.

Not with that wildly curling hair. Younger, perhaps? And less . . . solid? Not that he did not exude the same sort of power, but there was a . . . a greater maturity to the one who called himself Sergio.

Maturity? Was that the word? Not really, because the man she watched could, by no stretch of the imagination, be called immature. It irritated her that she could not think of just the word she wanted, but then the gaggle of males blocking her way shifted, and telling herself she was more of a fool than they for indulging herself with such speculations, she drifted beyond them and on toward that much to be desired doorway.

The doorway that led to a back hall that led to stairs and another hall that led to the Jerseys' library. Coming here tonight and rousing her mother's curiosity in the process had been the biggest mistake of her life. Especially since it seemed the man who had caused the aberration in her normally unsocial self had not had the courtesy to come as well.

Across the room, a tolerant look in his deep-set eyes, his arms crossed across his breast, stood that man. Sergio leaned against the wall and watched his cousin.

Stauss will have the time of his life while in London, thought Sergio. *Assuming he does nothing utterly foolish, of course. I only wish I found the world so new, so exciting, so full of adventure.*

He sighed and, pushing forward with his shoulders, found his balance and moved toward a door he had noticed earlier. It was half hidden behind potted palms which suggested it was not to be used by the Jerseys' guests. Which meant it led somewhere private . . . which was just what he wanted.

Why, he wondered, *did I come here tonight? What did that woman do to me? Mesmerize me?*

The sardonic thought brought a bark of laughter to the surface, a laugh that turned eyes his way. Only half consciously, he wiped knowledge of his existence from those observers' minds and turned their glances elsewhere as easily as he turned their thoughts elsewhere. But mesmerize? No one could mesmerize a vampire!

He continued toward that much to be desired means of escape. For half an instant Sergio swore softly. *What,* he asked himself again, *did that woman do to me? Why am I here?*

As before when he had asked himself that, he had no answer. At least he had no answer he was willing to accept. Besides, she had not come. Or if she had, there was no way they would find each other in this mass of humanity.

And at the exact moment of that last thought, Sergio and Tabitha came face-to-face with no more than the fronds of a palm tree between them. Tabitha's eyes widened. Sergio frowned.

"So you *did* come," he said.

"But of course. I thought *you* had not."

He glanced around, turned one young lady's curious glance toward Stauss, erased all thought of himself and the young woman with whom he conversed from another curious mind, and turned back to her.

"Were you looking for me?" he asked softly.

Tabitha felt heat in her neck and cheeks. Instead of answering his question, she said, "If you must know, I was berating myself for coming to just the sort of entertainment I most dislike and was about to escape this overheated room and the overpowering scent of too many bodies pressed into too small a space." She felt a trifle guilty at the acid note in her voice, but her mother was, eventually, going to demand a reason for her odd behavior . . . and there was none.

None to which she would willingly admit, that was.

"Escape? Two minds with but a single thought," he murmured. "Perhaps you would be kind enough to allow me to join you in your flight?" He wrinkled his nose in a most engaging and unexpected fashion. "I, too, find our host and hostess have squeezed too many guests into too little space."

Tabitha glanced around. No one paid them the least attention, and again ignoring common sense to say nothing of proper social behavior, she nodded. And opened the door. And slipped through it.

Sergio followed, giving the room one last look, wiping all memory of his presence that evening from the minds of everyone who had noticed him.

"So. A hallway," he said when they were beyond the closed door. "Where does your hall lead, my savior?"

Tabitha almost giggled. The notion she might do anything so inane as *giggle* shook her, and it took her a moment to remember he had not only called her his savior, of all things, but also asked where they were going.

"The Jerseys," she finally replied, "have a small library at the back of the house on the ground floor. We will find sanctuary there—assuming we reach it without running into servants or other guests who, for reasons of their own, have escaped the crowd."

He chuckled. "Reasons of their own? Is that a polite way of suggesting illicit reasons?"

"Oh, dear." She cast him a sharp glance and looked

way. "I must remember that you are better read than my usual acquaintance, with a sharper mind, and that I must not allow my tongue to run away with me."

"To me you may say anything at all and I'll not think the worst of you. Are your friends so lacking in intellectual accomplishments you may make jest of them in such subtle fashion?"

"I fear I am unlucky in my usual companions—not that that particular comment was so very subtle."

Tabitha stopped just before reaching the corner. She was about to peek around it to check that their way was clear when Sergio touched her lightly, stopping her. She glanced up at him, and he put a finger to his lips. She frowned. What had he heard?

And then she, too, heard it. The sound of approaching footsteps. And then a grunt of irritation and the same sound, the steps quicker, receding back down the hall.

Tabitha gave her companion a suspicious look. He returned hers with a bland, questioning one of his own. She sighed, telling herself it was nonsense to think her companion had, in some mysterious way, influenced the person to go away. The approaching individual had merely remembered something forgotten and returned for it. That was all.

Tabitha continued on to the library.

A small fire burned in the grate. Sergio went to it and added a few more coals while Tabitha took a candle from a candelabrum and lit it at a low-burning lamp. Candles around the room flared as she touched their wicks. She also lit the two argon lamps that stood beside chairs flanking the fireplace.

She caught Sergio gazing at her, and her chin rose.

"I mean to read until it is time to find my mother and insist we go home," she said, and realized her voice sounded a trifle challenging even to her own ears.

"I, too, will enjoy the quiet, a good book, and the knowledge I have an understanding companion who will not insist I talk of tonnish things, or ask that I jest lightly and flirt a trifle *less* lightly, and all those other nonsensical things that go on between a man and a woman at an affair such as this."

Tabitha stifled a touch of disappointment that he found the thought of flirting with her a bore, but nodded. Firmly. "I am glad you agree."

She scanned the shelves for a book that would hold her interest over the very tempting presence of the stranger with the odd eyes. Her gaze landed on one of Miss Austen's books, *Sense and Sensibility*.

"Just the thing," she muttered.

As she reached for it, she saw, just beyond it, something new to her, *Mansfield Park*, by the same author. With a tiny happy sound she drew out its first volume and turned—to find Sergio all too near. Once again she had very nearly bumped into him.

There was half a moment's hesitation before he stepped back. "I heard a happy sound. You have found something special?"

"It is merely a novel," she said dismissively, her mind on how he could possibly have approached so near and she not know it. "A rather new authoress. If this"—she raised the book—"is anything like her last, it will deal with real people and real situations, and all the while, she will be laughing quietly up her sleeve at the foibles of society." She turned and plucked down the first volume of *Sense and Sensibility*. "Here. If you have not run across her work, you might like to dip into this?"

They returned to the hearth, where they seated themselves. After a moment Sergio got up and found a footstool, which he set for Tabitha's feet. Glancing at him, she wondered how he had known she wanted one. But she was already well into the first chapter, and deciding she must have been fidgeting and thereby clued him to her need, she put the thought aside.

Every so often one or the other would chuckle. After the third time she heard his warm laugh, Tabitha asked Sergio where he had reached in the story.

"It is evening at Barton Park, and Marianne has been asked to play for the company," he said, and quoted, " 'Marianne's performance was highly applauded. Sir John was loud in his admiration at the end of every song, and as loud in his conversation with the others while every song lasted.' "

Sergio laughed again, and a feeling of warmth starting deep inside expanded to fill Tabitha's whole being. She looked up. Their gazes meshed and locked, and once again, both of them were lost in that odd feeling of connection.

With great difficulty, each returned to their reading.

Later Tabitha glanced at the clock, registered how late it had grown, and leaped to her feet. "Mother will be frantic," she muttered.

Or excessively angry, which, she decided, *is far more likely.*

Sergio got up, holding his book closed, one finger marking the place. "You must go?"

"I should have been gone half an hour ago. Or *more.* I don't know what my mother can be thinking."

"Then, perhaps we should find her?"

"No—"

Tabitha shook her head vigorously. A long curl wind-

g around her throat. Irritated by it, she pushed it away
Sergio reached to do the same. Their fingers brushed.
their gazes snapped, each to meet the other's. It was a
ng moment before Tabitha realized she was holding
r breath, blinked—and remembered what she had
gun to say.

"—that will not do. We have not been introduced,
d Mother would be angry with the both of us."

"How is she to know we have not been introduced?"

"I do not know how she knows such things," said
bitha shortly. "She just does. She says it is a mother-
ing." He chuckled, which drew a smile from her. "You
uld say I am too old to be worried about a motherly
old concerning some absurd form of propriety, but
u have not a notion how uncomfortable she can
ake one."

"Where will I see you again?" asked Sergio, and won-
red at the urgency he felt to discover the answer.

"I walk in the park some mornings," she said, a trifle
luctantly. "Not early. And only if the sun is well hidden
clouds. I find my eyes are bothered by too much sun."

"Do you, indeed?"

Suddenly suspicious, Sergio probed lightly into her
nd. Unfortunately, he found nothing that suggested
e, too, was of a vampirish persuasion. The sudden
easing thought that she might be dissolved into disap-
intment.

"I, too," he said, "am sensitive to the sun." He pushed
wanted regret aside. "By late, do you mean eleven or
ee or six?"

She laughed softly. "Tonnish time telling is a diffi-
lt art, is it not?"

"It *is.*" Then, to cover his sharp reply, he smiled. "At
st I have found it so."

"The trouble is that I do not know," she said. "I do not even know why I suggested I might be there. In fact"—she frowned at a new thought which suddenly drew her attention, the notion that this man was a danger to her peace of mind—"I am not even certain I remain in London longer than it takes to pack and depart. It is likely I return to the country tomorrow or the next day."

"Tomorrow?" That sense of urgency increased. "You would take the stars from my eyes, the moon from my heart? You would disappear from my life before I have truly found you?"

Sergio felt that part of him that controlled others reaching out for her. Let her go? No. He could not. He would not . . .

. . . except—Sergio cast an astonished look at her back. She *was* leaving. *Despite* his effort at control.

"I must go," she said, and silently upbraided herself for sounding sad. "I do not know what sort of eccentricity came over me, sir, meeting with you in this very odd way, but whatever it is, I must not give in to it further. You will enjoy your stay in London. Goodbye."

Hours later Sergio paced dark streets in a part of town rarely visited by anyone so well dressed as he. Unafraid, his every sense straining for what he searched, he stalked along, unseen, unheard, unmolested.

Sergio had decided the only way to get the strange woman out of his head was to feed. Newly blooded, he would have no reason to yearn for her, to feel this emptiness that she would be gone and far from him. He would, as Stauss so poetically put it, sip the nectar from an appropriate bud—or in this case, a well-blown

ose—and tomorrow, he would truly put his mind to
nding that one particular library where every clue sug-
ested he would, at long last, find the information he
earned for, the means for breaking the curse of his
resent existence.

I would be done with this . . . and on the thought, he
rew a woman dressed in rags from the shadows and
ito his arms.

A few moments later he tucked a five-pound note into
ie creature's bodice and turned away. As soon as he was
ut of sight, he drew out his handkerchief and rubbed
is mouth as if to wipe away the taste of her. He felt dirty,
epressed, and unsatisfied—although that last should
ot be the case. He had fed. Deeply. And she had money
› keep her until she felt up to her work again, the weak-
ess caused by his theft passing with time and good food.

Assuming the idiotic woman knew enough to eat
id did not spend every pence on gin, of course.

Half a block farther on he realized he had fed but
ad not taken the two-penny whore carnally. Was that
hy he felt unsated?

Why, he berated himself, *did I not?*

But he knew. In his mind a perky feather bounced
5ainst his nose. Silver-blue eyes locked to his in a mu-
1al gaze so heated it was like to burn the both of them.
bright mind, a sense of humor—oh, no!

Surely not!

At this stage of his life when he had given up all
›pe of ever knowing love, had he finally met the one
oman who would rouse him in that fashion? He had.

At least, Sergio was nearly certain that he had.

So there is no reason at all, is there, the vicious thought
in through his mind, *why I did not use the draggle-tail
hose business it is to be used!*

The next day Sergio found himself wandering lonely paths.

He had circled the Serpentine, had followed the bridle path from end to end, and traversed the whole of the wide pavement beside the carriage road. Only then had it occurred to him that if his silver-eyed beauty walked in the park, she would not look for the company of her peers, but would follow the hidden ways, the narrow paths, areas not normally populated by the *ton*.

Now he turned down still another well-shaded path and . . .

. . . was rewarded. He hurried his pace, catching up with his quarry. She looked up at him without surprise.

"You came," he said.

"So did you," she retorted.

"So I did. Have you decided you will not leave London after all?"

She sighed, looking straight ahead. "I must. I am achieving nothing here. I have found new material for my researches, tomes that were my reason for coming to London in the first place, but I cannot concentrate."

She cast him a quick sideways glance, fearing he would realize he was the reason she could not.

"Our town house," she explained, "is too noisy. Day and night there is traffic in the street. The servants begin their work early, and although they try to be quiet, it is impossible to clean grates and empty slop pails and make no sound while doing it." She frowned. "Worst of all, there is a dove nesting right outside my window who begins cooing at sunup. When I have not gone to bed until three or four, dawn is not an hour I wish to see."

"So you would return to the country where many birds chirp and coo with the dawn, and cows and sheep and dogs make more noise, and servants do their less than silent work?"

"The birds there are not just outside my window, and cows and lambs make a different, less troublesome, sort of noise than traffic over cobbled streets. And, except when Mother is in residence, which is rarely, our country servants do not begin their day at a truly ungodly hour. So you see, it is not the same at all."

"You sound vexed."

"I should never have come to London," she responded.

"We would not have met," he said, wondering what her reaction would be to that.

"Exactly."

That hurt. "You wish we had *not* met." It was not a question.

For a long moment Tabitha strolled in silence. "No," she said when he had given up hope of an answer. "No, it is not that I wish we had not met. Having met, it seems inevitable that it happened, and I cannot see how it might *not* have happened. If I were superstitious, I would go so far as to say our meeting was foreordained."

"I believe you said you study the supernatural," said Sergio, not quite certain how to respond, disturbed and distracted by a shiver running up his back. Foreordained? Such was not so impossible as she appeared to believe. It had not crossed his mind they might have—

"What field of interest do you study?" he added idly, his mind not on what he was saying, but occupied with the new and unwelcome notion.

—been fated to meet. But if so, then—

"Vampirism," she said.

—*why?*

"What?" he asked, her answer registering a trifle belatedly.

"I have recently taken up the study of vampires," she repeated. "It is a fascinating study. Many aspects of the myths surrounding the species date back to a Count Dracula who lived long ago in Eastern Europe. There is no evidence he himself was a vampire, only that he was an extremely vicious man, an evil man. Since vampires are thought to be evil . . . What is wrong?" she asked, turning to discover why he had stopped and was no longer matching his stride to her shorter steps.

"I fear," he said, his voice cool, "that I have remembered an appointment of some importance."

Foreordained? Is she to be my bane, then? he wondered.

"I will be unforgivably late," he continued, "even if I leave immediately. I wish you a good journey home and that your studies prove profitable." He bowed, clicked his heels, and turned away.

"Mr. Kuechera . . ."

He paused, debated, discovered there was nothing to debate, and, with great reluctance, turned. "Yes?" he responded, making his voice as distant as possible when what he wished was to take her to him, hold her, never let her go. . . .

"All best wishes to you as well," she said, her eyes flickering to meet his and dropping away—only to return.

For a very long moment there might have been no distance at all between them. That heated glance boiled something up inside each of them, pouring a molten force back and forth along the lines of their visual entrapment. Finally, as if a mutual decision had been reached, each looked away.

"Goodbye, sir," she said, her voice sounding haunted.

"I will not forget you," he said, the hollow sound of deep regret coloring his tone as well.

And then, before he could do or say something still more foolish, he turned and stalked off, determined to discover the owner of the library for which he searched so that he might quickly remove himself from London, retreat from the temptation to find her still again, or follow her to her country estate.

Assuming she returned to the country, of course. And assuming he could discover who she was, so he could find out where she lived. . . .

That thought made him frown. And yet, whatever his nameless blue lady said about leaving London, it was doubtful she would actually desert society. Anyone who had the entrée to the Jerseys' soiree was unlikely to forego this year's entertainments when hostesses would vie with each other, inventing new ways to amuse the visiting Lions and to celebrate the win over Napoleon.

Even a lady so blue as this one.

Yes, he would leave London. Leave the noise and bustle, the temptations. And he would forget the odd sensations coursing through him that insisted the woman was important.

Absolute nonsense.

No woman born of Eve was important. The short-lived creatures were a blessing without which he could not exist, but that some one of them in particular might be necessary to his well-being? Impossible.

And she *was* a woman, a child born of a daughter of Adam. He felt again the disappointment he had experienced the night before when his probing told him the truth of that. When the suspicion, the desire perhaps, that she was other than human would not go away, he had inserted a command into her mind that if she *were* a vampire, she reveal herself to him.

She had not. She was *not* his kind.

Whatever it was he felt for this woman must be an abnormality. It could, perhaps, be put down to the fact he was nearing the end of his search and was unsettled, in which case it was merely something of the moment and not at all significant in the scheme of things. It *must* be that. He had no business falling truly in love with a daughter of Eve. Not at this time. Not when his search might not end as he wished, not when he might very well face many more centuries of hiding from the suspicious, of seeking periodic sustenance by a means that disgusted him, and when he would continue to suffer intense world weariness, would spend his days attempting to avert it.

A short-lived woman could not possibly have a significant part in all that.

Still another unwanted thought crossed his mind. There was the problem that the woman could be *worse* than insignificant. The suspicion rose again that it was not impossible she was a danger to him. Perhaps that was what his instincts were attempting to tell him.

Yes, decided Sergio, *far better I leave London as soon as I possibly can.*

"Mother, I told you I would stay a week. Two, at the outside. I have been here for eight days, so why are you surprised that I have begun making arrangements to return to Detwood Hall?"

"You must not go," insisted Lady Detwood. When that made no dent in her stubborn daughter's determination, she added, "You do not understand."

"Then," said Tabitha with what patience she could muster, "explain it to me."

Lady Detwood sighed. "I had hoped to do this tactfully," she said, casting a resentful glance at her uncooperative daughter.

There is a man, thought Tabitha.

"There is a man," said her mother. "You would not remember him, but you and he met when you were very young. He was impressed by your"—Lady Detwood lowered her voice to a whisper, and her eyes flickered from side to side on the dread word— "intellect." She drew in a breath. "For the first year in a very long time he is coming to London. The celebrations, you know," she added as an explanation.

"Ah. I see. You believe we will meet, fall instantly in love, wed, and *you,* finally, at long last, will be rid of your troublesome daughter."

Lady Detwood had the grace to blush, the blood in her cheeks giving them much-needed color. "It is not that you are troublesome precisely."

Tabitha suggested an alternative. "Embarrassing, then."

"Nonsense." Her ladyship's deepening color acknowledged that there was something to that, despite her ready denial. "But, Tabitha, you know you will not always have the Hall as a place of residence. You know you must marry, as did your sisters, every one. You must acquire an establishment of your own so you will not be dispossessed when your cousin inherits!"

Tabitha smiled tightly and shook her head, holding back a chuckle that would have been unappreciated by her mother. "In the first place," she said gently, "Father is not about to stick his spoon in the wall anytime soon. The Jeromes are a notoriously long-lived family.

"There is also the fact," she added, "that my cousin and I understand each other very well. He will not push me out in the cold in my shift to fend for myself.

"And even if he did," she finished, "I have money in the funds that will provide for a comfortable life. If it is necessary," she continued thoughtfully, "I will take a lease on Ribble Cottage, which is near enough Detwood Hall I may walk over whenever I wished. My cousin will not forbid me the use of the library, which would be my greatest loss, beyond the loss of Father, of course."

"But . . ." Lady Detwood's expression was distorted fleetingly in a variety of ways by such a combination of contradictory emotions that they could not be read. "But . . ."

Tabitha had no trouble guessing her mother's prime concern. "Yes, Mother, that means I've no intention of marrying anyone, ever, so you need not be concerned by the fact that I will not meet your friend."

"Your father's friend," said Lady Detwood absently. "I knew you were excessively choosy, and your father has supported you in this; but I did not know you had something against the institution of marriage. Why?"

"But is it not obvious?" To her mother it obviously was not. "Am I to allow some man to take up the ordering of my money? Of my person as well? Have him be *responsible* for me? Are you unaware, Mother, that I could murder someone, and it is, if I were wed, *my husband* who would be tried and condemned! Do you think that fair? To either of us?"

"What nonsense is this? You? Murder someone?" Lady Detwood recovered herself. "But if you did do something so outrageous, it would be *you* who were taken up and hanged, of course."

"The law says a man and wife are one person and the man is that person."

"What?"

Tabitha sighed at her mother's confusion. "Never mind, Mother. That particular law is unlikely to bother you in any way; but I fear I am of a different nature, and I could not abide the knowledge I was no longer my own person in the eyes of my unfortunate husband or, if he were an understanding sort, then in the eyes of the law. I will jog along quite contentedly with no man"—a mental vision of Sergio Kuechera rose to taunt her—"in my life."

She turned away before her mother sensed there was something beyond what she was admitting. "I have a trifle of shopping to do if I am to leave in the morning. Are there errands I may run for you while I am at Harry and James in Regent Street? I mean to choose several dresses and have the lengths of material taken to my mantua maker, and then, too, I should choose material so that new dresses may be made up for the Hall's maids."

"The maids? Is it time again? But your own gowns! Your dressmaker will," said her mother scathingly, "make up the same simple design with no style and very little decoration, and you will look a guy! As you always do. It is unbearable that you dress worse than some charity child! Will you not," she coaxed, "just this once, go to my dressmaker, discover what it is like to wear truly beautiful gowns of the most up-to-date fashion?"

"But, Mother, at the Hall, who is there to see me?" asked Tabitha, barely hiding the humor she felt. "Mr. Munson? *He* does not see beyond the end of his nose. Or only so far as the surface of a book's page! Sidney does not care that I dress for comfort."

Lady Detwood threw up her hands. "Bah. I wash my hands of you!"

"Do not wash them so much they lose that lovely soft white skin of which Father is so proud," teased Tabitha. She could relax now she had gained her way. "I would hate that you are forced to wear gloves in order to hide that you have acquired chilblains from having them in water rather than because it is the mode to wear them."

Tabitha heard her mother growl in frustration and watched her stalk from the room and, finally, alone, chuckled softly.

"Poor Mother," she said, but then put the conversation from her mind and went to her room, where she collected not only her cloak and hat, but her maid, as was proper in London when one went out.

Soon they were in a hackney, called by the family's latest butler—Lady Detwood changed her town servants almost as often as she changed her bonnet—and on their way to Regent Street to patronize Tabitha's favorite mercers.

"Lord Detwood has given me permission to use his library," said Sergio to the roly-poly butler who stood at the door to the Detwood country home.

Sergio had arrived at Detwood Hall to discover the door standing wide to the warm, heavily overcast morning and no one in attendance. Finally, a footman had wandered into the hall, his chest and trousers covered by a leather apron, and his hands by thin work gloves. He carried a container smelling heavily of lemon and oils in one hand and a rubbing cloth in the other.

The poor man had looked excessively embarrassed to find a stranger standing patiently just inside the door and had immediately gone to find the butler, who was accoutered in much the same manner, minus the embarrassment.

"Yes, sir," said the butler, bobbing his nearly bald head. "And whom should I say is calling, sir?"

"My name is Sergio Dimitro Alexander Kuechera. I've a letter for whomever is in charge." He held out the missive Lord Detwood had given him. "Yourself, perhaps? Or a steward?"

"A member of the family is in residence," said the butler. "I will just give this to her. If you will wait in the blue salon, I will have refreshment sent in. Peter! Show Mr. Kuechera to the salon."

Sergio followed the footman. The doors were thrown open, and he entered the long, low room with tall windows looking out onto a pleasant prospect. He was barely inside the doors when he stopped.

"That scent," he whispered.

"Scent? Sir?"

Sergio turned. "What? Oh, I did not mean to speak aloud. It is merely I was struck by . . ."

"An odor?" finished the footman, looking worried. "I smell nothing but the lemon in the polish I have been using this morning, but I will open the windows if . . ."

Embarrassed, Sergio shook his head. "No, no, it is nothing offensive. I was merely surprised to . . . to find it here." He moved on into the room and walked to a window.

She is here. She is here.

Tabitha, her father's letter in hand, hurried into the salon. "Mr. Kuechera?"

He turned.

"It is you," she said accusingly.

Sergio bowed. He was glad he had had some small warning. Even so, he found his gaze tangling with hers.

Her eyes snapped shut, breaking the connection. When she opened them, she was looking over his shoulder. "Why are you here?"

Sergio sighed. "I came to England with my cousin who is beloved of the tsar for the reason that I had heard rumors of a collection of exceedingly old manuscripts and folios pertaining to a subject of interest to me. To you, too, or so you tell me."

"*Vampires?* You also study the mythology surrounding them?"

She cast him a suspicious glance—which was an error. Again their gazes meshed, were held in thrall. Footsteps called them back to themselves, and Tabitha turned to direct the footman and maid where to lay the refreshment brought for their visitor's enjoyment.

"Sir, my father says you are to have every consideration."

"Yes. He is kind to allow me a free hand with his treasures."

"I . . . you . . ."

Sergio smiled his rare smile, and the tiny gold flecks in his dark eyes gleamed. "You would accuse me of discovering your identity and following you, but have not discovered a way of stating your suspicion politely in case you are wrong?"

"Something of that sort," she responded, her voice as dry as the sherry he pointed to when she gestured at the variety from which he was to choose.

He watched her stiff spine. "I truly did not know you were a daughter of the house," he said softly. "I truly came here to do research of some importance to me. In fact . . ."

She smiled when his voice trailed off. "In fact, now *you* have the difficulty in choosing polite words?"

"Yes. And no." He chuckled, surprising himself. He was not one to laugh easily—but, he realized, it was not the first time it happened when with his blue lady. "I admit I did not believe you would leave London during the excitement of the Peace Celebrations. And I also admit that I left knowing it was the only way I could keep myself from hunting you down yet again."

She nodded, accepting his tacit apology. "We have something of a dilemma here, do we not? I suspect you would, if you dared, suggest I take myself off and leave you in peace to get on with your work."

"But I do not dare attempt to shift you from your own home. I could go . . ." He shook his head. "No. My work is important to me. Miss Jerome, can we not work this out? Perhaps if you were to study in the morning and I in the evening . . . No?" he finished when she shook her head.

"I am very much the night owl, sir. *You* study in the morning, and I at night."

Sergio grimaced and gestured. "You have not read the whole of the letter?"

She looked at him, then down at her father's words, reading to the end. She heaved a sigh. "This is impossible. If we are both such late sleepers, liking the dark of night better than the light of day, I do not know what to suggest."

"You once suggested," he said, feeling fatalistic, "that you would, if you were superstitious, think our meeting fated. We have met yet again when neither of us expected it nor sought it. What, my blue-eyed, blue-stockinged lady, do you say to that?"

She looked blindly at the pattern in the carpet, then out one of the windows, but blinked at the light where the clouds were thinning. She turned her gaze back— to meet his steady look. And again both were lost. Finally, when she felt herself about to take a step toward him, Tabitha blinked rapidly and broke the spell.

"My silver-blue, mentally blue lady?" he murmured.

She recalled he had asked a question. "Superstition. Such thoughts are nothing but superstition," she said, hoping she had hid the rather desperate feeling engulfing her. "There are coincidences all about us, but there is *not* some laughing god or goddess pushing us this way, pulling us that, making game of us—"

"Are you so very certain of that?" he interrupted. "It seems a very great coincidence when the both of us left London so that we would not meet and then find that we are once again face-to-face."

For half a second Tabitha considered it. Then she shook her head. "Nonsense." Then she sighed. "And if it is not . . . no, really! We must merely behave like the adults we are and *not* suggest a stupid coincidence is part of a greater plan. Come, I will show you to your room, and once you have washed off the dust of the road, I will take you to the library where I will introduce you to my tutor, who knows its contents in far greater detail than I ever will." She nodded and turned back to the door. "Ah. Jimson," she said to the butler who had returned just then, "where have you put Mr. Kuechera?"

Discovering the answer, she led the way one flight up and into the long hall to the left. "The family suites are to the right, sir. Guests stay in this wing. You have the Yellow suite." She added, "It is a great honor, you know."

Her tone was ever so slightly teasing, and Sergio felt something inside relax, which was strange since he had not known he was tense. "An honor?" he asked.

"Yes." She crossed the suite's sitting room and flung open the door to the bedroom. "In this room, in this very bed, a very long time ago," she said in a hushed tone that verged on laughter, "Good Queen Bess is said to have slept."

He frowned, and she chuckled.

"You are wise to be doubtful," she said, nodding. "The house is old enough, but, as you see, the bed is not. You will be quite comfortable." She glanced around, checking that all was as it should be while Sergio, speaking a language Tabitha had never before heard, checked with his valet, who answered in the same manner.

He turned to her. "Your family has been here a very long time," he commented and immediately changed the subject. "The library?"

Tabitha heard impatience. She nodded and returned downstairs and along the hall under the family's bedrooms.

"The library is at the end," she said. "It is two floors high, divided into three levels, two sets of balconies providing access to the upper areas. One of my ancestors built floor-to-ceiling stacks in the middle of the room, again with balconies.

"I have no notion when the oldest parts of the collection were brought together," she continued, "but I doubt anyone has ever thrown away a single thing, so you see why we have need of all the shelf space. There is even a smaller library where the more popular, more modern books are shelved—novels and poetry, and some biography. There are even a few books of sermons—although I have no idea where those last came from. Perhaps a Jerome wife or dependent brought them into the family."

Sergio wondered at her babbling and sensed a growing nervousness in her. "Miss Jerome," he said, bringing her to a halt. "I will not harm you," he said, when she turned to face him. "I swear it."

And then, as their gazes tangled and did that strange dance of power, he wondered, ruefully, if he could trust himself to keep his vow. But, after a long moment, she nodded and, turning, opened the double doors to a truly impressive library.

Sergio whistled softly. "Magnificent!"

"I do not believe it would be immodest, even as a member of the family, to agree," she said.

"No. Agreeing to the truth cannot be considered immodest. May I explore before you introduce me to Mr. Munson?"

She gestured, silently offering him the freedom of the great room. "I will be there"—she pointed to a deep alcove in the central stacks where a lamp glowed softly above a table piled with books and scattered papers—"working on a translation. My Latin is inadequate to the task, so it is slow going. You may find me there when you are ready."

Tabitha watched Sergio move through an arch in the stacks and disappear. She seated herself at her worktable, drew her book nearer, and opened it.

And stared at it. Blankly.

After a time she dipped her pen in the ink. It dried on the nib before she set the point to paper.

Finally, admitting she was too preoccupied for Latin, she closed the book and, so that it would look as if she were doing something, carefully turned to the first brittle page of a very old, rather thin, folio manuscript. A woodblock cut of the letter *V* headed the upper left-hand corner, an ornate beauty in which the leafy branch of a grapevine and tiny bunches of grapes, the whole colored and gilded and almost illegible, caught her eye.

The first word of the first sentence was vampires. Not, of course, in modern English, but the added *y* where the *i* should be did not change the meaning. She had found this particular manuscript stuffed between two books dealing with the lives of saints and had pulled it out, bringing it to her desk, thinking she would put it where it belonged when she had time. She had no notion why it caught her eye, but that first word proved she had been correct in thinking the vellum sheets had been misplaced!

Or not merely misplaced? Perhaps deliberately hidden away? But why?

A niggle of excitement wormed its way up her spine, and she bent her head to study the old and difficult English with interspersed Latin words and phrases and, here and there, equally old-fashioned French.

Halfway down the first page, she frowned. No. It could not be. Her head came up. After a moment she stood and tiptoed toward the arch through which Mr. Kuechera had disappeared.

Catching herself, she returned to her seat, berating herself for even a moment suspecting the man of being . . . something else.

But, she thought, *he did appear to call that Hatchard's clerk's attention merely by staring at him. If that* is *what he did, then is it not an example of the ability—*

She touched the line with one finger.

—to control others mentally?

She stared at the manuscript resting on the table, worked down to the bottom of the first sheet reading what she could easily read, and suddenly came to a decision. She rose and left the room. Fifteen minutes later she returned, a bulb of Cook's garlic hidden in her pocket.

If Sergio Kuechera happened to be a vampire, he would react to the presence of the herb. But vampires did not exist, were mere mythic beings. So, since he could not be a vampire because such did not exist, then, naturally, he would *not* react.

But either way, react or not, she would settle her mind once and for all and could get down to serious work.

Sergio, scanning shelves on the side beyond where Tabitha sat at her worktable, sniffed. He glanced at the ornately carved panel that hid her desk.

He grinned.

And then grimaced. What had he done that she already suspected him of being exactly what he was? How had he given himself away? Not that it made any difference. She would soon be satisfied that he was *not* what she suspected.

For perhaps the fifth time in his life, Sergio silently gave thanks to the brilliant ancestor who planted the myth that vampires were allergic to garlic. On more than one occasion he had been alerted to the fact his neighbors had, for one reason or another, developed suspicions of his true nature simply because they tested him in this particular fashion.

Not for the first time, it occurred to him that Naples and the southern reaches of the Peninsula below Rome were an ideal milieu for his kind: Every cook in the region steeped everything in garlic. And no one believed a vampire could survive the cuisine, so one was always safe there.

Actually, it was a rather nice climate if one could avoid the multitude of feuds and vendettas. Unfortunately, it was almost impossible not to become caught up in one or the other, so, although it was a haven for vampires in one sense, it was *unsafe* for very human reasons!

But why am I thinking about Italy? he asked himself. *You have been given proof this woman you find so attractive will be your bane. You should be thinking of how she will manage it and how to avert disaster.*

Not that anything need be done immediately, of course. She would accept her thoughts were nonsense the moment he came up to her and ignored the garlic she carried. Sergio frowned ever so slightly and reached up to rub all sign of it away. It seemed this ridiculous habit of frowning was growing on him. . . .

Should I ignore that she carries the garlic? No, he decided, *I will not. I will comment on the odor, but in such a way she will be certain I am merely a man like any man.*

A man like any man! Sergio grimaced. For the most part it was true, of course. He was a man. Not, however, quite like just any man. His life, for instance, would extend into a far distant future, although there were some who posited that it would not last forever, that one *did* age, but so slowly that once one was fully adult, it barely registered on the senses—despite what he saw in a mirror.

He rolled his eyes in a self-denigrating fashion. His comments aboard ship to Stauss concerning sagging skin and other signs of old age were, of course, an exaggeration. He was not old. Not for his species. And there was no proof he would ever age to a degree it showed in his face in the way he had suggested. So far as he knew no vampire had lived long enough to do so. . . .

Sergio continued along the shelves and around the corner while cogitating on the problem of dealing with his hostess, gradually returning to where Tabitha sat making no pretense of working. She leaned back in her chair and watched him as he neared her.

"There is too much to take in all at once," he said. "I have barely begun to see what is available, but will continue scanning the shelves every now and again." He changed the subject. "Would now be a good time to meet Mr. Munson?"

Tabitha rose to her feet and turned in such a way he walked on the side where the garlic rested in her pocket. He sniffed. She glanced at him, and he sniffed again.

"Do I smell garlic? It is, of course, not to everyone's taste, but I developed a liking for it when I lived in Naples some years ago."

Some eighty years ago, he thought, *and another time, more than a hundred years before that.*

"The peasants," he added, "use it heavily in their cooking."

For a moment Tabitha remained silent and then, drawing in a breath, she said, "A very good thing you like it—" She drew it from her pocket. "I had forgotten I carried it," she lied. "Cook always puts it in her ragout, and when I was in the kitchen warning her of your arrival, I picked up a clove. When we had finished discussing menus for the next few days, I must have walked off with it without thinking and then dropped it in my pocket until I could throw it away."

She held it up between finger and thumb, and Sergio took it from her. He rubbed off the papery peel and popped it into his mouth. "Hmm. Good." When he had swallowed, he added, "I have not had any for some time. It is thought to be good for one, you know."

"As are many herbs," she said, nodding, but she smiled and seemed to Sergio to have relaxed a great deal. "Here is the door to Sidney's cubby." It was a heavily carved door of age-blackened wood, rather low, and pointed at the top in the Gothic manner. She tapped at it, and muffled by the thickness, a voice ordered them to enter.

"Sidney?" she asked. "Is this a bad time for you?"

"All times are bad," said the old man testily. He looked from one to the other over the tops of gold-rimmed glasses. "Who is this stranger, Tabby?"

"Father has given him permission to do research here." She handed over the letter from Lord Detwood. Munson read it and nodded. "We are, as you see, to give him every aid."

"Happily. It will be good to have another scholar among us." He eyed Sergio, and his brows lowered over deep-set dark eyes. "Have we met?" he asked after a moment.

"Not to my knowledge," said Sergio—but seeing the man, he wondered if that were true. *Still, how could it be?* he asked himself and dismissed the thought. *Someone as famous as Sidney Munson—would I not remember if I had met him?*

"Hmm." Sidney was still thinking. "If I have not, then it must be that you remind me of someone. It will come to me. Now, how may I help you?" He turned to Tabitha and waved a hand gently. "You may as well run along, Tabby. You are working on that translation, are you not?"

"Sidney, you are no longer officially my tutor," she scolded, "and you know I am serious about my work. If it is that you wish me to leave you in peace with Mr. Kuechera, then say so."

"Tabby," said Sidney solemnly, "leave me in peace with Mr. Kuechera."

Tabitha sighed. "I will inform the two of you when dinner is served. I know you, Sidney. You never think to eat if you are not called to table. Have you the same problem, sir?" she asked, turning to Sergio. "Is it a failing among scholars?"

Sergio's brows rose to form inverted vee shapes. "But surely, my blue lady, you can answer that question yourself, can you not?"

"Because I, too, am a scholar?" Her lips pursed, and she stared at Mr. Munson for a long moment. Then she shook her head. "No, I cannot call myself a true scholar if my tutor is to be considered the ideal. I am still a student. Perhaps someday I will consider myself a scholar, but that is in the dark, distant future when I am old and crippled." She nodded firmly and left the men in peace.

"If she lives so long," muttered Sidney, and then glanced quickly at Sergio.

"I hope very much she does," he said politely. "Now, you will wish some notion of what it is I seek. My researches have reached the point where . . ."

He continued on for some time, gently outlining the work he had done toward a comprehensive work detailing all that was known, or perhaps one should say, believed, about vampires.

"I have," he finally said, "found hints that there are ways of . . . of curing? . . . a vampire of his sad fate, of returning him to the fully human condition? I would end my study by detailing such information."

"I see," said Sidney. He eyed Sergio, the end of his

glasses between his pursed lips. "Yes, I see exactly what you mean. Perhaps." Another silence fell. And then he nodded. "We have a certain amount of early work centering around your field of study. Are you aware that at the moment, Tabby has developed an interest in your field?"

"Has she long been a student of the supernatural?"

"Almost since she let her hems down and put her hair up and demanded a freer hand in choosing the subject of her work," said Sidney. He frowned. "I fear my studies may have influenced her," he added. "I cannot be certain, since there is always someone in the Jerome family who develops the interest. It has been so for centuries." He shrugged. "But it is no business of mine. I am merely fortunate to have such material available for my own work."

"Are you willing to point me toward the portion of the library most likely to contain that for which I seek?"

"Hmm." Sidney shoved his glasses back on his nose and hooked the earpieces behind his ears. "Yes. Of course I will. Follow me." They returned to the main room, and Sidney strolled around the central stacks to where a circular stairway led upward. "I fear the material is in the darkest corner and on the highest shelves, *not* where it is convenient."

"But then, it is material unlikely to be needed very often, yes?" asked Sergio politely. He followed Sidney up the stairs to the second balcony and along it toward where a crosswalk took them to a similar balcony surrounding the stacks. Sidney turned right. At the far end, where the shelves turned a corner, he pointed upward. "There. Those top four shelves contain that for which you look. Or perhaps I should say they contain the material which may include that which you seek."

Sidney's eyes were suddenly caught by a title a little

too low for Sergio to read. The elderly man struggled to pull the thick tome from the shelves, and immediately, Sergio reached to help him, taking the book into his own grasp once it was free. Absently, Sidney tucked the surrounding books, which had tried to come off the shelf with the wanted volume, back into place.

"They stick together when they have not been used in ages," he complained. "It is most annoying."

"I will carry this to your room for you and return to begin my search. Where may I work once I begin collecting material?"

His eyes on the book Sergio held, Sidney had to force himself to remember why he was there and what he was doing. "Oh. You require a desk or worktable. Hmm. Oh, anywhere." His hand came out toward the volume, but Sergio backed up a step. The tutor's eyes came up to meet Sergio's and, after an instant, changed from something approaching outrage to a look of extreme curiosity. But then he looked away. "1609," he muttered. "A narrow street packed with revelers behind the Globe Theater."

"What?" asked Sergio sharply.

"Hmm? What? Oh, just thinking of something I need to check," said the tutor off-handedly. "If you insist on carrying that for me," he added crossly, "then do come along. I've been away from my desk far too long as it is." He stalked off. "Always said we need more staircases. If only they did not take up so much space, we would have them, too," he added plaintively. "It is such a nuisance, having only the one. Come along now. Do hurry yourself a trifle," he added, although Sergio was very nearly on his heels.

Tabitha arrived at her tutor's door just as the two men came around the far corner of the stacks.

"Yes, Tabby? You, too, would waste my time when I have already wasted far too much?" Sidney spoke testily as he turned and took the book from Sergio. "Thank you," he said absently. "Well, child?"

"I merely wished to ask if you and Mr. Kuechera had discussed a work space. If not, I will."

"Very well, child," he said crossly. "Go right ahead. Waste your time, too." And with that the old man ducked into his paneled and book-filled study.

Tabitha shook her head. "His work is going very badly or very well. Those are the only times I ever know him to be cross."

"I wonder which it is. He has shown me where to find the material I need. If you will show me where you think it best I work, I will begin."

Sergio had tucked away the tutor's odd comment about the stews surrounding the Globe Theater in Shakespeare's London. That wild and bawdy era was the time of his first visit to London. That Munson mentioned it was something about which he needed to think, but *not* when he was distracted by Miss Jerome's presence.

"Thank you for carrying the book for him," she was saying as she led him along the stacks to another of the study areas built into it. "Here, I think," she added, gesturing to it. "Sidney is not a young man; but he refuses to make any sort of accommodation to his age, and I do worry. I know he was not particularly young when my father was a boy, so you can imagine the years he carries so well."

"I was happy to be of service," murmured Sergio, and added to the tutor's comment this further information: Mr. Munson was far older than he looked. Dared he probe the old gentleman? Discover who and what he really was? Sergio thought not. Not only was there something intimidating about Sidney Munson, but there was the fact that unless there was a very good reason, it was impolite to invade the mind of another vampire.

"Well," said Tabitha, hesitating, "if there is nothing else I can do, I'll return to work. I believe you will find sufficient paper." She picked over the implements available. "And, yes, you have a good penknife for sharpening pencils as well as ink and pens. If there is ought else you need, then you must just ask . . ."

"And you will," he said, smiling, "inform me when it is mealtime, is it not so?"

"Yes. Of course."

"You seem relieved by the thought?"

"Yes." She blushed. "I am in an odd mood, I guess. It is very strange, but there is something . . . something very . . . no—" She shook her head. "I cannot define it."

"You are," he said in a hushed and counterfeited tone of immense satisfaction, "falling in love with me!"

The blush deepened, and he touched her cheek delicately with one long, well-groomed finger, the olive-shaped nail a pearly color.

"You are quite lovely when you blush. I should apologize for my teasing, but the result is worth being thought an unfeeling brute!"

Tabitha shook her head. "You are incorrigible."

His brows rose to the odd tent shape they formed when he raised them. "I could be reformed. I am sure of it."

"Sir . . . !"

Again I flirt with her. This must stop.

He held back a sigh. "You are correct, Miss Jerome.

We both have work to do"—he recalled his fear she would be his bane—"and I have only a brief time in which to do it. You will excuse me?"

"Until the dinner hour," said Tabitha, wondering why she felt unsettled, almost *ill*, deep down inside. No, not ill exactly, but as if her interior was not . . . quite the same as it once was? It was very like when she first became a woman, was it not? The odd, unsettled sensation? The feeling that things were not quite right?

But that thought was such utter nonsense she took herself well in hand, settled to her work, and put all thought of their guest from her mind.

She read on in the ancient folio. And, becoming fascinated and therefore able to concentrate, she was surprised when a maid came up beside her and, once she had managed to make herself noticed, informed her mistress that Mr. Jimson was ready to serve dinner and please would Miss Tabitha inform Mr. Munson and the gentleman?

All three scholars were irritated that they must interrupt their work simply to remove to the dining room where the butler, Peter, the first footman, and James, the second footmen, served a four-course meal, each course involving several removes.

Munson, mentally going over a theory he had recently contrived, refused to be sociable, merely eating what was put before him with little or no notice of what it was.

Tabitha, too, was preoccupied by what she had learned from the work she had done that afternoon, but, well trained, she made an effort.

"Have you located the sort of material you hoped to find?"

"Little of what I have seen so far is new to me, but

there is one slim volume of interest. It convinces me I am correct, that the information for which I search exists. I will continue seeking it."

"Information. You speak as if it were something factual, something real, and yet did you not say your research involved vampires?"

"You have caught me out," said Sergio, recovering quickly. "I have studied the subject for so long, I speak of it as if it were real."

Sidney lifted his head and directed a blank gaze toward Sergio. He harrumphed, but said nothing, turning his face back toward his plate.

Tabitha stared at her mentor and frowned. "Now, did he hear your comment, or was that in response to something in his thoughts."

"Mr. Munson?"

"Yes. You never know. Sometimes he follows a conversation even when it appears he is deep in thought concerning some esoteric subject far removed from that under discussion. I am glad," she continued their earlier conversation, "that you believe your search will not be in vain."

Tabitha was not glad, however, at the odd, unsettled feelings inside her, nor with the odd ache in her teeth. It was not exactly painful, but it was constantly there. Irritating and interfering with her ability to think rationally. In fact, it was so irritating that instead of returning to the library and her work, she found her hat and cloak and, the sun finally set, went out for a long walk, praying she would not need to visit the local blacksmith who, as a sideline, pulled teeth.

It had not occurred to her that Mr. Kuechera had also opted for exercise before returning to his work, so she was startled when she heard his voice.

"Easy now. I'll have you out of there in just a moment . . ."

She moved off the path toward where she knew a charcoal burner worked.

"Steady. I know you are in pain, but you must make the effort. Now. Again. Careful. Slowly . . ."

Tabitha peered between the trees. Sergio had braced himself in order to lift a tree that falling, had trapped a man. Without thinking, only wishing to help, she ran forward.

"There now," she said, ducking under a branch and falling to her knees by the stricken man. "Careful. That's the way. Here, let me pull aside this branch and there you are . . . a bit more."

"Tabitha, move away. Now," ordered Sergio, his voice strained.

She glanced up, saw tendons along his neck tautened to the point there must be pain. Instead of following his orders, she pulled at the hurt man so that his legs moved to one side and then winced when he screamed.

"You can let the tree down now, Mr. Kuechera," she said, moving herself so that she would not be under the trunk or the branch that would drop very nearly where she had been crouched.

Sergio bent his knees slightly and heaved. The tree moved a bit to the side as well as dropping with a thud Tabitha felt through her bones. A smaller branch hit her alongside the shoulder and pushed her down.

Sergio instantly, it seemed, was there to break off the offending branch. "Are you all right?"

"I am likely to have a bruise, but other than that, I am fine. Old Rickets has passed out from the pain. Do you think I did him more damage when I moved him?"

"Very possibly. On the other hand, he is not dead, and I could not have held it up much longer."

"I do not know how you held it at all," she said, staring up at him.

He laughed harshly. "My dear, you have never been tested, have you? One finds the strength when it is needed. I once saw a man lift a traveling coach off a woman, reach down with one hand, and pull her from under it, and then, once he had dropped the carriage, he collapsed. Never afterward did he remember doing it, but he saved his wife's life."

"I have heard such tales." She looked at the tree trunk and compared it to a coach and shook her head, casting him an odd look.

"It is rotten inside and not nearly so heavy as you would think," he said dismissively when he guessed her thoughts were, again, turning in a direction he did not want them veering. "We must see to this man's care."

"Hmm?" The blank inward look in Tabitha's gaze faded, her normal intelligence showing through. "Oh. Yes. Of course. Will you remain here while I see to sending someone for him?"

"You know where to go, and I do not. Hurry, my dear."

She did, but in her mind she heard, over and over, that "my dear," words he should not have used when addressing her. She delivered her message and was returning with the grooms who carried a shed door on which to carry the old man, when she recalled that Mr. Kuechera had also used her name. He had called her Tabitha when ordering her to move.

Perhaps he can be forgiven since we were in a perilous situation, but does it not mean he thinks of me as Tabitha? she wondered. It occurred to her that she often thought of him as Sergio, not as Mr. Kuechera as she should. *But it is easier, is it not? Thinking of him as Sergio? It is merely that. That it is easier? Is it not? Or is it? Ah,* she scolded herself, *you are behaving like some silly chit in her first Season, attracted to an interesting male and dreaming silly dreams.*

They arrived at the clearing, and Mr. Kuechera supervised the careful lifting of the hurt man onto the door. Once the grooms were started back toward the barns, he offered his arm, and Tabitha, after only a moment's hesitation, took it.

"Will he be all right?" she asked, wishing to speak of more personal things, but knowing she must not.

"I have no way of knowing," said Sergio.

But he did know. At least, he knew more than he dared reveal. The man had been bleeding internally. Sergio had found the damage and corrected it, but he was not certain he had done so in time.

And, as always when he used his powers in the hopes of benefiting others, he wondered if he had done good or ill. Once he had saved a man's life, and days later a fire had taken the lives of the fellow's wife and children. Sergio had never been certain the man would not have preferred to have died those few days earlier rather than suffer the pain of his loss. Another time he had surreptitiously aided a woman having great difficulty giving birth—but the child was never right in the head, and he had always wondered if he had interfered only to give more pain rather than less.

On the other hand, there had been other occasions where his aid had clearly been for the good, so there was no solution to his dilemma. Should he? Should he not? He would never answer that question to his satisfaction.

"Mr. Kuechera . . ."

"Yes?" he answered, pulling his thoughts back to the woman walking at his side.

"I know you explained how you could lift that tree, but . . ."

"I would rather we not discuss it and that you not mention what you saw to others," he said. *I could make sure she does not. Why am I so reluctant to tamper with her mind when, with any other, I do it with nary a thought?*

"Very well," she said. *But you cannot stop me thinking,* she thought, unaware he had the ability to do that very thing.

They walked on, and once again that odd feeling between them surrounded them. This time they were not trapped in each other's eyes, merely walking side by side, but there was that . . . connection? . . . between them.

They both felt it. Neither acknowledged it.

But Tabitha's dreams that night were such that she was embarrassed to admit to them.

Sergio did not dream. Instead, he sat at his work desk and analyzed his feelings for Miss Jerome. That they were strong and growing stronger was something he could not deny. That they were wrong, unfitting, dangerous to both her and himself, was also undeniable.

He should leave.

But he could not leave. Somewhere in this library was the solution to his problem. At least, he was very nearly certain it was here.

In fact, he thought, *it is the solution to both problems. If I manage to break the curse and become fully human, then I may court Miss Jerome properly, win her love, wed her. . . .*

For some minutes Sergio thought with satisfaction of marriage to Miss Jerome. The years together. Their children . . . and the getting of those children.

Sergio looked around, discovered with his eyes—as he already knew with his mind—that he was alone. He made the color marring his cheeks fade and wondered at his embarrassment. The notion of making love to a woman had never before roused such emotion . . .

. . . but, this was different, was it not? Never before had he considered making love to a woman he loved.

Loved.

A grim feeling of determination filled Sergio. He *must* find that cure. He would not lose the only chance he had been given in more than three centuries to experience the joys of loving and being loved in return. He would find it.

Tabitha found she could not control a certain restlessness invading her whenever she attempted to concentrate. Finally, she gave it up and checked the weather. It was nicely cloudy, so, after retrieving her cloak and bonnet, she set out on a long walk. She would walk off this stupid irritation of nerves.

But walking did not make her mind stop circling around and around the stupid notion that had invaded it, settled, and however determinedly she told herself it was ridiculous, continued to burrow into her mind.

"It *is* nonsense," she told a sprightly robin sitting on a twig only a little above her head. "I have been studying such things for years, tracing the origins of the myths, and now attempt to determine when the idea of vampires first entered man's head . . . and this nonsense that Sergio Kuechera *is* such a one arose merely because I have spent too many hours at my studies. I forget that such terrible beasts do not, *cannot*, exist."

The robin sang a trilling, questioning note.

Tabitha smiled. "No. Impossible. I tell you the notion that Sergio Kuechera is a vampire is nonsense." She nodded firmly.

The bird twittered again in a very determined way and then, suddenly, flew away for all the world as if it were offended.

Tabitha chuckled. But even as she laughed lightly, her hands rubbed the region below her heart and up her throat, gently pressing against her jaws. The odd sensations she had suffered for some days now seemed to have intensified. It was not pain. In fact, in some ways she felt healthier than she ever had. It was . . . Was it life? New *life* in her veins?

But that made no sense at all. Of course she was alive.

"In fact, my girl," she told herself in a murmur, "if you do not soon stop thinking the odd thoughts you have recently had, you will soon find yourself chained to a wall in the nearest bedlam, your *life* as a decent human over and done! Now go home and finish transcribing into modern English that manuscript that explains how to cure a supernatural being of its affliction."

But, having decided to forget the whole thing, the notion Sergio might be a vampire, her rogue thoughts continued in a slightly different fashion.

You will admit it is a very interesting concept. The notion you might, if you were a vampire or a werewolf or another of the imaginary creatures man has invented, cure yourself of your dread condition . . . but, why would any such creature wish to do so? Does not it require a conscience for one to wish to forgo the terrible deeds perpetrated by such a being as a vampire? And is not a vampire soulless? In which case, how can it have a conscience?

Tabitha continued musing as she opened the gate to

the Hall's back garden. She was making her way carefully between the stakes up which the strong green tendrils of young pole beans twined when she heard an odd, rumbling sort of murmur that drew her eyes upward.

High on the back wall of the house was a narrow line of stone that divided the lower floors from the top floor and attic. Tabitha knew it extended away from the house a bare two inches, and yet, there, almost to where the main house jutted out to the rear of the wing, Sergio Kuechera clung to the bricks above, his toes barely pressing onto the tiny ledge.

Tabitha's heart flew up into her throat, nearly choking her. *He will fall,* she told herself. *He will fall and hurt himself. Perhaps kill himself.*

Paralyzed by her fear for him, she barely remembered to breathe.

"Now then, little malkin," she heard him say. "Easy now. I only want to rescue you, you silly creature."

Tabitha frowned. For fractions of moments, she would flick her eyes away from Sergio, searching for the cat to which he spoke.

"Easy, little one," said Sergio, and shifted his right hand as he gradually bent down, down, down . . . and scooped up a half-grown kitten with his left.

Tabitha watched him place the kitten on his shoulder. Instantly, claws stabbed through coat and shirt. Tabitha winced along with Sergio, but his rumble of chuckling laughter eased her tension.

"Little cat," he muttered, "is that the way you thank me? Setting your claws into me like that? Well, if it makes you feel safer, little one, then I can bear it. Hold on, then."

Tension returned to Tabitha as she watched him

inch his way back toward a window set wide. She tried to remember what room it opened from, but found her mind a blank, too preoccupied with praying for his safety to concentrate on something so ridiculous as the room beyond the window.

He made it, edged his way through the narrow window with difficulty, and disappeared. And then reappeared, to cast a startled look down at her.

"Miss Tabitha?" he called softly. "Did I worry you? I am sorry, but this ridiculous cat refused to move even when offered a few slices of the very best roast beef. Something had to be done or the creature would have weakened and fallen."

"Thank you for rescuing him. He is a bit of a pet, and I would not have liked losing him."

"Do I leave him in the house or bring him down to the garden?"

"To the garden, please. I do not know how he got up there, but perhaps he will have learned his lesson?"

Sergio smiled. "We will hope so. I do not wish to make a practice of walking along your outer walls like a fly on the window."

The words were trite and said nothing of what either was feeling.

"Wait there," he called, "and I will bring the malkin down to you."

He disappeared as Tabitha muttered, "That isn't his name. He is moonlight for that white breast against the black of his fur. His little white paws are stars. And his name is Nightcat." But Sergio, holding the cat against his shoulder, was long gone and did not hear her.

While she waited, Tabitha stared at the ledge he had traversed, the brick to which he had clung. How had he traversed that ten yards? At least ten yards.

She recalled how frightened she had been. When he suddenly appeared before her, she glared at him. "Do not ever do that again. Never. You might have fallen. You could have been killed!"

He blinked. "But, my dear Tabitha," he said, "I have gone mountain climbing in the Alps. This was a mere nothing, believe me."

She felt her breath heaving her chest as she drew air in through her nostrils, out, in. . . . Finally, she managed to control herself. "I repeat," she said firmly. "Never again. Nightcat is a good mouser and, when he wills it, a pleasant companion, but *not* worth your life."

"Now why," mused Sergio, "did I think you would be pleased."

"I have no notion. Oh, put the stupid beast down." She gestured to where the young tomcat sat on Sergio's shoulder preening itself.

Sergio lifted the cat down and presented him to Tabitha. The cat had other notions, turning in Sergio's hands and clawing his way back to the perch from which he had been removed.

Tabitha reached for Sergio's hand, looked down at the deep scratches. "Come," she said in a colorless tone. "We had best wash these and rinse them with brandy."

Again the words did not say what was in her heart. It was more than a natural reticence to reveal her feelings any more than she already had: The blood, welling up to bead along those scratches, was affecting her in a exceedingly weird way. The fact was, she wanted nothing so much as to lift Sergio's hands and lick them clean.

She wanted to taste his blood!

The realization frightened her badly, and she turned away, hurrying into the house. When she reached the door, she looked back. "Well? Are you coming?"

"Only if you insist. They are mere scratches. I heal quickly."

"But the dirt . . . I insist," she said firmly.

"Then, my dear Miss Tabitha, you must either allow this creature houseroom, or you can explain to it that it must remain outside. I have a feeling I will fail in any attempt to convince malkin myself."

"Nightcat!"

"Malkin Nightcat?"

His nonsense brought a smile to her lips.

"That's better," he said. "But what do we do about this cat of the night?"

The clouds began breaking up in the distance, and Tabitha found her eyes affected by the sudden increase in light. "Bring him in and pray he has been properly socialized. The sun is too bright for me."

Sergio, too, found the light more than he could bear and was glad Tabitha had decreed the cat could enter the house. He would have hated hurting the animal in order to keep him out. For one of the few times in his long life, he was less than happy that he could not control the minds of creatures other than humans. He would have had no need to creep along that ledge to rescue the animal if he could have called it to him. But if he had *not* crawled along that ledge, then he would never have known how deeply his Tabitha felt for him.

"I must get back to work," he muttered. "I must find it."

"As soon as we wash those scratches," soothed Tabitha, and for the first time, wondered what it was he hunted. "I, too, have neglected my work and must return to it," she said.

Sergio glanced down to where the scratches were already closing, healing. Where, within an hour or two, there would be no sign he had been wounded. "If I promise to wash them out myself, will you allow me to do it?"

Tabitha stared at him, her head tipped very slightly to one side. There had been a note in his voice that bothered her, but she could not determine why. "Very well," she said.

"I will see you in the library," he said, clicking his heels and bowing. And, as he walked away, he determined he must have as little as possible to do with Miss Tabitha Jerome until he found the cure for his condition, until he was freed from the curse of his nature and could woo her as would any mortal man.

He would not allow himself to think that that for which he searched was not there to be found.

Tabitha, over the following week, watched Sergio carry books for Sidney. She saw him tenderly lift a maid who had fallen from a ladder while cleaning the crystals in the dining room chandelier. She heard that he helped a farmer pull his cart from a mud hole after rain left the roads miry.

In fact, it seemed he made himself useful to everyone and anyone . . . except Tabitha herself.

He is avoiding me, she told herself when for the third time he refused to come to sit at the dinner table, but demanded a cold collation brought to him in the library. She said as much to her tutor.

Sidney looked at her from over the top of his spectacles. "Tabby, why are you so cross? The man is a scholar. He is searching for one particular bit of information. He is engrossed in work he has no desire to set aside. You have known me to behave in exactly the same way on many occasions. Once or twice you yourself have acted in that identical rude manner."

Tabitha felt her cheeks flush. "You would say he is not so much avoiding me as not interested in me."

"I would say no such thing." And then Sidney grinned a sly grin. "No, my dear Tabby, you will never find me saying anything of the sort."

"Then . . . ?"

"Then be patient. When he finds that for which he searches, perhaps he will be ready to notice your existence again."

"He *is* ignoring me!"

"Tabitha!"

She pouted and played with the portion of pigeon pie the footman had placed before her sometime earlier.

"Cook will be exceedingly upset with you if you do not eat," said Sidney, once again peering over the tops of his lenses.

She shoved the plate away from her. "I want roast beef. *Rare* roast beef."

Utter silence met her demand. She noticed and looked around to find everyone staring at her.

Jimson cleared his throat. "Did you say *rare*, Miss Jerome?"

She nodded and shifted her gaze to meet Sidney's speculative look. "Why are you looking at me that way?"

"My dear child, you never consume rare beef."

She frowned. It was perfectly true she preferred her meat cut from the well-done outer portions of a roast. She sighed. "Nevertheless, tonight I want it rare."

The rest of their meal passed in silence. In fact, after staring at her for quite some time, Sidney actually went back to his reading. Tabitha wished he had not. She did not understand the restlessness she felt and wished there was someone with whom she could discuss it.

But there was no one. Her mother had never understood her and was unavailable in any case. Sidney was preoccupied with his work. There was old Nan, of course, although Tabitha doubted the old lady, despite her reputation as a white witch, would know the answer to *this* problem, whatever it was.

But that was not why she did not turn to her old nurse. The real reason was that the person she *most* wished to talk to would allow her nowhere near him.

Tabitha stared at her plate on which nothing remained but reddish swirls of meat juices. For half an instant she wanted to pick up the plate and lick it clean. Horrified at such an odd urge, she pushed away from the table and rushed through the house to the back door. She had to talk to *someone.*

A maid's rough cape hung there, and she grabbed it, swung it around herself, and ran toward the stables, around them, and through a narrow gate. A path led across the meadow toward a copse nestled into a shallow dip in the hillside, a shallow rivulet running down it to the larger stream at the bottom of the valley.

Tabitha arrived at the open door to a neat little cottage. "Nan? Are you awake?" she called softly.

"Hmm? Is that you, Tabby, dear?"

"Yes. May I come in?"

"Of course, my child."

Tabby heard the sound of Nan's cane tap-tapping toward the door and, ducking her head, entered so the old woman would not have to come all the way. "You should not have got up," she scolded.

"When I cannot rise to greet guests, you can bury me," snapped Nan, frowning.

Tabitha giggled softly. "Yes, that sounds more like my Nan. Let me get the water," she added, seeing that her old nurse carried a kettle.

Tabitha soon returned and set the kettle on the hob, pushing it as near the fire as she dared. She straightened to find Nan staring at her with narrowed eyes.

"What is it?" she asked her old nurse.

"That is what I want to know. Other than the fact you are in love with a man you do not even know."

Tabitha felt heat rising up over her chest, up her neck, and into her ears. "I do not love him . . . do I?"

"Of course you do. Nothing wrong with that." The woman frowned, drawing graying, rather bushy brows down to shade deep-set dark eyes. "It is the other I do not quite understand."

Tabitha sighed. "It is that 'other' I was hoping you could explain."

Old Nan cackled. The crackly laugh subsided, and Nan motioned Tabitha to come close. Once Nan was seated and Tabitha crouched before her, Nan took her old charge's chin in her hand and forced their gazes to meet.

Tabitha felt like squirming but knew better than to move a muscle. She had known of Nan's witching abilities forever, it seemed, but had never entirely managed to accept them as real. Now it seemed as if her old nurse peered into her very soul before releasing her and sitting back.

"Hmm."

"What," asked Tabitha with what patience she could muster, "does 'hmm' mean."

"Just hmm. My dear child, when you return to the house, you will tell that idiot savant you call tutor he is to come to me. At once."

"I will?"

"You will."

"And if he does not?"

"If he demurs, tell him that unless he uses them to visit me, I will send a plague of warts to cover the bottoms of his feet."

"Nan . . ."

The old woman shook her head. "Get the tea caddy, child. And the pot and cups. We will have our tea, and you can tell me all about this man you do not know with whom you have fallen head over heels into love!"

Long knowledge of Nan kept Tabitha from both urging her to tell what she had seen in that odd way she had and from pouting that she would not. When Nanny was ready, then she would tell and not one moment sooner.

But why, wondered Tabitha, even as she described Sergio, *will she not speak of it? Whatever it may be?*

She was even less happy when Sidney not only rose at once to go to Nan, but returned, and he, too, would tell her nothing of what had passed between the two.

"You will discover soon enough," he said. Then his lips compressed into a thin line, and he stared at her as if he had never before really looked at her. "Why," he muttered, "did it not happen sooner? Why not at the proper time?"

Before she could ask what he meant by that cryptic comment, he was gone, ducking back into his study, and like Nan, she knew she would get not another word from him. She returned to her worktable, managed to translate into modern English all of two lines of the ragged, spotted vellum on which she was working, and then, feeling oddly itchy, exceedingly irritable, got up, and wandered back outside. She had discovered that long walks reduced the nervous condition permeating her.

Several days passed, and as the night of the full moon approached, Sergio seemed to take at least as many walks as she did. Twice they crossed paths, spoke a few words, and then, as if he could not wait to be rid of her, Sergio made some excuse and disappeared.

One evening he came to her, bowed and clicked his heels, and staring over her head, said he must leave for several days but would return to continue his work if it would not inconvenience her and her household.

"Would it be impertinent to ask where you go?" she asked.

"It would, of course"—he smiled a wintry smile— "but I will tell you. I must visit my cousin in London. I should be gone no more than two or three days."

"London." For half a moment Tabitha considered asking that she be allowed to travel with him, but then it occurred to her that with him gone, perhaps she could concentrate and could finish the exceedingly interesting manuscript with which she had been involved from the day he arrived. It was difficult, but not *that* difficult.

I will work without experiencing this odd restlessness while he is gone. I will not act like some young girl just discovering the differences between man and woman, but will put my mind to the work for which it has been trained.

But she did not. If anything, she suffered a still greater crisis of nerves, wanting nothing so much as to . . .

But that is the problem, is it not? she scolded herself. *I do not know what it is I want.*

She said as much to Nan when she stopped by the old woman's cottage on the day after the full of the moon. "My insides roil and rumble and ache. Perhaps I have come down with an ague?" she asked, but knew it was not that. It was not at all like that. "And my teeth. They feel as if they are *growing.*" She touched them with her tongue and blinked. *"Are* they growing?"

Nan eyed her and then sighed. "Child, you will not like the cure I will give you, but I promise it will make you feel more the thing. Will you take it if I fix it for you?"

"Have I not always done as you have said?"

Nan's teeth showed in a particularly nasty grin. "Do you really want an answer to that?"

"No." Tabitha had the grace to feel warmth in her ears, knowing that on more than one occasion, she had objected to one of Nan's doses. "I will take your nasty medicine. Anything to rid me of this . . . this . . . I do not know what to call it."

"A yen. A yearning. A need."

Tabitha tipped her head. "Yes," she responded after a moment, sounding surprised. "Yes, I think, now that you put it that way, that is very much what it is."

Nan nodded. "You return later. I will have your cure ready for you."

The cure was at least as nasty as Nan had said it would be. On the other hand, not long after she had forced it down, something deep inside seemed to unwind. For the first time in weeks she felt fully relaxed. "Nan, it worked. I hope I never have to drink anything so nasty ever again. Promise me I will not?"

"I never promise what I cannot fulfill. You go on back to the house and finish the work you have started. You may want it."

"I may *want* it? Nan, how can you say that? For that matter, how do you know what it is I am currently doing?"

"Sidney told me. Either you will or you will not, but you should have the option."

"Will you stop riddling me riddles and explain why I should want a ridiculous receipt detailing how one ceases to be a vampire? There are no such things. The recipe is merely one more bit of the mythology surrounding a hypothetical breed. I will refer to it in my essay, of course, but—"

Nan held up her hand.

"—surely . . ." She stared. "Why are you shaking your head?"

"Do not be so sure of yourself. Not about anything, my child."

Tabitha's eyes widened. She opened her mouth . . . and closed it when Nan shook her head, her lips a hard, narrow line that slanted rather than going straight across her face. Tabitha had not seen that expression often. She sighed. "Nan, sometimes I wish you were not quite so much the sphinx. Your riddles are harder than its. *Much* more difficult, in fact."

Nan shook slightly with silent chuckles. "You will understand in time. Quite soon enough. Just not all at once. It is better that way."

Tabitha, both unhappy that Nan would not explain and glad she no longer felt as if her body were a stranger to her, said goodbye and wandered back to the house, to her work . . . that finally, when she settled to it, seemed not quite so difficult after all.

Sergio did not return quite so quickly as he had hoped. When he did arrive, it was so early the sun had not yet risen when he let himself into the house. Exhausted, he went to his room with no one the wiser, having traveled all night.

His visit to London had been fortuitous, indeed, given the fire and Stauss's need of him, but all was well now. He had left his cousin in good hands. He smiled at the thought of the determined little lady. Miss Coop would see there was no relapse, that his cousin continue to recover from his burns.

He had arrived in London and found what he needed on a side street near the Pulteney Hotel, which was where he went next. There he found his cousin on the stairs leading to the foyer, ready to leave for a celebration in the park. Sergio thought back to that brief conversation, smiled at the memory, and then frowned. *What,* he wondered, *made me feel I must remain in London when I wanted nothing so much as to return here to my work . . . and to Tabitha.*

"I am close," he had said. "That for which I search is there. I can feel it. Almost taste it."

"And you will follow their directions and be lost to us." Stauss shook his head sadly. "Sergio . . ."

"Stauss, I have a new reason for using it. You once asked if I had ever wed, and I believe I said it was too much nuisance. But now I have found the woman I would take to wife, and I do not feel free to do so. I cannot go to her as I am. I will not. She must not know the torture of growing old while I do not. And I do not wish to lose her and be forced to live when she ages and dies. I must do this thing."

Later, Stauss stared at Sergio, who had healed his burns, a very difficult and tiring feat.

"I needed centuries to find my love. You have been lucky, Stauss." Sergio had smiled at Miss Coop, who sat on the far side of the bed holding Stauss's hand.

Stauss chuckled. "You required centuries. I have found the one I would . . ."

"Gobble up? Sate yourself with?" asked Sergio, chuckling at the obvious ending to his cousin's aborted sentence.

Stauss chuckled. "Not that exactly, but one I will keep with me so that I may nibble now and again." He had lifted Miss Coop's hand and kissed it, his eyes holding hers. "And again and again?"

Sergio, lying in his bed at Detwood Hall, wondered if he would ever again see Stauss and, at the thought, suffered a brief melancholy. But thoughts of Tabitha washed the feeling away, and he fell asleep dreaming of the day when he dared woo her as she should be wooed. . . .

Tabitha had worked long into the night, finishing the work she had set herself and then copying out a clean draft. She returned to the library late the next day after a long, healing sleep, headed for her desk where she would read through the whole and check it against the original—but just inside the doors she stopped. Her nose twitched.

"Sergio!" she breathed.

"Hmm?" Sergio, tucked into an alcove well away from where she stood, pushed back from his worktable and glanced her way. "Miss Jerome. You are looking well."

"Hmm," she said, unconsciously echoing him. "Was your journey successful? Did you find your cousin in good health?"

How trite, she thought, *when what I wish to do is to go to him, walk into his arms, and never leave them.*

"What?" she asked, realizing he had spoken and she had not listened.

Sergio, unable to resist his need to be near her, moved toward her. "Why do you ask if you do not wish to know?" he asked, gently touching her cheek with one long finger.

"I believe I only wished an excuse to have your attention," she responded, and then blushed at the revealing words.

"And I would give it to you," he murmured, distracted by the rosy color. *I should not feel this way, should not want, not feel need,* he told himself. *Not when I have just fed.*

"Would you?" she asked, thinking of how he had ignored her in the days before he had left for London.

Sergio blinked. Then he smiled. He nodded. "I would, my dear, but my work must come first."

"For what do you search?" she asked, thinking that if she helped him find whatever it was, then he would have time for her.

"You will laugh. There exists a procedure, a recipe if you will, for changing a vampire into a human. I would find it."

Tabitha's eyes opened wide. "But Serg . . . Mr. Kuechera! I have it."

"You . . . have it?"

She could feel a growing intensity in him, a tension, an almost menacing power trained on her as if his every sense was directed toward her. It distracted her.

"My dear," he asked softly, "do you jest with me?"

Danger. She felt it.

"You do not answer." He turned away.

No! He must not. "Come with me," she said hurriedly. "I have finished transcribing it from the ancient and extremely vulgar English in which it was written. At least, I believe I have an accurate translation. Perhaps you can help me check it?"

He followed her. Followed too closely. In fact, he realized, he was very nearly breathing down her neck . . . that exceedingly enticing neck!

She reached her work space and pushed the chair under the desk so that she could sort out the pages of her translation and collect the ragged vellum.

She turned, holding them in front of her, and found Sergio so close she could feel his breath on her forehead. He backed up, bowed, clicking his heels in that odd Continental manner she found more than a trifle intriguing.

"I have them here." She turned and moved to a table farther down the room where she spread out the original and the new version side by side. "There. You can see for yourself if this is not that for which you search."

Sergio seated himself, and Tabitha brought a second chair for herself. He was so involved he barely realized she was there, merely moving a trifle so she could set her chair beside his. Together they worked down through the monograph, paragraph by paragraph, with Sergio occasionally commenting on her choice of word or phrasing. When he did, they would discuss it, and sometimes he would come to agree with her, and sometimes she would carefully write in an alternate to what she had set down.

When a maid came in much later, they were very nearly to the end of it. Tabitha, when she realized the girl was there, muttered, "Tell Jimson to hold dinner for half an hour," and turned back to where Sergio pointed to a long, involved sentence.

Half an hour later the girl returned to discover her mistress and the gentleman still arguing. "Miss," insisted the maid, jerking at Tabitha's sleeve. "Mr. Jimson says you are to come at once if your dinner is not to be totally ruined."

Tabitha sighed. She looked at Sergio. "Perhaps if we take a rest from this . . . ?"

He nodded. "And then, too, perhaps we could consult your tutor."

Tabitha rose to her feet and went to Sidney's lair. She put her head in and told him he was to come to dinner on the instant if he did not wish Jimson to have his head for washing.

"In a moment," muttered Sidney.

"Mr. Kuechera is here, Sidney. And we wish your help with a bit of translation. Mr. Kuechera says it is very important that it be exactly right."

Sidney's head snapped up. "He found his cure, did he?"

"Actually, I found it. I have been working on it ever since he arrived. If someone had told me what it was he wanted . . . !"

Sidney chuckled. "I suppose that might have helped, but then, you did not ask, did you? Yes. Yes," he said more crossly. "I'll come. Run along and I'll be there directly."

Conversation at the table revolved around Sergio's visit to London up to the point Jimson took a last look around and, herding the two footmen before him, left the dining room and closed the door.

"The part we cannot agree upon is near the very end," said Tabitha, interrupting Sergio's description of how part of the prince's celebration had been spoiled when a fire broke out in the structure built specifically for some particular tableau. She did not know how near his cousin had come to dying in that same fire.

"It is a part of the directions that explains when the procedure is most efficacious, most likely to succeed," added Sergio, quite happy to turn away from thoughts of his London visit.

"Hmm. Yes, I seem to recall there was such a phrase, but cannot recall it exactly. I will look at it when we return to the library. Mr. Kuechera, in your travels, did you ever meet a Frenchman named Lamarck?"

"Jean Baptiste Lamarck? You knew him?"

"I was invited to a salon at which he spoke on his *biologie*, as he called it, and discussed his theories concerning developmental changes in creatures over time."

"I have, er"—Sergio glanced at Tabitha, who listened with interest—"heard of those theories." Sidney's reminder called back those days to Sergio's mind, but he could not place Sidney at the soiree. "My"—he cast another sharp look at Tabitha—"er, father may have attended the very same salon to which you refer."

"Ah yes! Your *father*, of course. That would explain it," said Sidney with a satisfied look.

"My, er, father said a wag asked Monsieur Lamarck how his theory explains the characteristics of vampires. Was that the occasion when you, too, attended?"

Sidney nodded. "Monsieur replied, as I recall, that their ancestors must have acquired those traits, but how and when were scarcely worthy of investigation since there are no vampires! I was traveling with a win—er, *group* at the time," he finished, looking at his nails.

When Sergio chuckled, Tabitha cast him a sharp look.

"Yes, with a group," repeated Sidney. "Mr. Kuechera, you are aware, are you not, that Miss Jerome's family history goes back a very long way?"

Tabitha tipped her head, frowning slightly at this further non sequitur. It was unlike Sidney to jump from topic to topic. She glanced toward Sergio, who frowned slightly, looking blankly at one of the bowls of nuts Jimson had set on the table at the end of the meal.

"I am not absolutely certain I follow your thoughts," said Sergio slowly, his eyes moving to meet Sidney's gaze.

"Do you not? We will discuss it again sometime," he said, pushing back from the table. "For now, I think we should return to the library where we may check your manuscript."

Sidney first read the original and then Tabitha's version. "Hmm. You did quite well, considering there is a brownish spot just where the most important word lies in the sentence with which you have particular difficulty. I can remember, however, from before the damage occurred, so I know the sentence should read, *At the height of the night when the full moon takes position at the top of the firmament,* which I take to mean when there is a full moon high in the sky at midnight."

"That is what I was afraid it said," said Sergio and sighed softly. "Have you an almanac which will tell us when the next such concurrence of moon and midnight occurs?"

Sidney cast Sergio a surprised look. "You do not just *know?*" he asked.

Sergio's eyes narrowed. "I recall a talk I had with my cousin not too long ago. We are not all alike. We do not all have the same abilities."

Sidney nodded. "I have isolated myself here at Detwood Hall for too many decades. Perhaps I will travel again, as I did"—he twisted so that he could look up at Tabitha—"for a time after your father had no need of me, Tabby."

"Now would be the time to do it, would it not?" asked Sergio, calling her attention from Sidney's near lapse into revealing too much. "Now Napoleon no longer controls the whole of Europe?"

Sidney tapped long, narrow fingers against Tabitha's papers. "I have thought, now and again, of going east. To our East Indies, perhaps. I would study new philosophies."

Tabitha, thinking of Sidney's age, of the difficulties of the long sea voyage, the dangers, opened her mouth to speak, but Sergio touched the back of her hand with a gentle finger and, when she looked at him, shook his head.

"I spent a few years in the mountains north of India," he said. "There are monks living there who believe their supreme monk has lived many lives, returning at the end of each life within a babe who is born just as his old body dies."

"I would talk to them . . ." mused Sidney, but then shook himself from such thoughts and rose to his feet. "The next moon full at the height of the night will be in two months. Why do not the two of you get to know each other? Nothing, after all, can be done until then."

"Done?" asked Tabitha sharply.

"Did I say done? Ah well. The meanderings of the old are not to be considered important." Sidney almost seemed to scurry to reach the security of his lair, slamming the door behind himself.

Tabitha stared after him. "Meanderings? Nonsense. Sidney has never rambled in the whole of his life."

"Still, I like his notion that we become better acquainted. We have discussed my business in London, but what did *you* do while I was gone?"

Tabitha thought of that awful potion Nan had given her to drink and shuddered slightly.

"Was it so very bad?" he asked softly.

"It? What do you know of it?"

He tipped his head, frowning. "I ask what was wrong since you seemed upset there for a moment."

"Well, it was bad. I was . . . unwell. Nan cured me, but for a moment I wondered if the cure was worse than the illness."

"I am very sorry to hear you were not well. What seemed to be the difficulty?"

"That's just it," said Tabitha, and accepted the arm he held out to her. As she described her symptoms—or perhaps the *lack* of specific symptoms—they moved out into the open air and set off for a long walk in the last of the dusk.

They talked of this and that, of Tabitha's dreams of visiting places Sergio knew well and could describe for her, of the difficulties of being a woman in a society that put hobbles on females and kept them from doing all the things men did so freely. ". . . and I don't think it fair," she ended what had turned into something very like a diatribe.

"It is not fair. I hope I would protect any woman in my care, but I hope, too, that I would not forbid her to stretch her wings in any direction she wished to fly. I would wish to aid her in her exploration and share in it, but I see no reason she should not use her abilities and talents, even if they are not normally thought of by society as womanly traits."

"Do you truly believe that or are you just saying it?" asked Tabitha.

"I truly believe it. I have known some amazing women—"

Tabitha felt a stab of emotion she realized was jealousy.

"—who have managed their own lives and done it very well. Of course, there are others who have done it very badly, as well. Do you know anything of Lady Hester Stanhope who lives in the Levant? I do not think she is a happy woman, and yet she lives exactly as she wishes, dressing as a man of that region, associating with Arab men as another man would do, and that in a culture in which women are mere toys and kept in harems."

"You have met her?"

"Yes. I traveled in the region and visited her for a few days. She is a strange woman by current standards. One who will not be dictated to. On the other hand, when she makes a decision which goes awry, she bears the consequences of her actions as would an honorable man."

"You admire her."

"She does not suit my taste, but I can admire her for who and what she is. I could not live with her, if that is what you mean."

Did Sergio read my mind? Did he realize I was jealous of Lady Stanhope?

Tabitha would not have been surprised to discover he could, if he would, do just that. And if she could have read *his* mind at that moment, she would have discovered a deep and abiding tenderness, his love for her deepening even as she spoke.

If she had known, she would have been glad.

* * *

Tabitha enjoyed the next weeks a great deal. She and Sergio developed an interest in owls and spent a great number of hours prowling the woodlands and meadows observing the silent hunters.

But then, once again, Tabitha began to experience that irritation of the nerves that had sent her to Nan very nearly a month previously. She was not, however, so nervy she did not notice that Sergio, too, grew more preoccupied, less attentive, in fact, less *there*.

"What troubles you?" she asked when, for the third time in the same walk, he wandered off and then, perhaps as much as an hour later, returned to her side.

"The matter? Should anything be the matter?"

"You seem . . . preoccupied."

"I have noticed you, too, are not so comfortable as you were. I wondered if I was upsetting you in some way."

"So, instead of asking, you take yourself off and away from me?"

"It is better so," he said, staring off into space.

"Better for whom?" she persisted.

Instead of responding, Sergio stopped in his tracks. "I have decided. I must return to London for a brief visit."

Tabitha stopped but did not turn to him. "To see your cousin?" she asked. She had learned of Stauss's burns but not that he had healed remarkably quickly!

"Yes. Of course. To see Stanislaus." His words burst from him in an abrupt fashion unlike his usual soft and soothing speech.

"And what, or should I say *who* else will you see?" she asked, suspicious and hurt.

Sergio hesitated a moment too long. When she ran off, taking a small path deeper into the woods, he did not follow, but returned to the house where he packed for his journey. If he rode through the rest of the night, he would arrive in London before the sun rose, before he need take care to avoid the weakening light of day.

"You would leave us?" asked Sidney.

Sergio turned on his heel. He had not heard the door open, nor had he sensed Sidney's presence. The knowledge the other man could approach him without his knowledge was worrying.

"Well?" asked Sidney, impatient.

"I must go."

Sidney tipped his head. "I thought you understood you were among . . . friends."

Sergio stiffened. "Friends?"

"I will take you to Nan. She will provide what you need."

"What I need."

"What we all need."

Sergio stilled still further. "All . . . ?"

"Will you come to my room? I have a tale to tell which you should hear. And to answer your question, it is not absolutely certain yet, but, yes, I believe *all*."

They soon settled in comfortable chairs in Sidney's sitting room, where they stared into the small, unneeded but decidedly pleasant fire and sipped from glasses filled with a very fine brandy. Finally, Sergio shifted, and Sidney smiled. "You would know my story," he said.

"I very much wish to hear this story," said Sergio, a trifle more determinedly than he would have wished, since it revealed emotions he would have preferred to keep hidden.

"It begins a very long time ago."

"All good stories begin a very long time ago," said Sergio when Sidney said no more.

"We will see if you think this story good or ill." Sidney sighed. "I have lived a very long time, Mr. Kuechera." He watched over his glasses. *"A very long time.* The centuries have come and gone . . . well, a great many of them." He relaxed when Sergio did no more than frown slightly. "But"—again he stared—"I was *born* a son of Adam, human, and of this family."

"Born . . ." This startled Sergio, but after a moment, he nodded and settled more deeply into his chair.

"More of that later. I returned to see this house built. I returned to it years later, applied for, and was given a position as what we would now call a steward. Any number of times I have left only to return to take up a new position. As has Nan."

"Tabitha's nurse?"

Sidney nodded. "Nan, too, is a daughter of Adam and of this house. She was my student during a period when I was tutor to the children. She was"—he smiled a rather wintry smile—"very like Tabby. When the change came upon her, when she became what we are, it took a great deal of tact and care to convince her of what had happened to her. We learned from dealing with her experience and since, the few times we have faced the problem in another, we have handled it with greater tact."

"Tabitha . . ."

"Yes, Tabitha." Sidney frowned. "What we do not understood is why Tabitha showed no signs until now. In fact, we have been far more cautious dealing with her than ever before. You see, the change, when it appears in a member of this family, occurs during the early to mid teens. I will admit I had hopes Tabitha would become one of us. She has the necessary inner strength, the inner resources necessary for living a life that stretches into the unknowable future. The only theory to occur to us, Mr. Kuechera, is that, in her case, *you* were the catalyst."

"I?" When the word erupted in a startled croak, Sergio cleared his throat. "*I* awakened the curse in her?"

"Why do you think of it as a curse?"

Sergio opened his mouth to reply . . . and closed it. "It didn't used to seem that way, but I have tired of forcing myself on the unwary only so that I may continue what has come to seem a useless life. I first thought of our situation as a curse over half a century ago, and at that time I began searching for the means of change."

Sidney nodded. "Which you recently found."

"Yes . . ."

"Which you mean to use?"

Sergio nodded and then found himself shaking his head. He cast a look of confusion toward Sidney. "I have wanted nothing else. Why, now it is at hand, do I feel differently?"

"Because you have no notion how Tabby will adjust to the change in her life, and you think it possible she will wish to remain as she has become. If you were cured, as you call it, you would lose her as surely as if the situation were reversed and she had *not* become one of us while *you remained as you are!*"

Sergio sighed. "If only one did not need to prey on the innocent."

"One need not."

Sergio half rose from his chair, sat back carefully. "I do not understand."

"I will have Nan explain." Sidney sipped the last of his drink, set the glass on the narrow hob before the fireplace, and rose to his feet. "I suspect we will find Tabby there. And, Sergio"—Sidney glared over his spectacles—"whether she remains one of us or returns to humankind, she must make her own decision, do you not agree?"

"Whether or not she will return to what she was before? Yes, of course."

"Then, shall we go?"

Nan smiled at Tabitha, who was frowning into the fire before which they sat. "You have begun to understand?"

"No." Tabitha realized how sharply she spoke and drew in a deep breath. "How can it be? It is nonsense. Surely I am making up stories and pretending they are real!"

"You make up no stories. My dear child, would you believe me if I told you I have lived for over four centuries, that I am fallen from a twig of the same tree that bears you?"

"That you are a relative?"

"Yes. It would be far too difficult to determine the exact relationship, so you may call me aunt if you wish. I believe you will find that your Mr. Kuechera calls his young relative cousin for the same reason."

"Sergio is, then, also a . . . a . . ."

"Say it," ordered Nan.

Tabitha drew in a deep breath. The words came as a breath of sound as she released it: "A vampire."

"Very good. *I* could not say it for days. Poor Sidney,

trying so hard to be gentle with me, helping me understand what I was experiencing." Nan smiled a soft, remembering smile. "But that was then and this is now. Tell me, do you find the situation frightening?"

"Yes. Well. Maybe." After a moment she said, "Nooo . . ." Tabitha pursed her lips before speaking further. "No, not *frightening*. Merely unbelievable." She smiled, but the smile was rather wobbly. Then she drew in a deep breath. "There is much I want to know. Much I would have you tell me, but no, I do not feel frightened, exactly."

"Ah. Exactly."

"You are laughing at me."

"Am I? Perhaps. And yes, there is much you must know, must be taught, must, perhaps, learn for yourself. But I think the first thing with which we must deal is the restlessness you experience. The need. It is a day or two early, but will you accept another dose of the cure?"

Tabitha sighed. "I have to, do I not? It was blood. I only just realized it, but that is what it was. Awful . . ."

"There is, of course, the traditional means of acquiring it which makes it less distasteful."

Tabitha felt prickles under her skin and wondered if she would pass out. "The vampire's bite?" she asked softly.

"You *will* wish to experience it, but first you need to learn to control your prey, to make them forget, and you have not yet acquired the skill."

"Mental control of others." Tabitha felt a shudder run down through her body. "Sergio *did* make that clerk come to my aid!"

Nan chuckled. "I have not a notion to what you refer, but need you sound quite so outraged?"

Tabitha blinked. "Perhaps not. You mean I can learn to do *that*? Oh"—she threw up her hands—"I do not believe this! Any of it."

Nan sobered. "My dear, *believe*. I do not know what talents you will have, what you will be able to do. We each are different in that respect, but what is true for all of us is that we live an exceedingly long time, are always healthy, healing rapidly if wounded, that sort of thing. Our powers tend to differ one to another." She raised her head suddenly, sniffed. "Ah! Sidney and your Mr. Kuechera will be here shortly. Push the kettle nearer the fire, my dear. I will get the box of good tea and my better cups."

"Good tea?" muttered Tabitha.

"My dear child," said Nan, pretending outrage, "I am a member of this family, as is Sidney, although up until tonight no one knew that but the two of us." She smiled. "We have always managed to acquire the little luxuries, the things that matter to us. But what am I saying? *Luxury*? My dear! Good tea is a *necessity.*"

They laughed, easing some of the tension Tabitha experienced. The tension returned the instant the men appeared, which they did as steam wafted from the kettle's spout. Tabitha poured water into the teapot as Nan bustled about assuring herself Sidney and Sergio were comfortable.

And all the while Sergio and Tabitha each found the other was casting surreptitious glances, one toward the other.

Tabitha felt her skin heat and hoped she was not bright red. Sergio felt a combination of amusement and chagrin. Amusement that she looked at him with such speculation in her eyes. Chagrin that she caught him, more than once, turning much the same look on her.

"Are we ready to admit to each other that we are a

wing of vampires?" asked Sidney after each was settled with cup and saucer in hand.

Nan and Sergio nodded. Tabitha bit her lip.

"Tabby?" Sidney asked gently.

"But how can any of this be true?" she asked, just a touch of panic in her voice. "Everyone but the superstitious knows vampires are mythic beings!"

"How, my dear, would we survive if people did *not* believe exactly that?" asked Sergio in a polite tone that suggested Tabitha was not using her head.

She nodded slowly. "Yes. That makes sense. As does the belief garlic adversely affects vampires. That is another false belief, is it not?" she asked, looking directly at Sergio for the first time.

He chuckled. "That day you wished to test me, even though you could not believe it possible? I was giving silent thanks to the one among us who began that particular rumor. Brilliant of him."

Tabitha shifted restlessly. "But surely I was born human. How am I then no longer human?"

Sidney cleared his throat, removed his glasses, and set the earpiece to his lips. "Do you," he said in his lecturing tone, "recall my speaking of Lamarck at table the other evening? He has theories about changes that occur in living beings. As in our case where some humans, if presented with the proper stimulus, make the change. I believe, in your case, Sergio was the stimulus," said Sidney. He smiled what was, for him, a whimsical smile. "I like to think of it as something akin to the butterfly. The larva closes itself into its cocoon and emerges as something quite different. Something wonderful."

Nan spoke. "Child, at the moment you are confused, unhappy perhaps, wondering what will happen to you. Much that is wonderful will happen, believe me. You will enjoy a long life, one that allows you to see as much of the world as you wish." Nan knew of Tabitha's dreams in that respect.

Sergio added to that. "Tabitha, it is possible to live among the others without rousing suspicions. You may take up the study of anything, go anywhere in order to seek pertinent information. Think, Tabitha. If you wish it, you have centuries before you in which you will grow and mature and learn and . . ."

"And I must begin at once, must I not?" She shifted again, crossing one leg over the other knee and, immediately, uncrossing them. A lady did not sit with crossed legs, after all, and the fact she could not seem to sit still bothered her. "Nan, I suppose I must . . . ?"

"Yes. I've a patient waiting. I'll not be long."

As the door closed behind her, Sergio turned to Sidney and asked, "This is what you meant? Her means of gaining the needed blood?"

"Modern medical treatments are a boon to us, Sergio. The poor among us have as much need of having their blood let as does our Regent, who has had I know not how many pints of blood removed from his system! The poor, however, cannot afford a doctor. Nan supplies their need," he said, and, after a slight pause, finished, "and they supply ours."

"Now, why did I not think of this as a solution?" asked Sergio.

"Very likely you retain other traditional urges which must be met in the traditional fashion," suggested Sidney.

Sergio, whose skin never showed color, turned faintly rosy. "You refer, of course, to the sating of one's passion as one satisfies one's need for blood." He avoided looking at Tabitha so did not see her eyes widen.

"You have never met a married couple?" asked Nan, who returned just then.

"I know several," said Sergio, his voice chill.

"But have not discussed this with them?"

"Of course not."

She chuckled. "It is simple, really. One still needs human blood, but the other need is fulfilled by one's mate."

Tabitha squirmed. "Nan, you embarrass me, speaking of such things."

"Nonsense," objected Sidney. "You are physically innocent, of course, but you will not convince me you retain a theoretical ignorance!"

"Still, I am embarrassed."

Sidney sighed. "I forget that the very young are easily shocked. I merely wish to point out that Nan and I have not felt a need to ravish anyone but each other for many centuries. I wed her, you see, as soon as she made the change. It has been to both our advantages."

"Sidney, I forbid you to say more," said Nan. "In fact, we have said enough and will not interfere to a still greater degree."

Sidney rose to his feet. "Will we not?"

The two glared at each other, and then, moving into each other's arms, they embraced.

"Careful," said Nan after a moment. "I must give this to Tabitha."

Tabitha drank down the draught quickly, gagging slightly now and again, but getting it down. She knew she would feel better shortly, that the draught would rid her of the twitches and aches and yearnings causing her such discomfort.

"Now that is done, will you walk with me?" asked

Sergio softly. He took the glass from her and set it on the hob. "I think those two would like some privacy."

Tabitha cast a quick look toward her tutor and her old nurse and felt her cheeks warm. "We will walk," she agreed.

They paced side by side for some way along the path before Tabitha broke the silence. "I think I dream. It is a nightmare from which I will wake. I will laugh about it all."

Sergio stopped her, turned her, drew her into his arms. "Then, dream more, my Tabitha," he murmured against her ear.

His mouth moved over her face, down her neck, back up, never quite closing over her mouth. Tabitha melted deeper into his arms, felt his hands mold her closer. New tensions took hold of her, and when she could bear it no longer, she moved her mouth and captured his lips with her own.

She had never felt this way. She wanted more and more from this man who bewitched her with his every touch, and did not know her own hands and fingers were rousing him equally. She moaned, wanting . . . wanting . . .

She did not know what she wanted—but Sergio did. He glanced around, saw where they were, and drew her from the path toward a glade carpeted in low-growing thyme. He laid her on the ground and settled beside her, holding his head up with one hand while his other touched her face, outlining her features.

Tabitha captured his hand and drew it down, pressing his palm against her breast. His fingers teased her, and she moaned. "Sergio . . ."

"Tell me to stop, my Tabitha. Because if you do not . . ."

"Do not stop. Teach me. Help me. Sergio, do not leave me needing . . . needing . . ."

"This," he said softly, and bent to take her lips with still more passion than when they had first kissed. His hands wandered more freely, gradually raising her gown, pushing it up farther and farther, his fingers burning along paths which, previously, no hands but her own had touched. "Touch me, *mia cara.*"

He murmured Italian words of love as she obeyed by pushing her hands under his coat and then, when that was not enough, tearing at his shirt until it came loose from his trousers and she could press her palms to bare skin. Hot skin.

Passion blossomed rapidly, forcing them to greater and greater intimacy until, finally, when Tabitha felt she could bear no more, he came to her, became hers, and with the scent of thyme enclosing them, the two found their release as one.

And then they held each other. Tightly. Silently. For a long time.

When Sergio gently began to move away from her, Tabitha did not wish to let him go. She clutched at him, buried her face in his neck . . .

Opened her mouth . . .

Set her teeth lightly to his skin, pressed harder—and experienced an ecstasy even greater than that just known.

When she released him, Sergio chuckled. "Will you allow me the same favor, little one?"

"What . . . ?"

"You have tasted me, my dear. May I experience the same joy?"

It had been joy, Tabitha realized. She had, instinctively, drawn his blood, taken it in through her newly acquired fangs, felt something rapturous as she did so. "I did not know . . ."

"How could you? May I?" he asked again, and touched her throat softly with a long, narrow finger that shook ever so slightly from the emotions he experienced.

Tabitha felt a trace of fear, but looking deep into his eyes, she knew it was what she wanted. She wanted the sharing of blood, the making one of two. She drew his head down and, only for a fraction of an instant, did she hesitate before pressing him to her.

When he lifted his head and looked at her, she saw blood on his lips. For a moment the sight roused the panic she had felt earlier, but, licking her mouth, she recognized the coppery taste on her tongue, realized her lips very likely showed traces of blood as well.

Carefully, Sergio sat up. He drew Tabitha up and straightened her skirts. "I wonder if your study of our kind has told you what we just did," he murmured and frowned. "I fear I've taken advantage of your innocence in more ways than the one, my dear."

"How so?" she asked, touching his cheek with her finger, gently, gently. She could not get enough of touching him.

"I will not hold you to it, child, since you do not know, but that, the sharing of our blood, was symbolic of the exchange of life vows among our kind."

"Life vows? A form of marriage?" she asked, backing away from him a trifle.

He nodded, holding her gaze with his own. "You will learn that a vampire loves but once. I was a very long time finding love, Tabitha."

"As it was happening, as I tasted you," she said, "it crossed my mind that by exchanging blood we were made one. Perhaps, Sergio, I did know. Somehow. As I knew how, without knowing *how*, to go about taking your blood."

He laughed, an open, free sort of laugh she had never heard from him before. "Tabitha, my dear, does that mean you take me for your own as I have done you? Are we wed?"

"I love you, Sergio, and between the two of us we are wed; but I have family. I must go to London and inform my parents. My sisters will wish to meet you. Can you accept a human ceremony as well, so that they need not know how it is with us?"

"It is often done. Others wed purely human wives, you know, but I could never accept that I would have to watch such a woman grow old, help her die, and all the while I would remain young looking." He rose to his feet and straightened his clothing before helping her up. "Shall we go tell the others? And make plans to go to London?"

Some time later they returned to the house and the library where Tabitha found the folio pages for which Sergio had searched.

She raised shocked eyes to his. "Sergio, you came here for a reason. You came to find this, to end your life as a vampire!" She looked at him, horrified. "Sergio . . ."

"Peace, child," he said soothingly. "Unless you wish to return to what you were, I will gladly forego the temptation. You see, when I began searching, I had not found you. And then I did, but thinking you a child of Eve, I was more determined than ever to break what I felt a curse. So I could be as *you* were, do you see? But now, with *your* change, life as it is takes on new meaning"—he paused, frowned—"but, my dear, if *you* would take the cure, as it were, so will I."

For a very long moment Tabitha thought of returning to what she had been, the comfort of the known, the assurance of traditional values and a life she understood. Then she thought of what the others had said about travel, of meeting new peoples and new ways of life, about living long enough that one could learn whatever one ever wished to know.

"Sergio," she said slowly, "the time may come when I wish to end this existence, but not . . . immediately?"

He smiled slightly, his eyes half-hooded, a look she had learned meant he was deeply amused. "Of course. In the meantime, however, I believe we must make these papers secure. Let us consult with Sidney. Assuming he and Nan are agreeable to company at this time?" He gathered up the pages and laid them between the leaves of a leather folder. Then, Tabitha on his arm, he returned to the cottage in which Nan made her current home.

It had never occurred to Sidney that some of their kind would ever wish to end it, so it had never occurred to him to send out copies to certain hidden places where their kind gathered now and again.

"But these. The originals. How do we keep them safe?" asked Tabitha. She thought and then said, "The circle."

"Ah yes. The very place," said Nan.

"The circle of stones?" asked Sidney, not quite so enthusiastically.

"It is high and dry, Sidney," said Nan. "People stay away for reasons of superstition. We can plant in certain minds an even stronger aversion to the place, and they will spread that dread. If we bury this thing, well protected, it could stay there for centuries and not be disturbed."

And that was what they did. It was buried, carefully

protected, under the altar stone in the middle of the stone circle high on a hill not far from Detwood Hall.

"This way if we ever change our minds and our translation was not quite accurate, we will not have to seek through piles of rotting manuscript where the thing will have become still more damaged and illegible! We can find it and use it for a new translation," said Tabitha gleefully as they returned from their visit to the ancient stone circle just as dawn turned the east the faintest of pinks.

The next evening Tabitha and Sergio left for London. Nan and Sidney would soon follow.

"Mother, make up your mind!"

"But it is so difficult," wailed Lady Detwood after some hours of discussing marriage plans.

She avoided looking toward her husband, who sighed, wondering if the thing would ever be settled.

"We will do just as you wish," said Sergio in a deep, soothing rumble, "but we must know what it is you would have us do."

"If only you were not so near your thirtieth birthday, Tabitha."

Tabitha blinked, looked at Nan, who smiled a tight little smile. Sidney merely shook his head. She looked at her father, whose brows arched in bewilderment. Finding no help from any of them, Tabitha turned to her mother. "What has that to do with anything?"

"It is obvious."

"Not to me."

"But, *Tabitha,*" said her mother in something very near a whine, "to be celebrating your first marriage at such an advanced age will make us a laughingstock!"

"Is *that* the problem? Then, of course, we will have a small private wedding for just the family."

"But then everyone will say we are ashamed of . . . of something." Lady Detwood's gaze drifted toward Tabitha's tummy and flicked away. "No," she said mournfully, "it must be Hanover Square." Suddenly she brightened. "Mr. Kuechera, will your cousin, the count, stand up with you?"

"Stauss will give me his support," said Sergio, nodding.

"Ah! A count in the wedding party! Then, we will do very well! Yes, indeed. Hanover Square it is."

Lady Detwood bore Tabitha off, saying they must choose her gown at once and *not* go to that silly modiste Tabitha insisted on patronizing.

"The gown must be truly exceptional if you are to wed a count's"—she closed the door to the hall—"cousin. Oh, if only it were the count himself. What a triumph that would be." She sighed and then again brightened. "Ah, but you are to actually take a husband when I thought you never would. That is good. I must just remember that you are to be wed, and perhaps I will manage to survive the coming weeks."

The unnatural hearing of three of the four remaining in the salon had the recipients of Lady Detwood's opinions very nearly unable to control themselves, inner laughter causing them to shake silently.

In order to change the atmosphere, Sergio turned to his bride's father, who had remained silent throughout his wife's vacillations. "You will wish to know something of my situation and arrange for marriage portions and new wills and all the legal matters a wedding requires. Do you prefer that we do it ourselves, or should I have my London solicitor contact yours?"

Lord Detwood waved a hand languidly. "If Sidney vouches for you, then I know you will be a proper husband to my little Tabby." He sighed. "I suppose I should not repine at losing her. As her mother so often points out, she has remained unwed far longer than most daughters are allowed to do. Besides," he added in a very dry tone, "from what I have heard, your family as a whole is wealthy beyond the dreams of avarice, so I have no fear you will leave her a penniless widow. My solicitor will meet with yours and draw up the forms, and we can sign them in a day or two." He turned to speak to Nan, drawing her away from the others.

"I must go, then," said Sergio. "I will see my cousin and then arrange for a new suit of clothes. I strongly suspect my love's mother will not be happy if I appear at our wedding dressed by a Continental tailor, no matter how good the man may be."

"I will come with you," said Sidney. "Nan and I leave for the Continent as soon as you two are wed, and I, too, have arrangements to make."

"We may all travel together for a space, then, since I take my Tabitha to meet my family before we go to some of the places she has most wished to see." He eyed Sidney's gray hair as they left the house. Since no one was near, he spoke freely. "Will you return to your proper form once we are away from London?"

"We have not decided. At some point we must in order to begin a new life, one which will allow us to return to Detwood Hall in whatever capacity we can manage."

Sergio's brows formed little tents.

"It is our home, Sergio," said Sidney gently.

"Ah. Home."

"But it will, I fear, be quite some time before we may

return to it this time." He looked sad for a moment. "Still, such is the way of things, and we will make the best of it. We have definitely decided to go far to the East."

Sergio nodded. "I was there in the not too distant past. I believe you will find one or two sons of Adam whom I called friend who will still live and can ease your path. Remind me to write you letters of introduction."

"I will do that."

Sergio asked the names of Lord Detwood's solicitor and tailor, wished Sidney luck in his doings, and walked toward Piccadilly and the Pulteney Hotel. Such nonsense, that they must go through all the ritual London society demanded of them.

Or perhaps, merely, he was selfish? He wanted his Tabitha to himself. Wanted them together and alone. Ah well, he had waited more than three centuries to find her. He could wait another two or three weeks.

It was more like five, but finally the two stood before the altar, again taking vows of eternal oneness. Sergio glanced up and down his bride, noted the lace-trimmed gown with its low-cut bodice and the fact his Tabitha suffered the indignity of tight lacing beneath the pale rose-colored silk. He touched her cheek in that way he had, and she smiled at him, a gloriously radiant smile, before turning back to listen to the vicar's words.

But even when the ceremony was over they were not allowed to escape: There was the wedding breakfast to survive, the introductions to what seemed a horde of relatives—one of which, an elderly gentleman, claimed to have met Sergio's father when he had visited Paris many years previously. There were sly hints that his "father" had been something of a rake.

"A rake?" whispered Tabitha when the old man, a

distant cousin of her father's, left them and there was no one immediately to take his place.

"A very long time ago," he whispered back. "Before the French king and queen lost their heads."

"You will no longer go raking, my love. Will you?" she finished on a less assured note.

"Only if you wish to go a-raking with me," he whispered into her ear. "How much more of this must we endure?"

Tabitha glanced around. She caught her father's eye, and he joined them. "We wish to go."

Her father took her hand and held it tightly. "I will miss you, child."

Tabitha felt surprise. Her father had never been one to show emotion or to demand her attention, although quite often they had enjoyed long and involved arguments.

He smiled. "You *must* go, of course, and you mean to live on the Continent, but I hope you will return to England at least once before I depart this earth."

"Perhaps you can join us once we have settled ourselves," said Sergio, wondering how they would manage that. Lord Detwood would notice if they showed no signs of aging, assuming it was some time before he visited.

"I doubt I will. I have never liked travel. So difficult and tiring." He gave his daughter another sad look. "Have a good life, my child."

"We will," she said.

Ten minutes later they were in their carriage—only to have it pull over a little way down the street.

"The only good thing about your English wedding breakfast was that there was time for one last talk with Stauss and his Miss Coop."

"I like her," said Tabitha.

"That is good, because I think, in future, when she and Stauss wed and return home, you will have much to do with her."

Another handful of minutes and they were joined by Nan and Sidney. And, after what seemed all too many hours, to Sergio at least, he finally had Tabitha alone in their suite in Dover where they would await the packet for France.

"My one and only love," he said and opened his arms.

They tucked their faces into each other's necks and, once again, experienced the ecstasy of reaffirming the vows they had first made in a thyme-scented glade near Detwood Hall.